B

Ma... ...outh... ...ho, The Daily Mirror and the *Sunday Times*. He is the author of eighteen crime novels in the Harpur and Iles series, which are published all over the world. *Protection*, the fourth in the series, was televised by BBC 1 as *Harpur & Iles*, starring Hywel Bennett. Hollywood is currently negotiating for *Halo Parade*, number three.

James lives in his native South Wales and divides his time between his home near Cardiff and a caravan on the Pembrokeshire coast. He also writes under the name David Craig, most recently a series set around Cardiff docks, where he grew up. The Warner Brothers film, *The Squeeze*, with Stacy Keach, Edward Fox and Carol White was adapted from the David Craig novel, *Whose Little Girl Are You?*

He is married with four children. At present he is working on a sequel to *Split*, again featuring Simon Abelard. James is a part-time tutor in creative writing at the University of Wales, Cardiff.

First Published in Great Britain in 2001 by
The Do-Not Press Limited
16 The Woodlands
London SE13 6TY

Casebound edition: ISBN 1 899 344 72 1
B-format paperback: ISBN 1 899344 73 X

British Library Cataloguing in Publication Data. A catalogue
record for this book is available from the British Library.

1 3 5 7 9 10 8 6 4 2

Printed and bound in Great Britain by
The Guernsey Press Co Ltd.

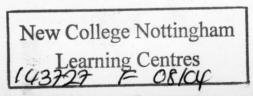

Bill James
Split

I

ABELARD GAZED AT his present setting. He had been there a while: long enough for some heavy thematic thoughts and satisfying moments of mild self-pity. It was a filthy but nicely deep shop doorway off Praed Street, close to London's Paddington station. From here he could watch the lit-up windows of a first-floor flat almost opposite. The side streets in this area had a pattern: small shops, cafés, fast-fooderies and the occasional restaurant at the busier end of the street, near the main drag, and then, further up, big, elderly properties that had long been turned into apartments or bed-and-breakfasts. Fast-food cartons made up the bulk of the litter, but with plenty of help from papers and other debris.

Abelard's spot was the entrance to a card, fluffy toy and souvenir shop, closed now. From here he watched and wondered if he was being watched: the same old twitch, the same old threat, despite so many shifts and amendments lately in his job. Cars parked nearby gave him worry. They shouldn't have been there, anyway. This was double-yellow country, no parking, even at night. Perhaps they weren't parked, only stopped. All the cars seemed occupied. They might be punters about to kerb cruise for girls, or punters and girls on a short time, or pimps ready for girls to return with the takings, or vice police keeping a fatherly eye. After all, this was Paddington and Paddington was still Paddington, despite the odd clean-up. Possibly one vehicle might hold a deputation waiting for Abelard: a big old Rover seemed full of shoulders, wide necks and sharp chins, the faces turned his way, most likely not balletomanes.

He kept alert but also continued with the heavy thinking and self-pity. Lurking like this was not really his kind of work.

So, adapt, Abelard. Pampered, elegant, pissed off, misused, nervy, black – or at least half black – he reckoned he'd already begun a transformation, in fact. There had been a time when he was… all right, the crude and melodramatic word would do… when he was a spy: yes, crude, but a word people understood. And, it was more or less accurate. More than less. As a young graduate he'd joined Her Majesty's security services and was deftly trained to preserve the secrets of his country; or, if he switched squad, to lift the secrets of other countries. Now, though, as was famous, secrets at home and abroad had dwindled. *Now* meant post-Wall. *Now* meant almost a decade post-Wall, plenty of time for secrets to dry up, or to become irrelevant, and for idleness and redundancy to set in among spies; dangerous idleness, serious redundancy. This was 1997.

Somehow, Abelard had held on to his job, even advanced in the career, but knew that it and he were changing, were getting modified. He had become a policeman: a sort of detective – plain clothes, no helmet or silver buttons, but a policeman, all the same. Officialdom did not call him that, of course. Nominally, he remained, as ever, an agent, a spy. The duties defined him as something else, though. It was not what he had joined for.

So, what *had* he joined for? To preserve the realm? This sounded large and flatulent, but, yes, to do that. Perhaps the realm did not need Abelard or the workmates of Abelard to preserve it any longer. In those years since the Wall collapsed – *was* collapsed – the realm found it could look after itself, because fewer enemies threatened. Political certainties had faded, and the hatreds that went with them. Bloc thinking, Bloc subterfuge, undercover Bloc gallantries were obsolete, and doctrinal wars involving Britain unlikely now the greatest secular doctrine of them all had been as good as buried by the Berlin rubble. Northern Ireland was still active, naturally, but that made up a special corner with work for a very special cabal. Except in Africa and South America – remote, remote – coups grew rare; for-your-eyes-only plans about new weapons were still around and pinchable, yet scarce; international defections hardly mattered any longer because nobody believed anything wholeheartedly enough to make a betrayal rate as much. What was a security services boy, or girl, to do?

Well, today, instead of secrets there were crimes. Greed, theft and the attendant violence and killings continued as ever in the world, or better than ever. And this was the point, wasn't it: some former spies found their skills could be converted to new uses, now that in these fine pre-millennium days such skills were unwanted for espionage? Here and there, in this country and overseas, such underemployed operators had turned their schooled, risk-taking minds to brilliant international embezzlement, consummate fraud, indomitable trade in drugs, titanic steals, epic corruption. Abelard's current job was to stop such abuses, or as many as he could, when they were attempted by one-time colleagues, and bring those colleagues back for settlement. He had become a crime and punishment man, no longer an unseen guardian of the nation's soul, entrails and destiny.

Tonight, here, near the handsome old railway hotel, he was seeking the girlfriend of a colleague who might have turned law breaker in one of those profitable ways, and possibly not just one of those profitable ways. This colleague had, in fact, been more than a colleague. Julian Theobald Bowling and Abelard used to be friends: not exactly close friends, but definitely pally, as pally as people ever got in their kind of work. Now, Abelard did not even know where Julian was, not town, not country, not continent. Abelard *ought* to know where Julian was, and *ought* to be able to nail him and bear him home. The new job said so. This girl might give a pointer. Of course, she could give pointers to others, also, and might have already done that. Abelard did not know a great deal but he did know Julian had apparently cornered a fine stack of illegal funds lately, perhaps by smart illegal deals, perhaps by hi-jacking cash profits meant not just for him but for sharing between him and his new associates. Abelard considered this later possibility the more likely. Julian's views on loyalty had always been cloudy. A lot of other people might be looking for him, none much interested in righteousness, as Abelard was, but very interested in the commandeered funds. Julian would be a target, and not just for Abelard. Almost certainly Julian wholesaled drugs, possibly shipped drugs by the ton. If you ripped off lads in that game you were in big and brief peril, brief because you would not be around for it to last. One of Abelard's objectives was to reach Julian and reach Julian's girl before rivals in the quest did. He could not count on this. The missions had two sides. One was to catch Julian and bring him back to judgement. The other was to save him. On the whole, Abelard considered the second more important, but it was a near thing. Hard to give Julian much sympathy.

Of course, Abelard would admit that spying and policing had overlaps. Whichever it was tonight, though – espionage or *flicery* – at his pampered and elegant rank he should be above this peasant task. And so, yes, he felt pissed off and misused. But also nervy. In his doorway, he wondered again whether any of the loitering cars were police. If so, they were almost colleagues now, weren't they? Maybe, but not colleagues who could be told what you were about because you were not really one of them; and not colleagues who would feel obliged to offer protection if things went bad, also because you were not really one of them.

Abelard missed the old job. It had owned a grave and slippery grandeur. In those days, even the method of recruitment was a glamorous mystery, implying an élite, a club, and a club that was fussy and autocratic about whom it admitted. You did not apply to join. You were approached and asked very privately whether you might be interested in a certain sort of work. You could not apply because posts were never advertised. Abelard had been approached while still an undergraduate. People recommended you and you did not know who they were or how they had noticed you or what they had noticed. Abelard supposed he had been named by someone on the university staff charged to spot likelies. It was flattering, and sinister and frightening. You felt part of a shady but socially very OK tradition: Graham Greene was in Intelligence, and Ian Fleming. Even the traitors – when treachery mattered – even those three or four or five had been at good schools and Oxbridge.

As Abelard understood it, none of these hidden, unique, class criteria applied when joining the police – though promotion there might depend on equally unchartable qualities. Lately, then, Abelard had begun to feel the old job was sinking. He knew there would not be much sympathy for him and his colleagues. They had become less because they were needed less, and they were needed less because things overall had grown better. In any case, if you lived in Britain, decline had been the national mood since the death of Victoria and was especially potent now among the thoughtful, as an antidote to imminent millennium turdery. *You're on the slide? So? Hold my hand and we'll all go together.*

Anyway, here he stood tonight, watchful, tense, bloody minded. The flat was above a restaurant which would soon close. Two waiters stood at the back sharing out tips. Every light in the flat seemed on, with all the curtains drawn back. But, in the three hours he had watched, nobody moved across the windows. Time to get closer. A side door was part open to the street and he saw a corridor with stairs at the end probably leading up to the flat. Half way along the corridor was a door to the restaurant kitchen. He picked his way in the near dark through food smells, cat smells and sacks of peelings and tins. Decline, decline. One of the waiters appeared from the doorway and asked what Abelard wanted. If he had really been the police he could have said so and that would have been enough of an answer. Instead, he pointed up the stairs to a mauve door: 'Miss Francis – is she in?'

'Sometimes she not here,' the waiter replied.

'The lights?'

'To keep out burglars.'

'I'm concerned about her,' Abelard said.

'Oh, concerned. You know her, you?'

Even though Barbara Francis was not all white herself, the waiter meant, *I didn't think she had blacks as friends, or clients.* On intonations Abelard reckoned himself as sensitive as a drama coach. He had more than most drama coaches to be sensitive about. Through the restaurant window he saw the old Rover was still there. Possibly a couple of the faces inside had shifted to look towards the restaurant now: substantial faces and, no, probably not balletomanes' faces. Were these folk here to see Miss Francis? Had they already seen Miss Francis and were waiting to discover who else wanted to see her? They hadn't found what they had come for and needed a new lead? Did they think Abelard was it? He said : 'I must talk to Miss Francis.'

'Robert in the kitchen has a key,' the waiter replied, 'to look after her plants and a brown animal in a cage, not a rat but—'

'Hamster. Could you get the key?'

'I must go home to sleep,' the waiter replied. 'And would it be right, sir, for me to take someone I don't know into her flat?' Abelard pulled out a five, but this jerk's scruples went deep and eventually it took ten. A basic in that fine early training had been the methodology and scale of bribes: giving, not getting in those days. Were police detectives coached in this sly art? Did they have the same sort of budget and reimbursement procedures? The waiter returned to the kitchen, came back with the key, then led upstairs. Handling the door's big lion-head knocker he giggled: 'Here the brave king of the jungle. Inside, the little brown rat.' He opened the door and stood aside. Abelard paused, surveying what he could see. The things were cheap but tidy. Nothing said violence. He went in. Progress. He ought to feel pleased. Yes, he ought to.

'Anything look different?' Abelard asked.

'Different?' The waiter crouched over the hamster's cage, which seemed empty.

'Does she have many visitors?'

The waiter seemed obsessed by the cage. Abelard did not like obsessions, others' obsessions, especially when they were aside from the main business, or appeared to be. 'A moment,' the waiter hissed. The cage was circular, with a separate smaller compartment on top as sleeping quarters, like two spacecraft joined. The waiter drew his finger softly across the bars a couple of times. He looked strained, as though this creature had become a kind of omen, and if it were not here, or if it were dead, everything must be wrong. Or was that how Abelard felt? Good Christ, where had that dozy idea sprung from? Just the same, his nerves sang.

The waiter grinned suddenly. In one smooth movement the hamster glided down a plastic chute from the bedroom, stood up on the sawdust with its paws against the bars and pushed a busy muzzle through, sniffing ardently. It was a mixture of browns – dark on top, a lighter waistcoat across the belly: plump, a little rat-like, yes, but dumb looking. Abelard left the two of them and went swiftly through the whole flat, searching for anything that might show him the next step, trying to keep away from windows. Opening a couple of drawers in a bureau, he found a few old records and some empty chewing gum wrappers. A colour picture of Barbara Francis, known also as Melanie and Roxana, stood framed in silver coloured metal on a radiator shelf. The brightness of the frame seemed a bit cruel now. *Oh, bollocks, Abelard, ditch the mush.* The photograph showed her in fancy dress as an astronaut, beaming with fun, two rows of very bright and exceptionally small teeth on display.

From the other room, where he had left the waiter, there suddenly came a high, angry, unbroken whistling. Abelard hurried back. The waiter had gone and the hamster was clinging suspended on the bars, making this shrill, meaningful din. Someone bright and very impatient might be reincarnated there, fed up with the cage, condominium or not. *Oh, bollocks, Abelard, ditch the cheapo mysticism.* He bent to look more closely for anything non-hamster in the eyes and while crouched heard a footstep behind, maybe more than one.

He did not have time to turn and see. Something metal and unfragile crashed against the side of his head. As he went down the pet was still at it, like an intemperate kettle.

*

Consciousness came back at a gallop and as soon as he opened his eyes he knew he was in the locked boot of a moving car, big enough to be a Rover. Blood had run down his face and dried on his lips, sticking them together. His nose seemed blocked – perhaps more blood. His chest was heaving for lack of air and he broke his lips apart and desperately sucked at what was on offer in this fume-filled box. Exactly how old was the crate? Did it leak poisons?

Other terrors queued, like, if he did not die here, now, how long would he live when they stopped? He was being freighted somewhere – to be finished and dumped? When they opened the lid oxygen would enter, but was he going to get time to savour it? Or they might never lift the lid at all. They could fire the car or drown it and him in a dock. Christ, yes, they would need to get rid of the vehicle. His mother and all the training had stressed that when you went into the car of an unfriendly you were very likely a deado. And all this for asking questions about Barbara Francis, who might have shown him a step forward. There still were steps forward, even in an age of decline, decline.

They were making some speed. It was motorway driving. He had no idea how long he had lain unconscious. They could be anywhere now. He was on his back. Reaching up he pushed at the boot lid with both hands and when it did not yield used his feet as well and shoved with them and shoved again. It still did not budge and sweat flooded him. Divers in trouble some-times panicked and struggled and ate up their air. Briefly, he tried to lie still, but the procession of dreads would not let him. Were these the reactions of an inspirationally chosen and ruth-lessly instructed secret officer of the Crown? Fuck that. This time he turned on to his hands and knees, then pushed up with his arched back, a desperate, prolonged pressure, slackening when the car swayed and broke his balance, and when the pain of breathlessness grew too much. As soon as he strengthened again he resumed.

He thought he felt something begin to give – a tiny movement as if a lock bar had bent a fraction and could be bent more next time. Then, as he was getting himself together for another last shove, the car's speed began to fall rapidly and for a moment he paused, still arched and gasping, terrified he had left it too late. The vehicle stopped. He heard voices and doors slamming. Footsteps came to the rear of the car and he realised that if they pulled up the lid to take him out now he had no chance of defending himself, head and hands and feet all pointing the wrong way and exhaustion dragging at him. Shouldn't there be tools here, maybe a tyre lever? Why hadn't he felt about, tried to arm himself? But he just hung there now, bent up, petrified, fearful of making any sound that might signal he was conscious. Perhaps they were not ready to deal with him yet. He heard other vehicles nearby, quite a number, and there were voices, including what seemed to be children. Wherever this was it might be too crowded for them to show what they had in the boot.

The lid stayed down. Slowly his mind began to function fairly fluently again. Possibly they had turned into a motorway services station, and some of them had gone for a leak and a coffee. The footsteps must be those of one man left on guard. Occasionally now he heard whoever it was take a few paces, as if to ease the boredom.

Abelard had to break out while the car was parked here. The odds might never be as good again. If he had read things right, it would be one-to-one and he should have surprise on his side. For a moment he relaxed his body. He had to rebuild his breath and strength. With one hand he explored the side wall of the boot in case something as suitable as a cosh were strapped there. But perhaps they had already helped themselves. What had hit him as he tried to commune with the hamster could have been some meaty item from a tool kit. He found nothing now. He thrust upwards with his back against the lid again and for another second felt that all his worry about a weapon did not rate because the boot would stay shut until they chose to open it, and there would be no surprise and no fight and no hope. Metal struts on the underside of the lid cut into his back and he could not be sure whether the moisture he felt running across him was sweat or blood. But he kept the pressure on and struggled to make it more.

There was another small, sharp sound, like metal yielding and the lid groaned and flew back. No longer jammed, Abelard jack-knifed up and then collapsed sprawling. He half dazed himself as his temple hit the spare-wheel hub. He heard a man swear and step towards the car and, as he forced himself back to full consciousness, saw a hand reach up to the boot lid, about to bang it down again.

Abelard struck out, a sweeping, upward blow at the man's arm, attempting to knock it away and stop him. At the same time he yelled for help and began to get to his feet in the boot, so everybody could see. Once in a while people would ditch their indifference or fear and lend a hand. He had to try. *I'm a soldier of the Queen, for God's sake!* A thought only, not a cry.

The guard had lost his grip on the lid after Abelard's blow and now, like an idiot, was reaching up again to pull it down. He left himself beautifully open, his body and neck stretched and tensed and inviting. With his spare hand he groped for something in his jacket pocket and Abelard did not wait to find out what. Half upright now he chopped fiercely at this extended neck – a cultivated, precise blow, much practised on dummies; possibly a non-police blow. He watched all cohesion abruptly leave the man's frame so that the arm which had been reaching up tumbled back, brushing against Abelard's face. The guard's legs folded. As he went down his chin hit the car's bumper and he hung there for a moment like someone on the execution block, then eddied to the ground. He would be about twenty-eight, not big but powerful looking and in a good suit and silk tie, most likely a purchased, heavy-duty lad.

A couple of middle-aged women had watched as they stood by their Nova and now one of them bellowed at Abelard as he jumped from the boot: 'I say, who are you?'

'Jack-in-the-box.' Yes, Abelard was that. Despite the changes, he had lately sprung high in the newly shaped and newly toned security services. As they had shrunk, they were also required by law to become increasingly open and competitive and subject to scrutiny. More of that self-protective secrecy and class clannishness had been loosened. Admission of a few people like Abelard had not been deemed enough. Democracy was getting a run. The Chiefs' names were actually published now, and their pictures appeared on television and in the Press. Even political correctness had edged in to departments, and that old public school/Oxbridge dominance was also crumbling. It had *seemed* to weaken a little with Abelard's recruitment all those years ago: he was neither public school nor Oxbridge. In a way, that had made his invitation even more flattering and mysterious. He used to wonder what they saw in him. The wondering did not last long. He discovered that even in those days the clever folk who ran things realised that their image might go against them eventually, or sooner. They had decided they needed a prole or two, and even a black or two. Abelard had been twice qualified. He was a double gesture, and had been meant to remain at not much more than a gesture. But recently the attempts at some sort of further egalitarianism had brought Abelard's accelerated rise to somewhere above middle management, oh, yes, definitely above. A Labour government helped, even a Labour government led by a public school, Oxbridge laddy. Abelard adored positive discrimination and if he'd had a cat he would have called him after it. Not even positive discrimination could keep him entirely out of rough sequences like this one, though, sod it.

Now, he saw he had been right and they were in the car park of a services station, though not one he recognised. He had been right, too, about the car: this was the Rover spotted outside the restaurant. For a second he stared towards the station buildings, in case the others from the car were on their way back. He saw only the customary crowd for these nowhere places, the men in Littlewood's cardigans and aglow with mileage pride. Abelard bent down and went through the pockets of the guardian. He was still breathing, though with occasional long pauses. Next of kin would have worried, and so did the two women. 'Stop it, oh, stop it!' one of them yelled. She hurried to their car and leaned on the horn to call help. Both began screaming. They would not necessarily be racist but, if a black was hitting a white, British whites would side with the white, unless the black were Joe Louis and the white Max Schmeling, in 1938.

Abelard kept working. He found keys in one pocket and a short barrelled FN .38 revolver in another. There was a bit of money and nothing else. These boys knew who they were and carried no identification. The din from the women must have worked and three men rushed out from the building, all of them youngish and fit looking, the last in a homburg hat. One of his mother's other chief observations about the world to Abelard as a child was, Never trust a man in a homburg. He pulled the boot lid down, praying it would stick. It did. Then he jumped into the Rover, praying again, this time that one of the keys would fit. One did. As the three sprinted towards him he reversed the Rover, turned and, waving to the two women, made for the motorway, the elderly engine sounding loud but bonny and ready for almost anything. They weren't bad old wagons, thinking about it from the driving seat, not the boot. He joined the motorway.

In a couple of miles he picked up signs and found he was on the M1 going north, not far from Luton. He took the first exit and doubled back towards London. He thought he smelled dawn and this pleased him. In a little while he must pull off and choose a country corner where he could search the car. Daylight would help. After another fifteen minutes he took an exit, found a country lane and pulled in at the gate of a field. By now there was enough pale, grey light. At once he began sifting through the thick litter of cigarette packets, old maps, wrappers and tattered newspapers. It was all very anonymous and he might have been digging through the muck in his own car, except for the smoking mementoes. Finding nothing around the front seats or in the glove compartment, he moved into the rear. Again it struck him that these were trained people: men who discarded all kinds of rubbish, but nothing that told a tale.

Then, in a corner of the back seat, he discovered a Marks and Spencer carrier bag which he at first thought empty. Feeling around inside, he located what seemed to be a large postcard. When he brought it out, though, he was appalled to find a photograph of himself. The shock dazed Abelard. It was a wedding picture, more than twenty years old now, but still a passable likeness, give or take a top hat. He had become a bit heavier and his eyes were less cheery and amiable today. All the same, anyone could have recognised him from the snap. Anita beamed on his arm as if she might truly mean to stay. He turned the photograph over and read what was written in pencil on the other side:

Simon Abelard, age 44, Senior Principal (Personnel), HMISS. Heads search for Julian Bowling, and currently operates clandestinely from offices registered as Anstey Financial Consultants, 318 High Holborn, London, not MoD.
Married 1978, Anita Selby Sawyer. Divorced April 1984. No children.
Private address: 15A The Hawthorns, London NW11. Mixed race. Welsh mother (lives with him). West Indian father (dead). Born, Loudoun Square, Docks, Cardiff, 1956. Educated Manchester University (Upper second, science, 1977). Post grad. work, Columbia USA. Recruited originally as Whitehall token black.

Find and bring. May have leads to Bowling. Approach with care. To be kept in adequate state for questioning.

The writing was very small and very neat – female? – and the information very accurate. Yes, token black sounded spot on, spot on for then: 'Not just black but Cardiff Tiger Bay working class,' the chiefs could chortle, when citing Abelard: to rebut the unrebuttable charge that the Outfit was a costly, silver spoon, self-perpetuating cabal.

For a moment, Abelard recalled one of his earlier jobs. Properly, that religious rural trip should have been handled by Special Branch, but the call came for Abelard. So, even then the blur between security work and police work had started. It was in apartheid days and he had been ordered to a huge inter-denominational rally on a show ground in mid Wales to make sure the visiting South African cleric, Desmond Tutu, was not done on British soil. There had been a half hint that a talented Johannesburg cordite team might smuggle themselves near and take out the then bishop, subsequently arch-. The Brits, not the Boers, would thus catch the blame.

As a witty race gesture, Abelard, very much the solitary black in the Outfit, had been ordered to get his wide, trained frame between Desmond and fusillades. Verdun Cadwallader ran these matters then and now – another to dodge the pruning – and it was the sort of malign man-management touch he adored. Of course, no SA execution squad turned up and no bullets. Once or twice that day Abelard's eyes met Tutu's and he had seen a mixture of amusement and mystification in the bishop's. Perhaps it shook him that a man like Abelard could make it into one of Britain's passionately exclusive Intelligence services. Perhaps it shook him that a non-white should want it. In a packed exhibition hall, Tutu was given a reception like the Beatles in their pomp and made a joke, probably standard. Aglow in his purple, grey curly hair gleaming under the platform lights, he had said: 'One thing about being black: nobody can see you're blushing.'

There had been moments under Tutu's scrutiny when Abelard had felt like blushing himself for having landed in this career. But he *had* landed in it, and landed in it brilliantly early. A while after the Tutu duty, events had started to make Abelard promotable. He climbed. For instance, he could have been directing this search for J Bowling from his decently furnished, not unspacious, subject-to-audit office.

Why the hell wasn't he?

2

'MOVE?' HIS MOTHER protested. 'I'm too old. I mean, move *again*? I like it here. Now.'

'Only for a while, most probably,' Abelard said.

'What's that mean, "most probably"? Move up here from Cardiff to be with you, OK, very kind, very like a good son, but now move again?'

'This address—'

'Someone's got your address, Simon? Some woman?'

'No, ma.' Or perhaps yes, but not as she meant it.

'You're afraid?'

'Some folk have been spending time on my background.'

'So you worry about me?' she replied.

'You're often here alone.'

'What do they care, whoever they are, about a widow of seventy-two from Nowheresville, lodging with her boy?'

'People like these, whoever they are, don't always think straight when they're looking over a property.'

She stood up, as though ready to defend the property right away. 'This government job you've got – oh, still so nice, plenty of money, lovely suits, but is it worth it? What I mean, you could have been a teacher, your qualifications. There's a call for black teachers. Or a pharmacist. Their shops don't just smell great. There's loot in pills and corn cures.'

'It won't cost us to go from here for a few weeks. Till it's over. My boss approves. The office picks up the bill.'

She paced slowly across his living room and back. 'So they're scared, too? This to do with that beating you had?'

'I was hit once. 'It might have come to a beating or worse if he had not escaped from the Rover, though. He was being taken somewhere quiet where he could be asked and really asked about where Julian Theobald Bowling and his appropriated gains might be. Abelard would not have been able to answer and might have tried not to answer even if he could, which would have meant a bigger beating, or worse. At least one very formidable firm was looking for Jules. They could attempt the heavy stuff and seemed gifted on research and neat dossier preparation, too. To warrant such efforts, Jules must really have conned major major people out of major major takings.

Mrs Abelard said: 'All right then, is this move to do with that beating that wasn't a beating? What do they do, put you on all the sharp end jobs because you're—'

'There aren't many sharp end jobs these days. Everyone gets a share when they do come. I spend part of my life dishing out tricky assignments to whites.'

'Smarty boots.'

'Not what I meant.'

The telephone rang and Abelard turned away with relief to take it. A slow, West Country voice, quite possibly real, said: 'We might be able to help you. Well, it would be reciprocal, as you'd expect.'

'Help me with what?'

Abelard's mother began banging cutlery down as she laid the table for lunch. 'You work from a caff, Mr Abelard?'

'What help?'

'With the search for Julian Bowling, that charmer. Call on us. No need for cloak and dagger.' He gave an address off Belgrave Road in Pimlico. 'Tonight? 7pm? You're handling this alone? You boys crave kudos. We can watch you come up the street, so do be solo.'

'He'll be there?' Abelard asked.

'Jules? Oh, not impossible. But a talk would be valuable, even without him. So many want Julian Bowling, don't they? We all know why.'

Yes, we all did. 'Do we?' he replied.

As Abelard and his mother ate their meal after this call, she continued her questions and tireless commentary. She sat very straight, her eyes bright with the reasonable suspicion he would try to soft-soap her. Towards the end she said: 'How can they understand you, your mind, these powerful white people you work with?'

'Are you asking because they're white or because they're powerful? You're white. You understand me. Some of them I trust, some not. It's not because of black or white, though. Just what I know or half know or don't know at all, only feel.'

Mrs Abelard sighed.

'They'll get us a fine flat, not too far from here and nearer the park,' Abelard said.

'What park? Can I walk there alone? In a London park? You going to permit that? When?'

'What?'

'When we got to move? This afternoon?'

'No, no. They're not unreasonable.'

'Tomorrow morning?'

'That OK?'

After lunch Abelard looked up the Pimlico street on his ABC guide. 'You'd obey a voice from who-knows-where on the telephone, Simon?' his mother asked.

'My work's not the higher mathematics, ma. Some uncertainties are always present.'

'I'd say you've got a death wish.'

'Great meal, I'll wash up.'

'Eventually.'

He left not long afterwards, although it was still only late afternoon. Abelard liked to give a lot of time to surveying the ground. From inside his Escort he inspected the house, a well-cared for terraced cottage, curtains open upstairs and down. During the half hour he watched he saw no movement. He withdrew to a pub, had a gin and decided he had better break in and do a real inspection before the meeting time. As his mother had said, a voice from who-knew-where? Mad to walk into that kind of setting without an advance peep. So, here might begin one of those remaining differences between cop work and the other.

Leaving the car at the pub, he walked back towards the rear of the house. No lights showed, although it was growing dark. He could not spot an alarm box, which might mean anything or nothing. He entered through the back garden and tried a few sash windows until he found one where the wood was going. He forced the catch with a knife. No bells sang. He climbed in, leaving the window open behind. Although he carried a pencil torch he did not use it yet. Instead, with his nerves and his nose and his ears he felt out the house. *Bollocks, Abelard*: he meant he tried to guess if he was alone in the place. The training said that when a break-in went so easily keep alert for a trap. Mostly the training got things right. For a second he risked the torch.

The first room was poky and over-neat, as if never used. It had a lot of pink in the décor and furniture. Christ, had he mistaken the address? A door, half open, led to a hallway and, putting out the light, he edged gingerly forward. There would be time for only a swift and general tour: no drawers or cupboards and nothing to be disturbed because at 7pm he must come back and act as if he had never seen the place before. How were his theatricals lately? He had about two hours, so he needed some speed. On the ground floor, he found another sitting room, similar to the one he had just left. Increasingly the place looked like something run by two dear old ladies. How in God's name did it connect with a delinquent agent, on the run and turned highest level drugs trader? Because this was the front of the house he could not risk the torch, but street lights revealed further pinkness in wallpaper and easy chairs, a sedate glow.

More edgy than ever, he started to climb the stairs and paused on a small landing, listening again. He could make out four doors, one ajar, leading to bathroom and lavatory, the others all shut. Suddenly, for no reason Abelard could pinpoint, he became certain the house was empty, and he caught himself beginning to relax – sliding into the kind of daft confidence that might be one step from death, whether this was a spying game or a police game: drugs were hazardous cargo. He decided to stop and do nothing for a few minutes. Then, very gently, he tried the first of the closed doors. It opened on to a bedroom, the kind he expected after what he had seen downstairs, everything innocuous as far as he could tell in the dark, the bed made and turned back, like in an hotel.

Moving across the landing, he tried the other two closed doors and found the same depressing spruceness. This house was turning out so normal he felt defeated by it and prepared to leave. He went back to the first bedroom and from frustration as much as anything shone the slender beam of the torch inside. Leafy wallpaper gleamed palely. Then, as he moved the light across the floor, something glinted more brightly between the edge of the fitted carpet and the wall, something minute with a shiny surface. As first he thought it a bit of imitation jewellery, even real jewellery, but when he went forward and bent down he picked up a blood-flecked front tooth, so small it could have been a child's.

It was not the image of a child that rushed into his mind, though. He recalled the picture of Barbara Francis in her Paddington flat, dressed for a party and displaying that remarkable smile. He wrapped the tooth in a diary page and put it in his pocket. Then, keeping the torch alight, he systematically searched the carpet on hands and knees but found nothing else.

He left through the same window and sat for a while in his car, wondering whether he should call it a day, or call up help. Bowling would show, would he? Abelard had a terrifying picture of himself tapping the front door in that dinky little porch, spot on time and an even more beautiful target than when he body shielded Tutu. Yes, there was a very rough gun culture in the drugs trade. Ask the police. Right. Julian might have learned it. He knew about guns, anyway. But he might have learned new money – centred uses for them. His colleagues might have known the uses for years.

His mother's onslaught had made him especially jumpy, though. While they were eating she'd said: 'As soon as you joined your dad told me you'd finish up star of a very secret funeral, the only mourners a couple of men with good-school faces and cashmere overcoats. No union jack or sad trumpets.' And probably his dad *had* said something like that. But he had also spent a lot of time telling Abelard that the two of them were as much a part of what he always called 'the current GB' as everyone else, so they might as well look after it. Abelard had come to agree and, here he was, trying to look after it, in a way, but not the way he had expected.

Although he would never have admitted it to his mother, he often felt the kind of division in himself she hinted at. After all, everyone was entitled to an identity crisis. He had known one throughout his life, even at home in the comparative innocence and multi-racial peace of Cardiff dockland more than thirty-five years ago. He was a bit black and a bit white and a bit Welsh and a bit British. So, which was the biggest bit? Possibly the British bit had taken over. He was not sure he liked that.

Over the rhubarb tart and custard his mother had snarled: 'Last night I watched that *In the Heat of the Night* on TV again. Sidney Poitier, slim and gorgeous and clever, flashing his bright police badge, and Rod Steiger, so fat and white and scruffy, working at his gum.'

'Police. Yes, ma?'

'Racialism, all that – in the police. I'm not sure what I'm trying to say.'

'Unlike you.'

'They mess you about. It mucks up your home life. You can't blame Anita for walking out – not altogether. I mean, what are you supposed to be doing, looking for some defector, like in dramas? Only thing, what's any British agent got to defect with? Oh, I know there was another lad from Loudoun Square who went into your kind of job way back and did all right – Stephen Bellecroix.'

'Entirely different department. Not the Outfit.'

'Same sort of work.'

'Maybe.'

'They made a special place for him, to show they could be broadminded, like they made a special place for you later.'

'Me, I'm the only one in the Outfit.'

'But Stephen Bellecroix – that was in the days when this country needed looking after, and was worth looking after.' Abelard could never be sure who did the telepathising: he from his mother, or his mother from him. The message sounded strong, whichever of them launched it first.

In the Pimlico street now an estate car carrying two men passed, driving towards the house. They varied their vehicle? Were these two of the faces last seen in an old Rover? Or perhaps these people hired the old Rover crew. Would they have carried Abelard somewhere to be questioned by these two about Julian Bowling's whereabouts and loot, as if Abelard knew anything about his whereabouts and loot?

For a moment longer Abelard hesitated, then left the Escort. He had decided against summoning aid. The man on the telephone was right: score alone, grab the *gloire*. As his mother had said, this was a trawl for a defector, until lately a prized and admired colleague: one reason for handling the search personally. Defector? A term from history? His mother was right again. Since the Wall came down, where could anyone defect to? And why? And, as his mother had also said, what with? Jules had split – bolted – true, but split with a lot of money, not a lot of injured ideals. He should more simply be described as a thief – the spy who sloped off with the gold. No conscience crisis. Those were no longer the mode. That famous falling away had occurred. Most of the people hunting Julian would be hunting him for the money they considered he had pinched from them, not because he had betrayed his calling. One reason Abelard wanted to get to Jules first was to prove – prove somehow – that what Jules had done was at least in part from principles. Julian Bowling had always possessed one or two of those, hadn't he? Had he? Otherwise, the career really had become meaningless – not just Jules' career but Abelard's, too. Everyone's in the Outfit. The rot had taken over.

At 7.02 he returned to the house and walked up the small front garden to the door. The estate car stood outside. He knocked heavily, an Old Bill greeting designed to soften up. At the back a light burned now. Approaching the house, Abelard had scanned the windows for signs he was under scrutiny, but if so it was someone good. Now, at the door, he kept a fraction of his mind on the house but the bigger part on the road behind: so sweetly easy to sandwich him here. A light came on in the hall and after a second the door was opened. But the middle-aged, large-faced customer who answered was not Julian Bowling, of course. Abelard found himself once more encompassed by that comfortable and comforting West Country voice. 'Wonderful to see you, old son. Do remind me of your name. I can't keep pace sometimes. I'm Paul Matson.'

'Abelard. Bowling about? Or coming?'

'I hope so, Mr Abelard. With Julian it's – well, you know him. One has to cross one's fingers.' He led Abelard into the small room at the back of the house where now a couple of table lamps burned. Another man of about Matson's age was seated in an armchair, better dressed, just as friendly and jovial looking. Had either been in the old Rover? Weren't they both too old? How would Matson look in a homburg? He chortled as he made the introductions. 'Here's a visitor, Richard. Richard Field, Mr Abelard. Rest assured, Mr Abelard, that we both know Julian.'

Beaming, Field stood and shook Abelard's hand with that special warmth people use to show they don't baulk at contact with black skin. 'Please do sit,' Matson said. 'Many's the stimulating hour of talk we've had in this room with Jules and others.'

'It's vital I locate him,' Abelard said.

'It's vital we locate him,' Matson replied.

'They seek him here, they seek him there, that damned elusive globe-trotter and junky's friend.' Field's voice was

surprisingly light and skittish: Oxford Union against
Mevagissy. Some sort of act was under way.

'Is it your house?' Abelard asked. 'Is it Julian's?'

'We're here to tell you to lay off, you know, Abelard,'
Matson said cheerfully from his armchair.

'No, I didn't know,' Abelard said.

'Oh, yes, that's our role.' Matson nodded pleasantly. 'Draw
away now, would you?'

'I've been ordered to find him and bring him back.'

'Like the Mounties,' Field said. 'You're confused, Abelard,
and I don't blame you. This is an opaque situation.' Neat and
square faced he sported plentiful hair which was just beginning to grey and had been tastefully cut in a style meant to
assert life began at forty-six. With an extraordinarily fine navy
three-piece suit, which Abelard's mother would have loved, he
wore red and white trainers, which she would not have.

Matson guffawed for a while in a large Atlantic breakers
way: 'Opaque? Fucking occult, I'd say.' He had on a scruffy
woollen waistcoat, a deeper pink than the furniture, very
loose, very thick in weave, very well able to conceal anything
he might have fused to his shoulder. 'I don't think we can offer
to buy you off, Mr Abelard, but we should at least offer you
something to drink. We have a little ginger wine or limeade. To
me you look like a limeade man.'

'That would be delightfully refreshing,' Abelard said.

'So, you see, Mr Abelard,' Matson said, pouring the stuff and
bringing him a dire little table from a nest of them, 'you see we'd
like you to put Julian Bowling out of your head now. There we
are – all the virtue in the bubbles, they say. I'm going to have one
myself. For you ginger wine, Rick? If you can't find Julian you
can't, Mr Abelard, and those above must not complain, surely.
You've certainly put the time in. All those visits to his haunts and
so on. Are you to blame if you run against a brick wall?'

'How you see yourself?' Abelard asked.

Field smiled, a wryish smile: 'Not us. Circumstances generally.'

'Things aren't too bad, as it happens,' Abelard replied. 'I regard you two boys as progress. Finding this bijou property is progress. I can't back out when doors are beginning to open.'

'Which?' Matson asked.

Field said: 'They hand you the shitty jobs, do they? Tutu. This. It's like them, even though you've given their gang fine loyalty. They probably think they should be canonised for taking on a, well, non-white in the first place.'

'My mother believes the same.'

'The Outfit were very slow on that,' Matson said. 'A long time after Bellecroix, across the quadrangle.'

'We have an interest in Jules just as much as you,' Matson said.

'You've had a damn good look around this place already,' Field said. 'Fucking cheek.'

'Your high-ups – Cadwallader *et al* – probably think it's no end of a juicy jape to put you on the trail of a gilded high flier from a loaded home, such as Jules.' Matson had another big chuckle. 'A kind of police job, really. Except it has to be hidden from the police at this stage at least, because your people don't want the stink. The Outfit is already suffering, isn't it – cuts, cuts and more cuts? Enforced accountability, piss of that sort. On top of all this, do they want one of their people proclaimed a drugs baron? Oh, scarcely, I'd say. So, they get someone like you to do the dragnetting, the cop role.'

Abelard said: 'Not someone *like* me. Me. For Christ's sake, is he still alive? There are people I should notify. He's got parents.'

'Have you met that pair?' Matson asked.

'We don't understand why you're interested in Jules so obsessively,' Field said. 'We understand why you're interested, but not so much. All right, he is, was, one of your guys, and he used his job as cover for the trade. So you're peeved, all of you from Cadwallader down. But can he damage you? Is he stuffed with big secrets? What big secrets, for heaven's sake?'

'My mother says that, too.'

'Can't you leave him to us?' Matson asked. 'It would be so much cleaner. Certainly he's alive. Where do you get these ideas?' He stood up suddenly. 'But excuse me, would you permit Rick and myself to withdraw for a moment and talk in private?' They left the room immediately, closing the door behind them.

For a second, or less, Abelard felt as if he had achieved a victory. Carrying the limeade he crossed the room and poured it into a desk drawer. Perhaps he had these two buggers on the run. Training shoes was what they both needed, not just Field. They talked about Abelard's confusion but might be in a worse state themselves. He changed chairs when he sat down again, so he was to the side of the door, no longer in a straight line of fire And then, almost immediately again, his sense of triumph began to ebb. Jesus, were they still in the house? He could hear nothing but the dripping of the limeade, no sound from beyond the door since they went out. If he had been left here alone, what had he been left *for*? All sorts might imagine he knew more than he did – or knew anything at all – and want him taken out. Were they trying to put right the failure with the old Rover? Very anxious, he looked about. This was the first room he had entered on the earlier visit. It had two windows, both with curtains drawn across now, but he suddenly felt exposed from that direction. They could break the glass, tear the curtains down and there he was, boxed in this little square pink room.

The door opened briskly and Matson returned alone. 'Rick had to go on.' He took Abelard's former chair. 'He thinks you've had contact with others about Julian before you came here. We need every possible lead to him.'

'Julian had a girl, an easy-going girl at the Bête Noire who might know something about what he was up to. Barbara Francis. Also called other things. Has she been brought here to talk?'

'To this house?'

'Upstairs,' Abelard replied.

'Julian owes us. What he's pulled is not decent. But we'll catch up. What we don't need, with respect, is people of your sort in the way, however proper your motives.' His voice kept ample chumminess.

'Which sort?' Abelard asked.

'What we meant by draw away.'

'Fragile,' Abelard replied. 'She wouldn't take a lot of knocking about.'

'Julian's taste! I think I know the piece you mean. Boys from fine families often end like this – dirty business, unimpressive women. I doubt whether she's been here. This is an area of quiet charm.'

'She wouldn't be missed, I suppose, if she disappeared.'

Matson suddenly seemed to revert to an earlier line. 'Know where Julian is? Of course we know. He asked us to meet you, asked Rick and me to plead with you to drop the search. It embarrasses him.'

'You haven't got a fucking clue where he is, have you?' Abelard replied.

'If Rick's right and you've had contact with others about all this we would be ready, *might* be ready, to consider an exchange of info.'

Abelard said: 'This girl died on you too soon?'

'Look, we might be able to arrange for you to talk to Julian, in due course.'

'I considered going back to Paddington and camping on Barbara Francis's door,' Abelard replied.

Matson gave a minute shake of his head. 'It would be as well you recognised you're dependent on us. I admire your confidence, even cockiness. It's not all colour compensation. However, don't underestimate Richard Field.'

'Where is he?' Abelard stood suddenly. Matson got up as well, reaching urgently under the pink cardigan. Maybe it was only for a locket of his grandma's hair but Abelard wondered and hit him full and square in the middle of his genial face: an honest, rich punch and British all the way, none of that karate crap. It had to be like that: this was a Brit mission, about old Brit values, wasn't it? Was it? Matson crashed back into the chair and blood spurted from his top lip and skidded off the upholstery like rain off a brolly.

His fall made a din and now Abelard heard hurried even violent movement from another downstairs room, as if somebody had been alerted or frightened by the sound. Matson was half stunned and his hand dropped away empty from under the thick wool. Abelard made a grab in there and came out with some kind of biggish foreign pistol he did not recognise. It felt nicely heavy, which meant loaded. The whole encounter so far had been a plus, a nice harking back to old routines. Gripping Matson around the neck where he sat, Abelard crouched behind him, the pistol aimed at the door. Blood dripped warm and comforting on his wrist from the broken lip. 'Oh, we're in here, Ricky, boy,' Abelard fluted. Nobody entered. Instead, there was a swift scuttling sound in the hallway and then the street door was pulled open so hurriedly that it must have banged against the wall and Abelard heard a glass panel fall and splinter. Someone ran.

Leaving Matson where he was, Abelard dashed into the hall and stood at the open front door. He saw nobody in the street, but there were a score of driveways where a man could have hidden, and two turnings off. Suddenly, Abelard realised he had already played this hopelessly wrong and hurried back inside, pistol ready. Matson had gone. Specks of blood on the carpet led to a rear door, now swinging in the wind.

Abelard began a genuine search of the house. He learned little from the clothes and possessions he strewed about the floor. Only men seemed to have lived here, despite the maidenly blushes of the décor and furniture. The suits were all pretty good, but no better: Austin Reed reach-me-down. Matson might have worn them, Field never. Pockets had been cleared and told him even less than the ties, tobacco tins, sun glasses and fishing gear in drawers and cupboards. Nothing anywhere bore a name, except Austin Reed's and to start there would be a long, long trail a-winding. Of course, the absence of information said plenty.

In the front bedroom he smashed through a boarded up fireplace, part for the broad joys of vandalism, but also because he had once missed a safe located in a concealed grate. Turkey Latimer swore this ludicrous slip was what held up Abelard's promotion for so long, nothing social or ethnic. He was wearing only suede creepers now and it took him a dozen kicks to mash the board.

There was no safe but, as the fragments of papered-over three-ply flew all ways he suddenly found himself looking once again at his own wedding photograph. He actually groaned with shock and the noise startled him so much that he swung around with Matson's huge pistol ready in his hand. God, was he coming to pieces? The picture had been stuck to the underside of the three-ply: still those two stupidly blissful faces, his and Anita's, with a typewritten sheet fixed alongside. His hand shook from a mixture of rage and dread as he hardened himself to read that cold, know-all biog again. Those shits downstairs had been fooling with him, and he had let them go. He was a trained security services officer. Honestly?

But this profile was not a duplicate. He read quickly:

Simon Abelard, Senior Principal (Personnel), HMISS. Conducting probably official search for J Bowling. Possibly unpurchasable, at all but highest amount. See earlier dossiers.
At least one other apparently authorised security services search for Bowling active. Possibly former colleagues involved with Bowling in trade and seeking to recover hi-jacked profits. Unlikely Abelard aware of this.

He read it three times. 'Possibly unpurchasable, at all but highest amount.' Insolent sods. Insolent accurate sods? 'Unlikely Abelard aware of this.' And how. When Turkey and Cadwallader briefed him about Bowling there had been no mention of a parallel hunt by others from the Outfit. But it was the sort of trick that would come naturally to both. Or, conceivably, they did not know of this extra team, either.

The piece of three-ply he held had been broken off under the last word. Perhaps there was more on another fragment, and he started to go through them carefully. Instead of more about himself, though, he suddenly came upon a picture of Julian with its own blurb. The photograph showed him alone, a carefully posed studio job. He looked very young and charming, dark hair nicely tousled, chin set to signal at least decency and quite possibly honour. His eyes gleamed with hunger for the future and with what could have been mistaken for a wish to serve by those who liked to believe the best.

Abelard read:

Julian Theobald Bowling, age 36, Intelligence recruitment 1989 or 90. From at the latest April 1997 has been expanding trafficker within international syndicate. Government salary as last notified, £37,877. Duties: Liaison Paris, Brussels on mainly Mid East security policy. Syndicate's trade profits estimated at:
1996 $25,400,000
1997 $35,600,000
1998 $43,200,000
1999 $51,000,000+

Bowling absconded with approx. $9,000,000 syndicate profits.
Bi-sexual. Connections with following:
1. Barbara Francis, aka Roxana and Melanie. Shop assistant, hostess, singer. Octoroon. Flat 11, Vassingham Place, Paddington, London. Regular at Bête Noire club, Pitier Street, Hoxton, London.
2. Lucy Mary McIver. Nominally clerk US Embassy, Paris. Likely Intelligence status.
3. Peter Glass/Graff, Paris, address unknown. Bowling has trade and sex connections with.

4. *James J Ovalle, New York, significant trafficker. CIA connections?*

Bowling schizoid (in-patient at least thrice). No recent contact with parents (8b Colm Close, Marble Arch, London). Graduate (languages) Oxford. 7.65 PPK pistol.

Abelard sat on the bed and re-read this several times, too. It baffled him, even though he had known in outline the case against Jules. How many of the world's redundant spies went moonlighting, bored with the unlucrative and footling secrets they were supposed to guard or steal, intent on stout personal gains instead? Was this how the enterprise culture of the 1980s had developed? Were the KGB and the former East Germans part of it, too? Perhaps the ultimate cynicism had taken over. These spies worked not at fooling one another but at concealing from their chiefs in London or Washington or Moscow or Paris or Tel Aviv what was going on in the field. And among these far-flung chiefs were there some who were unconned and who knew very well what was going on? They liked their share of the proceeds, too? No wonder Abelard had come to think of his job as policing.

He felt terrified. He saw crazy elements in this situation. What Abelard's mother often hinted at about his status in the system, remained unpleasantly vivid. Was he mad to think a half black from the ghetto could take on some of the world's most slippery and potent vested interests? When his father told him to look after 'the current GB' did he realise how hairy the job would grow? Did Abelard owe that much to 'the current GB'? Did he care enough? His father believed all things a man might reasonably want could be achieved by steady hard work and a clean nose. A lot of the blacks of that generation had somehow believed the same, despite endless evidence of the opposite. They believed it because the alternative was despair. Steady work was not going to crack this one, though, nor a clean nose. Abelard would need a ton of luck, and luck was something his father certainly did not hold with. Luck meant gambling. He and his friends buckled to their jobs, lay low and hoped their kids would somehow get on and get out. A few like Simon did. And there had been Bellecroix, 'across the quadrangle' from the Outfit. Another former neighbour's lad, Glyndwr Jenkins, also black, younger still, Oxford educated, was apparently doing fine in the police. Yes, but when they did get on and out wasn't it likely people like Abelard, Bellecroix, Jenkins would come to look at things differently, find a new life philosophy? God, he had started to deny his upbringing now.

He made a heap of the bits of three-ply in the grate and put a match to them. It soothed him a little to see the picture of Anita curl and flare. Abelard's dad used to quote a Bible line about sticking to it once you put your hand to the plough. Abelard felt this plough had suddenly acquired a Ferrari engine and might very soon go out of control and dig him into the ground. All the same, he could not junk his father's teaching on duty to the nation without making some fight. From his US student days at Columbia he had a British friend called Charlie Tate. Charlie had stayed and was now a distinguished New York investigative journalist. Perhaps Abelard would ask him to raise discreet inquiries about JJ Ovalle – but with a warning to back off fast at the least trouble. Charlie would have to do instead of Interpol.

3

YES, PERHAPS CHARLIE Tate would do the New York inquiries, and Abelard himself might have to visit Paris later to locate those named acquaintances, Lucy Mary McIver and Peter Glass/Graff, supposing the fireplace archive was accurate. He *had* to suppose the fireplace archive accurate. He didn't have much else. For now, though, he decided he must go back to Barbara Francis's flat over the restaurant at Vassingham Place in Paddington. Last time, he had learned next to nothing there, except that the carpet was thick enough to let someone, or more than one, get up pretty silently behind while he communed with a hamster. Definitely more than one. After all, he had been carried blotto downstairs and stored in the Rover boot. The waiter helped? Another tip? Or was this waiter more than a waiter? Had this waiter been waiting, waiting for Abelard to turn up?

Abelard saw that to return to the flat was another sign he might be moving out from the methods of his original job into something else. No HMISS-trained agent on an Outfit assignment would risk revisiting the spot where he had been discovered, identified and catastrophically defeated. An inculcated flair for secrecy made that unthinkable. If you tumbled into error, the taught priority was to gallop away from it, supposing you could: disappear and reassemble as much as was feasible of that precious, laboriously constructed, painfully fragile anonymity. You were a spy and the first requirement of a spy was cover. *Spies spy until they are spied spying*: possible epigraph for the training manual. If you had endangered your cover or lost it you did not go back, attempting to put things right. You went out of view and stayed out of view until it seemed safe-ish to let your disastrous face sneak into sight again, preferably a long way from the fuck-up location. It was a ruthlessly narrow, expertly defined role. You were hired to protect the State, the State as concept and holy historical idea, and this might be not much to do at all with protecting individual members of the State, such as Barbara Francis, aka Roxana and Melanie, or even Julian Bowling, HMISS. When you worked for HMISS you looked after HM and her nominated causes.

Now, though, Abelard found he felt concern for Barbara Francis, especially after that discovery of the tiny tooth. And after Matson's signal that a return to Vassingham Place was pointless, Abelard felt concern for Julian, too, but this was routine: he had been a team-mate, a colleague, a blood brother, whatever he might be now. It was the wider worry for this woman he did not know which convinced Abelard he had entered a career break: did not know and had never even seen except in a comical photograph. She might be only marginal to the search for Bowling, but this did not matter. He felt an inescapable duty towards her. Perhaps this was too late. All right: if so, he felt an inescapable duty to find out what had happened to her. He knew this would have been so even if she were not a link to Julian Bowling at all. She pre-occupied him on her own account. He had read of detectives growing obsessed with a case, like the original Popeye Doyle of *The French Connection*. Barbara Francis stuck in his consciousness, harried him like toothache.

Toothache. Standing in the doorway of the closed-down shop opposite her flat again, he brought that miniature tooth out of his pocket, unwrapped it from the diary page and had a gaze for thirty seconds or so. *Oh, worthy, all-compassionate Abelard*. He had always possessed an awkward and powerful visual imagination, and for a while he could picture this thin girl getting mashed with tyre levers in that leafy, pleasant bedroom, clobbered back and forth between Matson and Field, both of them in overalls because of the flying mess, and Field with a blue plastic elasticised bath hat on to keep his distinguished hair from getting distinguished by blood flecks and bits of bone. She was dressed, but not in an astronaut's gear. They were asking questions, of course, as she lurched and stumbled and tried to keep her arms up to protect her face. Once she went down near a wall, perhaps banging her mouth and dislodging the tooth. Matson pulled her up again and batted her across the room with his tyre lever to Field. Matson's burr was still homely and warm, Field's tone still all playfulness and *jeunesse dorée*. 'You're bound to know where Jules is, you dear companion, you,' Matson said. 'He's cut you in for how much, you sweet helpmeet, you?' Field asked. Seemed to say, seemed to ask, in Abelard's brain. He stared at the little open package in his palm. *Oh, come on, Abelard, get sane again, right? What are you, the fucking tooth fairy?* He deliberately tipped the diary page and let the tooth slip off and go out of sight among the cans, old take-away curry cartons and trampled newspapers on the ground. Then, immediately, he bent down and rummaged delicately among this timeless rubbish in the dark until he found it again, nestled in phlegm. He picked the tooth out, re-wrapped it carefully and put it back into his pocket. He had felt a kind of guilt when he discarded the thing, as if committing a betrayal. For a second, its slide and fall had seemed to symbolise so much that had slid and declined: Julian Bowling's degeneration, for instance, from guardian of the domain to druggies' pal and thief. *So sensitive, Abelard, so empathic, so soulful, so symbiotic.*

He could make out the same two waiters in the ground floor restaurant. It was an hour earlier than his previous visit and they were still serving the tables. Above, all the lights in Barbara Francis's flat were on again, still repelling burglars, maybe. And then, as he watched, a woman walked across what he thought must be the room where the hamster had its plastic den. Her head and profile appeared in the window briefly. She did not seem to look into the street, appeared unaware of the outside. Not Barbara Francis, Abelard felt almost sure of this. The women was dark like her, but seemed more heavily built than the girl in the picture – more solid in the neck and shoulders – and possibly older, as much as ten years older. Her features could be sharper, the nose forceful and perhaps aquiline.

Abelard left the shop doorway and approached the flat. This time he did not take the service entrance to the restaurant but went around the corner into the main street where he reckoned the front door must be. He found it and a cluster of voice boxes, one marked Francis. He pressed the rectangular call button and a woman answered on the intercom. 'Yes?' It was spoken amiably, almost a welcome. A business operated from the premises, besides the restaurant?

'Barbara Francis?' Abelard asked.

'Not here, I'm afraid. Who seeks?'

'Name of Abelard.'

'She know you?'

'She knows a friend of mine.'

'Barbara knows a lot of people's friends. Which friend?' The voice was half estuarial, half educated, like Bowling's.

'Can I come up?

'Is this someone whose name can't be shouted from a doorstep?'

'Why not?' Abelard replied.

'Can it be?' She seemed about to giggle.

'What?'

'Shouted from a doorstep.'

'Certainly,' Abelard said.

She was silent for a while. So was Abelard. He heard the lock on the mauve front door click. He pushed the door open and walked up carpeted stairs to the first landing and Barbara Francis's place. There had been bulk buying of mauve. Abelard saw the uncovered concrete stairs, which joined the landing on the other side from the passage by the restaurant; the ones he had used last time, and perhaps the ones he was carried down later. The door of the flat opened and the woman smiled and stood back for him to enter. 'From Julian Bowling, I suppose?'

she said, as he passed her. She was almost as tall as Abelard and strongly made, but not burly. She closed the door.

'You don't sound pleased,' Abelard replied. They went into the hamster room, though the hamster was not in sight.

'*Barbara* will probably be pleased – relieved to hear from Jules,' the woman said. ' That's what counts, isn't it?'

'Is it?'

She had on dark trousers and what could be a man's beige striped shirt with open collar. She wore flat-heeled black patent shoes. She had a hate for Bowling?

'Julian can be a worry,' Abelard said.

'Barbara tends to go for men like that when she does.'

'Does what?'

'Goes for men.'

'Where is she?' Abelard replied.

'I think I'd recognise you as from the same sort of career as Julian. I mean, even if I met you in an ordinary social situation, not prowling.'

'How?' Abelard asked. It pleased him and annoyed him: pleased him because the job and the work had been worthwhile; annoyed him because the job was obsolete and he did not want to be stuck with its style.

'The way you stand, perhaps,' she said. 'And then… oh, what – call it a *thoroughness* in what you do, a concentration and intensity. I don't deny he's got those.'

Abelard glanced down at himself. 'How I stand? Feet on the ground?'

'No, I mean when you're in a shop doorway, watching. That patience and casualness, or what seems like casualness. Plus, the cover behaviour – bending and fiddling with the refuse on the floor like a tramp looking for dog ends. It's as good as a one-act play. I think *thoroughness* is right. Julian has that, also. I'm not sure it's good in him, though. Gets mixed up with selfishness. How you see him? What, a message for her from Jules?'

'"Same sort of career?" Which career?' Abelard said.

'Oh, you know, an *official* career. I think it's a wonder to you that Julian in such a job goes for a girl like Barbara. I expect you think of her as dubious? I could understand that. I'm her sister, but I could. Barbara has her uncharted aspects.' Abelard thought the woman would be about thirty-six or seven. Did he have an age for Barbara Francis?

'If he wanted to get a message to her he'd telephone, wouldn't he, not ask someone to call?' Abelard asked.

'It might be... it might be *awkward* for him.'

'Awkward how?'

'To get to a phone,' she said.

'Mobile?'

'If he can use it.'

'How do you mean?' Abelard replied.

'I've had people here, looking for her.'

'Which people?'

'People like you and like him. What I said before, that kind of job.'

'Did you see them in the shop doorway as well?' Abelard replied.

'I come here now and then to clean out the hamster cage and squirt a bit of air freshener.'

'There is a hamster is there?'

'You've been here before, have you?' she replied.

'How many people?'

'Utterly civil, but disbelieving. Your work does that, doesn't it? Appreciative of the furnishings and décor.'

'Well, they're very nice.'

'Who? The people who came? You know them, I expect.'

'No, I meant the furnishings and décor. I like the flower prints. The whole layout. Comfortable and airy. Asking what?' Abelard replied.

'Didn't you know they'd come and were asking? Is this right, now? You're not teasing?'

'Or, better still, describe them.'

'Jules is very autonomous, isn't he? He'll do what he wants.

That's how I see him, anyway. I didn't know whether Barbara would be able to cope with Julian, to be frank. But I wouldn't interfere. What point? I'd only get told to stay out of things.'

'Big Sis.'

'Or, on the other hand, if not in the same work as Julian, I'd have guessed a cop. Of course, the two jobs are close.'

'Why a cop?' Abelard asked.

'Coming with a scenario already prepared. Making things fit.'

'Which?'

'And yet a listener,' she replied. 'It's like talking into a well. You know it's all still down there and can be pulled up in the bucket any time it's wanted.'

' I thought people from the restaurant looked after the flat,' Abelard said.

'On the other hand, Barbara can be very autonomous, too. I'm not suggesting she might get dragged into something without being aware of what was happening. This wouldn't be an innocent bystander situation.'

'Have you looked for her?' Abelard said. 'The club in Hoxton, and so on. She's been gone for a time, has she?'

'Don't kid me a hamster can tell who's looking after it,' she replied. 'Barbara reckoned it knew her. I'd really doubt that.'

'Simon Abelard.' He stood with his hand out to her. He had been seated in one of a pair of armchairs, both in dark blue cloth covers. There was a matching settee. She had the other armchair, opposite him across the carpet, also dark blue and, yes, probably thick enough to muffle footsteps if they were managed carefully. She was near the hamster chambers. She did not stand herself but moved slightly forward in her chair and took his hand.

'Veronica Rombarde.'

'Is that a professional name?'

'Is yours?' She released his hand.

'What exactly is the relationship between your sister and Jules?' he said.

'I'd say you know Barbara's dead,' she replied. Her voice was blank, almost matter-of-fact but she began to weep. She kept her head up, her eyes wide and swimming. Her mouth was open and lop-sided, uncomely.

'You're really her sister?' Abelard asked. He was still standing close to Veronica Rombarde and put his hand gently on her shoulder. He couldn't tell whether she noticed. She continued to weep silently, staring towards one of the framed prints, but probably not seeing it. He took his hand from her shoulder 'Relationship?' she said. 'You're asking did he ever stay here – do more than sleep here? You're asking would there be things of his that you can look through?'

'I'm interested in your sister as well, not just Bowling.' He found he longed for her to believe this. It was more than the Outfit looking after its own. Oh, sure, the Outfit *would* still look after its own, but Abelard could see wider now.

'Or was there something important on the floor?' she replied.

'Where?'

'In the shop doorway. You looked frantic to find it.'

'Important? How could it be important? No, just theatre, as you said. Where were you watching from?'

'Not a lit window.'

'They're *all* lit.'

'Not the one on the landing. When you were here before did you search – drawers and wardrobes and cupboards?'

'Here before?' he replied.

'*Somebody's* been through. Your kind of work – very neat, very careful, but somebody's been through.'

'How do you know?' Abelard asked. 'Stuff taken?'

'Too neat and careful for that. But a damn good rummage. Were you going to come in and have a damn good rummage yourself, if I hadn't been here?'

'I'd be afraid of the hamster,' Abelard said.

'It's dead.'

'What? How?'

'Oh, tragically.'

Abelard drew a couple of fingers across the bars.

She said: 'That cage is in two halves, one on top of the other. Possibly I didn't put it back right after cleaning. It pushed the top bit enough to the side to get out when I wasn't here. I suppose it ran around and then climbed that door curtain, but they're not great climbers, not like a proper rat. Didn't know how to get down. *Hurry on down.* Remember that song at all? Everything is hurrying on down. I found it on the carpet, still alive, but its back broken. Luckily I was able to finish it all right.' She had stopped crying.

'Luckily? How?'

'There are scissors. I washed them off. Barbara would hate to find its blood on the blades, if she were ever going to come back.'

'But the hamster's body?'

'You don't contradict. You don't say, "Of course she will come back."'

'If the animal's body's in a kitchen waste bin she's liable to see it, isn't she?'

'This is a first floor flat.'

'Yes?'

'I mentioned the landing window. Hurry on down.'

'I didn't see it on the pavement.'

'Were you looking for it? The sweeper guys will have removed it.'

'Barbara will be upset about the death?'

'Yes, she would have been. But at least she'd have believed the thing would know it wasn't her with the scissors, wouldn't go into Vassingham Place and the Beyond blaming *her*. Killed how?'

'Well, you said – with the scissors and then thrown out of the window? "Gardez l'eau, and a hamster."'

'I meant Barbara. You can get her phone records? But that's only outgoing.'

'She had a lot of calls?'

'You mean punter calls, don't you?'

'Others.'

'She knew people abroad. People who didn't care about the cost. On at her to get fax and go e-mail. I know she didn't want that. Too much of a commitment. Beck and call situation.'

'Abroad where?'

'The United States.'

'France?'

'Could be France.'

'Paris? Did she know these people through Julian?'

'Ah. I thought you said you were interested in her as her, not just as someone who might point you to wherever Jules is. You people – lots of contacts overseas, obviously, through the job. So easy to use them when you move into something else.'

True, true. 'What something else?'

'Barbara didn't like it very much. She could be fussy on moral matters, law and order matters.'

'That right?' Abelard replied. 'Any organisations involved, that you know of? Say in the States?'

'Organisations? What sort?'

'Well, we're talking about security organisations, aren't we, security organisations that have become perverted?'

'Deep word.'

'That have been turned from their proper job,' Abelard said.

'The only security organisation I've ever heard of in the United States is the CIA.'

'So, the CIA?'

'Barbara Francis involved in perverting the CIA? Wow. You really think so? I think you know more than you're saying. What a stupid remark. Of course you know more than you're saying. You're trained to it.'

'Was she involved with Julian in the business – I mean, as well as being a girlfriend? Accounts? Looking for markets? People wanting her to get fax and get on to e-mail – this sounds as if she was important in the organisation.'

'Organisation again? Which organisation now?' she replied.

'But she didn't go for all that, right? She just wanted Julian to clean up, get some good funds together, and then she and he could split?'

'Barbara was very business conscious.'

'I'm sure. She'd have a lot of contacts, too, wouldn't she?'

'Which contacts? You've got names? America, Paris? Germany?'

'No, no names. Not at this stage. Germany? How come Germany?'

'Oh, I don't know. Don't rely on me. I thought I heard something about Germany. A syndicate involved with a slush fund there, maybe?'

'A political slush fund?' Abelard replied 'Are you saying the drugs syndicate Julian fell into was helping to back a German slush fund? Slush fund for elections? Whose slush fund?'

'Fragments of fragments of gossip, that's all. You've got a list of names, have you? Surely, as her sister, I'm entitled to know them?'

'You certainly would be, if I had any,' Abelard replied. So, hey-fucking-presto, here comes secrecy again, that old, narrow instinct and habit and discipline.

'What I can't make out is whether you *know* she's dead because you've found something, discovered where it happened, or whether you're just assuming it's what the disappearance must mean.'

'Did she ever talk about getting away somewhere, somewhere secret and secure, once he had landed enough money from the syndicate?' Abelard asked.

'Which syndicate? You mean in case Julian has gone there alone?'

'I'm concerned about both.' Leaving, he went down the service stairs to the passage alongside the restaurant. Maybe he would come back yet again for what she had called a rummage, but when she was absent. He didn't want to do it with her looking on. He would not expect to find much. If others had been here, and she had examined things enough afterwards to detect they had been here, what chance? Through the windows, he could see the waiters as they were that first time, dividing tips. The one who had taken him to the flat then seemed to sense he was being watched and glanced up. He appeared shocked to see Abelard. You bet he was. Abelard ought to be dead or at least locked up and possibly defaced. The waiter did not panic, though, or not instantly. He turned back to the split and in a while pocketed his share. Then he went, no rush, into what Abelard supposed would be the kitchen. Another exit through there? Abelard walked out into the street and stood on a corner opposite from which he could watch the front and rear of the restaurant.

After about ten minutes the waiter appeared from a back door. He saw Abelard at once and hesitated, as if considering a return into the restaurant. He must have decided this would only postpone the problem and suddenly started to run up towards Praed Street and Paddington Station. Abelard ran, too. He kept pace with him easily. The weight of coin might be slowing the waiter. Plus, those compulsory, recurrent, Outfit sessions of physical fitness training were bound to grow useful one day. The waiter seemed to be making for the station, perhaps the Tube. Abelard had been trained never to let a quarry get into the Underground system of any country or you were fucked. All those movies about the horrors of trying to tail someone there were spot on. Not far from the entrance, Abelard sprinted a bit harder. He put a hand on the waiter's arm and stopped him. For a few seconds, the man tried to resist.

'I can give you back the £10,' the waiter said. 'Gladly.' He put a hand into his jacket pocket and brought out a crowd of one and twos, showing them in his palm. One coin rolled off but he did not try to pick it up, though it might have been a two. He did not want to take his gaze off Abelard. 'Or more than ten. Yes, not just ten. Fifteen? Like interest, you know.' He tried to giggle.

'Put it away,' Abelard said.

'I must get home, you see.' He still held the money out.

'Yes, to sleep.'

'To sleep, yes.'

'Who hit me? Abelard asked.

'Hit?'

'In the flat, by the hamster.'

'Ah, the little brown rat.'

'Who carried me down the stairs?'

'Carried?'

'When I'd been hit.'

'I don't understand. I have to go.'

'I think it was you who hit me,' Abelard replied.

'No,' he yelled. 'This is not true. No, no.'

'And helped carry me down and shove me into a car boot.'

'No, so not true,' he shouted.

'Are you all right, mate?'

Abelard turned, about to say he was, when he realised the question had not been meant for him. Four beered white lout prowlers in nicely matching football shirts had come up close. Some London club, probably. Abelard knew nothing about soccer, except it spawned simpleton heavies like this. He had better remember the colours. One of them with peroxided hair and pumped up shoulders had spoken to the waiter.

'Fucking blacks think they can mug anyone, anywhere because of that fucking what-you-call report,' he said.

'Macpherson,' one of the others said.

'Yea, that. Scotch git. Listen, black boy, you think you can mug anyone anywhere because that fucking what-you-call report about the Lawrence case says all the fucking blacks are great and only the police are bad. Well, the fucking police *are* bad but that don't make all the fucking blacks great.'

'It's not like that,' Abelard said.

'Who's talking to you, black boy?' Peroxide said. 'How about you, mate. You all right, mate?' he asked the waiter.

'Only I want to go home to sleep.'

'What are you, some wop?' one of the others said. 'Wop but white. Can't have everything. He tell you to bring out all your money, did he, wop? All them coins in your hand? What you do, hit the fucking jackpot on the fruity?'

'So what you still holding him for, black boy?' Peroxide said. 'Didn't you hear him, he wants to go home to sleep.'

'This is an inquiry,' Abelard said.

'What inquiry?'

'An inquiry,' Abelard said.

'Don't tell me you're a bit of black Old Bill. Don't tell me this is some fucking racial equality stuff, you in the Old Bill, I don't believe it. That's a fucking new one for a black mugger that is. That's the best I heard from a black mugger yet. Didn't I say let him go?' He punched down on Abelard's wrist, trying to break the hold. Abelard kept his grip. One of the others punched at the side of his head from behind. Abelard felt his senses slip for a second. He realised he must defend himself here and he could not do it with one hand. He might have been able to do it with one hand and his feet, but he wanted to do it without kicking. This was the new millennium, different work. He let go of the waiter and said, 'Now, you wait.' Immediately, the waiter ran again, the coins clutched in his hand. He still did not recover the dropped one. Abelard turned with his fists up to deal with the slob who had punched his head, that untrained booze-weak blow. The four grouped around Abelard to give a hammering in private, or at least as private as could be managed in a street busy even so late. Not that anyone would intervene.

Of course, Abelard could dispose of soccer toughs full of drink, or not full of drink. He put one on the floor and smashed the nose of another who yelped and then stood sobbing with two hands up to his face and a cascade of blood flowing to the ground and down the sleeves of his mindless soccer shirt. Abelard kept it to fists, as he'd promised himself, an absolute ban on footwork. The remaining two, unhurt but gutless, hung back, offered no obstruction when Abelard turned away and ran after the waiter.

Abelard did choose the Underground, and in the Underground chose the Circle line going east. No reason, but why not? Why not? – because he found an empty platform and could not see the man he wanted in the crowd on the opposite platform, either. He tried all the other platforms, but no waiter. The knuckles of his left hand were bleeding and he thought there might be a swelling on his temple from that head blow. People backed off from him. They could not know he had fought a fight that was clean and virtually noble, Rorke's Drift with the colours reversed. To many of these Tube travellers, he was a marauding, big black bloke who looked as though he had seen some action and could want more.

He thought the waiter might be off work for a while sick. Stress.

4

'WE ALL FEEL you could be happy here, Mrs Abelard,' Cadwallader declared. 'Simon especially thinks that, and we don't want him fretting about you, do we? He has to go away for a while and he's understandably very concerned that his mother should be comfortable and so on, aren't you, Simon?'

'What's that mean – "and so on"?' she replied.

'Comfortable. Relaxed.'

'Safe?' she said.

'Secure, yes.' Cadwallader began to show her again how to operate the front door intercom.

She spoke into the system. 'Who dat down der? And then he replies, "Who dat up der saying who dat down der?"'

'A jazz number, yes? Louis Armstrong?' Turkey Latimer laughed with true generosity. 'Grand to see you make a joke of things, Mrs Abelard.'

'People make jokes about things when they are scared of the things, Mr Latimer. Which things, anyway?'

'I mean in general,' Latimer replied, no longer laughing.

'"Things" means I'm in peril because Simon is?'

'"Peril." Such a charged word, don't you think?' Latimer replied.

'Who's going to charge me?'

'Here's a nice view over the garden,' Cadwallader said.

'Looking a bit bleak now, but things will soon start to buck up with the sunshine.'

'So how long will I be here, sunshine?' she said.

'It's for the best, ma. I've had to move my office as well. Elementary precautions when addresses get known.'

'Don't most people want their office address known? How else to do business?' his mother said. 'Harley Street doctors.

They *like* people to know the address. Think of 10 Downing Street.'

Latimer took her to see the rest of the new flat. Cadwallader, short, slight, almost spectral, smiled at Abelard. His power was big and possibly growing, or slipping. He was at a level where he might be asked to draft a policy paper on the future role of the Outfit now people had come to accept the Cold War was gone: it had only taken almost a decade. In any such projection Cadwallader would certainly include a place for himself. It might work. Or, he could be on his swan song task. 'Wonderful woman, your mother. No fooling her.'

'What's it mean, that ply-wood dossier I told you about: a second official team looking for Jules? I'd find that damned objectionable – back to *A Small Town In Germany* – our departments working against one another.'

'You take after your mother, Simon, and why not? "What does this mean, what that?" Admirable thirst for precision. Second team? Search me. I don't know anything about it and nor does Turkey. Do I expect you to believe this? Please believe it. This is colleague speaking to colleague. Oh, shit, that does make it sound like stinking lies and fobbing off, doesn't it? But, these people with their secrets in carrier bags and fireplaces, could be guessing, couldn't they? They're just drugs runners stalking stolen loot. They're organised, sure, do their little bits of research, and possibly pinch bits of ours, of course. But they can make mistakes.' Cadwallader was a bowling-green nut and had his club blazer on and grey flannels. He came originally from south-west Wales and spoke the lingo. Not only urban Welsh blacks could do well in the new enlightened Intelligence *apparat*, Welsh Welsh as well. He had come on a more usual type of route than Abelard: Llandovery College, Cambridge, Harvard and Bologna. 'Turkey suggested you were the man for the job, and probably would not object to what is, let's admit, a kind of policing aspect to this task. I agreed. No more to it than that, Simon. It's below your rank, admittedly, but if you want to do it, fine.'

'Yes, I want to do it,' Abelard said, 'though I know fuck all about drugs and trafficking.'

'None of us knows about them, Simon. From our point of view, Julian Bowling is simply AWOL, a defector, and even in these relaxed times we don't let our people wander off without trying to bring them back. If we did we might as well pack up. It would be an admission our work is nothing. You really can't believe that, Simon, can you? Can you?' He sounded desperate for a bit of comforting, not like Cadwallader. Or perhaps it was like Cadwallader when Cadwallader emerged now and then from his Little Big Man act.

'Going away where?' Mrs Abelard asked, coming back into the room with Latimer. She sat down in a big armchair, stretching her legs.

'I can tell you're going to love it here,' Verdun Cadwallader replied. 'Could I show you one other thing? On the phone here, if you press this key you go straight through to my office, no operators and no exchange. There's someone to answer twenty-four hours a day. We can get here swiftly.'

'What's called a panic button?' Mrs Abelard asked.

Turkey Latimer raised another laugh. 'You'd never panic, Mrs Abelard.'

'I'm near it right now.'

Cadwallader said: 'But Simon's not going away immediately, of course.'

'Going away where?'

'Oh, no,' Cadwallader replied. 'Simon, in his new position, liaises direct for us with Her Majesty's brightly fresh government on many aspects. He has an agenda which will keep him in this country for a while, certainly. Important meetings very imminent.'

Abelard knew of none but tried to look as if he did.

'When you say "for us" who's "us"?' Mrs Abelard asked.

'He's a son to be really proud of,' Cadwallader replied, 'if I may say, without, I hope, being patronising. I expect you little thought when Simon was small that he would be in one-to-one touch with a Minister of the Crown, if not more than one. And yet, why shouldn't you?'

'My God, are these some of those big mouth people who keep diaries, like that Benn and Alan Clark?' she said. 'They'll put Simon in the public domain?'

'Simon has been chosen for this liaison work because of his known presentation skills,' Cadwallader replied.

'You mean these Ministers of the Crown will give him and your outfit an easy time because he's half black and they're scared of being tough on Simon, in case they look racist?' Mrs Abelard asked.

*

In Cadwallader's office later in the day he said: 'The Foreign Office – Ministers and functionaries – have begun to ask for any pointers we have to Monsieur Jospin's even more brightly fresh French government's stance on Mid-East things, Simon, to augment their diplomatic soundings. It's not clear whom you're to see in the FO, but you're to see one of them. Probably not Robin himself, he's hopping about the world, trying his sturdy little legs, but it will be somebody unnegligible.'

'And I'll tell her/him, shall I, Verdun, that we're a bit short of stuff because our best boy on such matters has lately gone into trade?'

'You'd think one Labour government – ours – would be happy to see another one in place, wouldn't you? But they're fretful about the Communist grouping behind Jospin. More fretful, I swear, than the Tories would have been. The old terror, Simon. Even these days, Pink is always scared by the sight of outright Red because Red looks like what Pink was meant to be but couldn't make it.'

Cadwallader had a double room suite furnished in cheery light oak, part office, part conference area, with a vast wall safe in the office section big enough for a bank. Or, as Verdun said now and then, big enough to take a folded body. Perhaps in the era of the new openness the safe was preposterous. It might be history, like the Wall. So far, though, nobody had tried to demolish it. Maybe the whole building would collapse if they did. Cadwallader said: 'My guess is they'll get young Beal to interview you, number four or five over there, but with a bit of expertise on security, so we're told. Nice lad. Rampantly Blairish. My own MP, as a matter of fact.'

'I stall him?'

'We want a disclosable reason for your going to Paris. It's a part of the new openness, Simon, that details of such trips must be available for scrutiny. As you know, I've always been hugely in favour of openness.'

'Yes?'

'Oh, hugely. A policing function would not be disclosable. Get your briefing from Beal and I can sign your travel warrant. Only then. As a matter of fact, Julian did file some general forecast material a while back on what was likely to happen in the French elections and the possible Communist gains. This was not long before he went. Sharp, remarkably accurate speculation. Profiles of most of the Reds, with details of their links. Jules's got some good sources. He's a sound operator. Was. You can use some of this material on Beal, enhanced and updated a bit. He'll probably buy it. Of course, conceivably whispers about Jules have reached the FO. I don't think leaks would come from the Outfit, but if I ever find they have I'll fry the sod who did it.'

'It might have been done as a contribution to the new openness.'

'I'll fry him and possibly his wife and children. Then you say to Beal that our devoted man, Jules, is into ticklish follow-up inquiries at present and we do not want to pressure him. When I say Beal's got a bit of security insight I mean a bit. A *Teach Yourself Espionage* paperback. He won't understand yet about how these things work – what kind of pace he should expect from us, what hindrances and metallic risk an agent in Paris on Mid-East affairs might run into. Well, you needn't invent the risks. Paris, an Open City for hit men. With luck and no leaks, Beal won't give you a hard time. He's always been noisy against race prejudice and hot for non-discrimination in employment. You'll be right up his street.'

'As my mother said.'

'A fine woman. A pillar for you. Yes, charm him, stall him. Charm you're high on. I'm always conscious of it.' He gave a small, unprepossessing Carmarthenshire smile and held it for a time. This had probably pulled people in Llanelli. 'As a matter of fact, Simon, I do wonder sometimes whether this undoubted rapport that exists between us indicates something more than a mere work closeness and I'd like to—'

'If I can stall him, that's all it will be. We're going to have to find Julian and bring him back damn fast.'

The smile dropped into some Celtic pit. Wearily, Cadwallader said: 'Indeed, yes. See Beal and afterwards get deeper into Julian's connections. Not just women. The women are always a start. You've done well with the tooth and the hamster and Barbara Francis's sister. But wider material? His Oxford days? Some don might have taken him on a reading holiday in France. Perhaps there are places Julian would have a sentimental attraction to and use as a bolt hole. Experiences at that age can stick and endow spots with what seem special, protective qualities. We do urgently need some geography, Simon, and a return of our wanderer. It wouldn't do us any good at all to have it known that a frontline lad has slipped into trafficking. Some folk think the changes in the security services – the relaxations and disclosures – are all very fine, as one does oneself, obviously, but there are those who allege they are still not enough. Critics could use the case of Julian Bowling against us. There might be more troublesome questions about what we cost. Some would like to chop us even lower. Some would like to see a woman at the top here – at the Outfit, as well as overall. Where's your future then?' He frowned. 'But you'll despise me for appealing to your selfishness. All right, where is my future then? My grandfather survived the battle of Verdun in 1916. My father was named after it, and he passed the name on to me. I would have passed it on to a son of mine had I been into all that. We are a family who look after ourselves.' He did a little strut about his enormous room, less than ten stone of him, still in his bowls blazer, tinily formidable, stuntedly ruthless.

'I don't know much about my grandfather,' Abelard replied. 'A mahogany plantation slave in the West Indies.'

'Oh, God, really? This is great. Give Beal plenty of that. You'll have him weeping and beautifully ethical and pliable. Mow that corn, gnaw that tree. It's Roots all over. He might persuade Blair to do a mahogany apology after the one he's going to make to the Spanish for British bad weather hitting the Armada.'

5

BEAL SAID: 'I suppose that in a sense spying has in fact become not much more than an extension of normal diplomatic activity these palmy 1997 days. And since diplomacy is for most of the time only an extension of international commerce, espionage skills are now not far off salesman's skills.'

No, crook skills, police skills. But Abelard only thought this. He did not fancy an identity discussion with Beal. 'I hadn't ever considered things that way,' he said, with a good smile and comfortable nod.

'Oh, you'll say something other than – and more than – salesman's skills are needed for keeping an eye on Sadam or Arafat or the IRA and one could hardly argue. Or Loyalists, of course. Or Tel Aviv. There's still nitty-gritty around for you boys and girls, I expect.'

'So much, Minister, that there are strict demarcation rules about who handles nitty and who gritty.' He was here to charm this jerk, but not charm him non-stop.

'The politician can allow himself the luxury of a generalisation now and then, though,' Beal replied. 'Don't confuse me with the facts, as it were! On the other hand, Simon, the broad sweep approach is possibly more than an indulgence: is sometimes very necessary, when it comes to formulating policy. One has to have a *direction*, and that direction will be chosen with reference to the largest and most patent landmarks. When Aneurin Bevan was creating the Health Service, medics of the day tried to obstruct him with all kinds of very powerful argument on detail, but Bevan sailed on. He had set himself a course. He did not know exactly how he would reach his destination but he had a destination and was not to be diverted.

Any Minister, no matter how lowly, can learn from this.'

Bevan? God, a history seminar? 'We'll have full material on the Paris changes very soon,' Abelard replied. 'And we hope this information will take matters at least a little beyond what could be achieved by standard diplomatic methods.'

'Please!' Beal said, holding up one hand in a kind of half surrender and coming on with a mild chuckle. 'No need for a defence. You must allow me to tease a little! I think you could say it's my way. Yes, my way. You and yours will never be undervalued by this Department and its new leadership. I know Robin hugely admires the work you people handle, as do we all.' He was lean faced, thin bodied, tall, dark quiffed, unnaturally lively about the eyes, like the hamster at Barbara Francis's place on that first visit, or a gospel preacher. Hustings he would probably be damn good at, but a bit unnerving on close-up TV. His voice was undiffident and nearly merry, his accent streety and touched by Newcastle. He had had coaching. The suit could have come from the same pretty shop as Blair's. 'I glanced at the list and see that your laddy in Paris is a Julian Bowling,' he said.

'We're fortunate to have someone of that calibre in post at a time of what might otherwise have been rather disorientating *bouleversements*.'

'Without drawing you into the politics of the matter, I have to say, of course, that we welcome the Jospin victory. In general.' He lightly knuckled a file on his desk, glanced down at it, and did some lean wryness with his face. 'I imagine that a few years ago, before we moved into sensible openness, I might not have been permitted, at my level, even to see this schedule of agents. *For Your Eyes Only* would not have meant mine. A Foreign Office Minister and yet excluded from key knowledge about this country's activities abroad! Desperate.' He backhand-stroked the file again. 'Bowling may be said to have come up on what used to be called "the golden road" to the security services. Public school, Oxford.'

'Did he?' Abelard replied. The sudden move into character

discussion of Julian and his background: did it mean Beal really had been leaked something and was coming at it slowly, obliquely? This meeting was supposed to be about France and the French, wasn't it?

Beal's voice boomed: 'Entirely acceptable – don't get me wrong, Simon. How could it not be? Tony's the same, for heaven's sake. Indeed, I am myself, but not Oxford – the other place. You yourself climbed an alternative rope, and that's fine, too. Manchester University's fine. Its own totally decent traditions. Anthony Burgess. And a true public school – public. What this government is about. Across class. It speaks for everyone. Bowling's people pretty loaded?'

'I've never met them.'

'I've nothing beyond the dossier, but I thought I smelled money.'

'His pricey education?'

'And mine, you mean? And Tony's? Fair enough. But really heavy money in their case. Place near Marble Arch. Houses abroad. Dad's companies where he seems to be virtually sole owner.'

'Julian didn't speak much of them.'

'The rich can be like that, the sly, garnering fuckers. But I imagine you're trained not to talk much about your backgrounds at all, of whatever nature.'

'Yes, mine's a bit whatever,' Abelard replied.

'All that question of upbringing rot. We'll make it irrelevant.'

'Great.'

Beal said: 'I do look at someone like Julian Bowling and wonder what it was, is, that brought him into this kind of work. He's used to wealth at home, so the salary must look derisory. He's thirty-six years old and still earning only £37,877. Do I remember these things right?'

'About that.'

'You see, I can do detail, when it's important.' He struck himself a minor congratulatory blow on his narrow chest.

Abelard had become uneasy and made sure he sat as though pleasantly relaxed and kept his face as though pleasantly relaxed. He said: 'Verdun Cadwallader regards Julian as a natural. "Built for the espionage game as the Globetrotters are for basketball," he said. That might be why Julian joined.'

'A vocation? Certainly it might be so,' Beal said. 'And there's a well-known tradition for the sons of rich upper crust families to go into the army or navy for a spell. Well, Prince Andrew. So, why not the security services?'

'It's worthwhile work. I think that more than anything would appeal to Julian.'

'Yes,' Beal replied. 'I'm sure. I'm sure. This must have been true when the safety of the country seemed menaced by potential enemies. One does wonder now, though, whether the career can still keep a hold on people like Bowling.' He was on a black leather settee, not behind his desk, and leaned back now, eyes closed, before speaking again. 'One does hear—'

'It's still worthwhile,' Abelard replied. Oh, God, why had he done that, trampled whatever it was Beal might have said? Wasn't it important to know what Beal had heard? It was important, but Abelard found he could not bear to have this jaunty piece of politics begin talking Julian down, especially if when talking him down he was talking the truth, as he probably would be. Abelard knew this was lunatic squeamishness, daft loyalty. Julian, the gilded sod, was a villain, wasn't he, and Abelard had the cop job of proving it? Wasn't it mad to guard the link with Jules as though it were still holy? Of course it was mad and not just mad but passé. Yet it was trained into him and it hung on, especially when the option was to let a ponce like Beal spill his rumour tray and invite Abelard to contribute to it. 'Still many compulsive aspects of our work. There are the areas you mentioned. The Middle East is no less challenging than it ever was. Julian yearned for stability there, yearned, and wished to help. He knew a lot about T E Lawrence.'

Beal leaned forward over the desk towards Abelard, eyes really working. It was a small but pleasant room and Abelard once more thought of the hamster shut up in its smart cage before the break-out and multi-stage death. 'You are in touch with him all right, are you?' Beal replied.

'Julian? As I explained, we're into security silence for the moment. You'll know this is an entirely standard drill, Minister, when an operation becomes a little sensitive. He would prefer not to be contacted at this stage. We wait for him to call.'

'Sensitive how?'

'Julian is skilled and careful, but he has to try to open a few potentially dangerous doors. All kinds of difficult groups have their headquarters in Paris. You'll appreciate that I, too, must be careful, even with you.' *Especially with you, you supremely gifted, high flying bag of shit.*

'Oh, absolutely. This could be a good man's life. How long would you say this silence will be necessary?'

'Our conversation might truly be straying into operational regions now, Minister. Even in the age of openness, you'll appreciate there have to be borderlines.'

Watching him with what Abelard had arranged to be exceptionally friendly eyes, he could see that Beal was minded to say, but only minded: 'You're shielding this degenerate, you slimy black thug.'

'Oh, inevitably,' Beal replied.

'I know Verdun Cadwallader is very aware of your need for updating as a matter of priority.'

'Is Verdun another one?' Beal replied.

'Another what?'

'AC/DC?'

'Another?'

'Like Bowling. Not that this is in the least material. I've always wondered about people who play bowls. All that bending, you know. Beryl Cook got it, didn't she – the picture of one lady bowler with her finger up the other lady's arse?'

'I might get over to Paris myself, to see if Julian needs any back-up,' Abelard replied.

'That's the purpose of this fucking visit, is it?' Beal said. 'Clear it without actually saying what it's about. Any come-back and the meeting's there in my log.'

'Minister, I understood the meeting was called by the Foreign Office. I've been sent in response.'

'And told to make what you can of it. Although we've demystified you people, we're still conscious you have to be kept an eye on.'

'We might be asking too much of Julian on his own. Quite often two people on something can produce much more than twice the results, as you know,' Abelard replied. 'In government, for instance, it's Alastair Campbell *plus* Tony Blair, isn't it?'

6

HE WAS STAYING in something a fraction up from a flop-
house in a rough part of Montmartre, not far from the *Folies*:
like grimmest bits of old style Soho and then more, the streets
full of young gangs looking for antics, and police about in
threesomes, stiff with boredom and guns. After a couple of
working visits Abelard knew Paris inside out and liked it. He
had the language pretty well and on the whole the people were
all right about colour: they despised all non-French equally,
white or black. He liked their indifference, though he realised
this might be only a Paris characteristic, a capital city characteristic, not much different from the way of people in London
or Rome or New York. They did not want to know. He
approved of folk who did not want to know. They were safe.
He was someone who *did* want to know, was paid to want to
know and drilled in the ways of finding out what he wanted to
know. He was aware of what a scheming, ruthless sod this
wish and determination could turn you into; had turned him
into. It comforted him to be among people who did not seem
to share the same drive, though, of course, some of them here
did. As Cadwallader had said, Paris, Open City, for hit men.

French grub had made him upchuck a couple of times naturally, and probably would this visit. But food anywhere could
make him do that these days. If you were a sensitive little thing
you were a sensitive little thing. Since the divorce his digestion
had grown fallible: it was not that he missed Anita's cooking,
but he still missed *her*, even thirteen years after. Turkey maintained that not getting your end away often enough could jinx
the gut: something to do with spare fluids coursing. Abelard
supposed he did not get his end away often enough. His
mother also worried about this, although she would word

things differently and speak only about the absence from his life of female companionship of his own age, or younger. That was fair enough, though Abelard was not sure how she would take it if he brought a girl home as a permanency, to share the flat with him and her. Girls had stayed with him now and then for short spells – days, not weeks – and his mother behaved all right. But he had the idea she knew things were only going to be very temporary. He might think about something long term any time now. Perhaps when this dismal problem with Jules was over.

Tonight, Abelard did eat the hotel dinner, to prove he could. Then he left on the Métro for the northern suburb of La Courneuve. The research trip suggested by Verdun Cadwallader into Julian's undergraduate days at Oxford had produced two Paris addresses. Abelard had found the Careers don who first recommended to someone in the Outfit that a student called Julian Bowling might have the due qualities. That's how things were done in those days. The Careers don had made up his mind by watching Julian's Oxford life over his first couple of years and by reading a poem Bowling had written in a college magazine. 'A poem?' Abelard had said. 'You turned him into a spy on the basis of a poem?'

'Not only because of the poem, obviously. The poem was a summation, in my view.'

'I don't do poems,' Abelard replied. 'I wonder how whoever picked me did it?'

The don had kept a copy of Julian's work and brought it out for Abelard. It was called *Going Straight*.

I wear head-waiter's tails by choice:
these orderly, lickspittle years.
Then, mornings, I take breakfast late
and read the *Mail*. Last night came lordly
praise and unextravagant
aggrandisement, in cash and hand to hand;
'Oh, thank you, sir.'

Indigo dreams defoliate
my afternoons: those mid-life blooms
of fright and safety first slide off.
Pub lunchtime lager works the trick,
plus snorts of anything at home;
a gorgeous, through-blue coma until five,
then think of work.

'No other *maître-d* takes care
of us as well as you, Jerome.'
'Oh, thank you, sir.' Their folded, unmissed
tens and twenties glide my way.
This crew have mansions which ten years ago
I'd raid and strip with tact when they dined out,
no bulky stuff.

I wear head-waiter's tails by choice:
my rectified, lickspittle times.
Tomorrow, sleeping prim till noon
I'll dream-do crimes. Tonight come lofty
praise and unextravagant
aggrandisement: we're stung for tax on tips;
'Oh, thank you, sir.'

'It showed me he could move into other identities, you see,'
the Careers expert said. 'What a spy does. Julian could write
like a crook and like a reformed crook and a reformed crook
who might slip back.'
    'That's shrewd.'
    'Is it? *Has* he slipped back?'
    'Back?' Abelard replied. 'Was he a crook before? Did you
believe the poem?'
    'Why are you here? Did I make a mistake with him?'
    'He got through all the selection boards.'
    'Did I make a mistake? Are you the sort of police?'
    'Police?'
    'You have that air.'

Abelard found to his astonishment that this almost pleased him. 'It's the width of my cutaway collar.'

The don looked back at the poem. 'I saw a fine amorality, a wonderfully adjustable identity. I thought, This man is a born spy. I can still remember that. Why should fucking Cambridge produce all the people with those qualities?'

And, as literary criticism went, Abelard would admit it was not a bad sketch of Julian. The Careers don put him on to a French lecturer who had taught Bowling and who had made one trip to Paris with him, though probably not for the kind of reading week Verdun mentioned. She talked easily about the past, seemed still to take pleasure in the visit with Jules. They had done some 'mildly recreational' drugging there and the lecturer could offer two addresses where stuff used to be to hand. 'No real secret about it. They were known, tolerated. Probably are now,' she said. She had been back to both spots several times since Julian disappeared from Oxford and her life – one visit quite recent – and this kind of genial trade still went on. One was a print works in the suburb, La Courneuve, from where a talented dealer and graphics expert used to function in dual roles. The other was a café. Possibly Verdun was right and one or both of these places would have a sentimental pull for Julian now, maybe a business pull. Everyone liked familiar ground. Verdun was certainly right on that.

At La Courneuve the works looked closed for the day. Or he hoped it was only for the day. Perhaps the place had been shut down. The structure seemed in reasonable shape but it stood on the edge of a half-abandoned industrial estate, and for a while he waited near the perimeter wall of what had once been the parking space of a big neighbouring factory and watched the print works. La Courneuve was seriously short of glamour and rated no mention in the *Welcome to Paris* brochure dished out on the plane. Near him, infinitely aged graffiti, political posters and some tattered old film bills showed now and then in the lights of a car: *Sharon, Begin, Assez de Sang... Dressé Pour Tué avec Angie Dickinson...*

Fête de l'Humanité... Usine Occupée, only no longer occupée by striking workers but falling to pieces. Wasn't there once a French economic miracle? Perhaps if the print works still functioned as a distribution post, Julian would be drawn back here, possibly as a dealer himself now, not a punter? Had he cornered some stuff, as well as the money?

The faded name over the works was Chandon. Possibly he had switched careers decades ago, centuries ago, and gone to make a fortune with Möet. It was a chilling, utterly silent place, a dark puzzle, which almost persuaded Abelard to do nothing now and come back in the light. But bugger that: he could not face the idea of trekking to La Courneuve again, night or day. He found a way to the rear of the premises, walking on rubble. He tried a yard door which to his astonishment opened – not like the French. Perhaps, after all, this building had been abandoned, too. The place looked dead, and dead for a while. He saw no lights inside and heard nothing except a window or door flapping somewhere. Eventually he made for this noise and found a disintegrating door hanging on one hinge and dragging forward and back now and then in the wind. For a few moments he stood and did a bit of a survey. The French lecturer had not said exactly how long it was since she last came here. There were what seemed to be several rows of tall machines under sacking. As printing equipment they would have been obsolete for an age, perhaps even when Julian first came here. Yet although the place appeared unused Abelard no longer thought it had been abandoned: the floor looked recently swept. The building still had a role. Snorthead revisited. He felt like a crude intruder, poking into bits of Jules's almost innocent, undergrad., pre-HMISS days. *So, crudely intrude, Simon. He might need you. And, even if he doesn't, you and the Outfit need him: need him helpless in a net.*

Abelard took a few steps inside and half crouched, listening and trying to locate stairs. If trafficking continued it would be on the upper storey. He could still not make out any lights inside, so presumably no business was under way now. All the same, he would look around. He edged forward a couple of yards and then paused for a moment, listening again. Abelard was unarmed, another fruit of Cadwallader's contempt for bureaucracy. Verdun refused to bother himself with the formalities needed for getting his people through Heathrow's screening tooled up. Laziness: Cadwallader would not wilfully put a man or woman at risk, Abelard felt sure of that, not even when $9,000,000 might be involved, or even especially when $9,000,000 might be involved. Cadwallader seemed to despise money. He spent next to nothing; his only excess, green fees at the bowls club. As to clothes, Heavy Neville reckoned Verdun bought some of his at Oxfam – the children's section. Cadwallader's abiding fault was not greed but destructive impatience with all administrative rules and procedures. He regarded these with a classy disdain, not bad for a jumped-up south-west Walian, even one with his education, but now and then impractical. Abelard had considered looking around for one of these new plastic handguns which went undetected on the screens but which would do the job. They were not in the Outfit yet, as far as he knew, and it might have taken him a long while to locate one in the free market. But not bloody free, anyway.

From the upper floor Abelard thought then he heard a small sound repeated twice, like someone shifting position very carefully. Christ, where were the stairs? He could be suddenly confronted by someone coming down, and worse than confronted: if he moved away from the wall he might be surprised from behind. He knew how to get surprised from behind, didn't he? All the same, he did go forward a few more yards, eyes straining in the poor light, ears straining, too. He stopped abruptly. As he passed the first of the shrouded machines he saw behind it one of the sack coverings on the ground and even in the dark realised at once that this sacking shrouded a body. Such strange delicacy.

He approached slowly, his eyes everywhere, and gently

pulled the material away. It was a man, on his back, about thirty, burly, fair-haired, well-dressed, probably English, not Jules. Beneath the back of the head the floor was stained and although he could not be sure of the colour he felt it had to be blood. The face was the sort of face Abelard thought he should recognise, not because it was dead and in an evil setting, but because the neat, assertive features were the kind he was used to seeing around the corridors at work, or in the quadrangle outside, on top of capable shoulders and at least reasonably fit looking lower bodies.

He had begun to search the man's pockets when he heard the kind of sounds that came from upstairs earlier. This time they were closer, and he stared to his left, trying to penetrate the darkness. He thought he saw movement fifty metres away, a man using the machines as a shield and slipping between them quickly, seemingly on his way towards the wrecked door where Abelard had come in. Still straddling the body he yelled: 'Julian. Stop, will you? It's Simon.'

Calling the name was a gamble, nothing more. The physique looked just about right, and maybe the age. The man took no notice, anyway, and in a moment was dashing towards the door. Christ, it was like Harry Lime in *The Third Man*. This man went out of sight. Abelard hesitated a few moments, wondering whether he should stay with the body and discover what he could from it, as he should have stuck with Matson in that Pimlico house. But Bowling was the target, and this corpse could not leg it like Matson. Abelard ran for the exit himself, reaching it just as the yard outer door swung shut after whoever it was. Abelard covered the yard at a sprint and emerged into the street, but saw no running figure ahead. There were three directions to choose from. He picked the one which looked as if it must eventually come to a main road and kept going.

He had it wrong, again. The streets grew darker, more miserable, meaner than mean, but with dogs that barked as if they guarded a fortune; so French. What would Bowling be doing in such a thumbs-down area, if it was Bowling? This boy had cornered $9,000,000, plus, perhaps, a ton of substance. Why waste his time and risk himself in Merdesville? Abelard slowed then stopped. Had he fucked up his second good chance? He must get back to the man in the machine room and find what he could.

In one of the narrowest streets a car passed him, a barge like Peugeot estate, made for the unreconstructed, expanding Catholic family and all their camping gear and patent medicines. It pulled up not far ahead. There seemed only one person in it, a fat, elderly, very manageable grey-haired man. Abelard tensed just the same. What was someone's old uncle Pierre doing cruising here so late? Cruising? For what, whom in this spot? Why had the car stopped? Nobody left it and there were no traffic lights. Abelard had been hurrying back to chez Chandon, but now dropped his pace. He felt hemmed in. Except for this driver the street was deserted. To avoid passing close to his door, Abelard moved out and walked in the middle of the road. Would this be his first chance ever to call for help in French? Which of the sods in these little dark, dank fortresses would take any notice?

Just before he reached the car and when his attention was entirely on it he became aware suddenly and too late of someone walking behind him. Two sharp, generally painful thoughts came to him and he almost cried the first of them aloud: *I'm sole supporter of a dear old mother, a white mother, and acting not so much as an agent, but in a police capacity here.*

Of course the second was that this whole thing felt like a replay. Hadn't he been felled before from behind, finishing in the Rover boot? Yes, he was getting used to being taken from behind, as it were. Spinning around he raised his fists, all he had to raise because of Verdun Cadwallader and his Carmarthenshire grandeur. Something cracked against the side of his head, half stunning him, but only half, and he was able to see the face and build of a man too old to be Bowling and glimpse the butt of a pistol that looked like a British standard issue .38, not a PPK. Then came the second blow from a different direction altogether, and he was aware of his mind packing to leave him and of the darkness growing darker. He did get his lips around 'Au secours' but it seemed to come out sounding like 'You sucker' and could have been meant for himself.

7

HE CAME TO seated in what felt like a big and good leather armchair, head back, mouth hanging open, his brain for the moment slow and clouded, neither an Outfit brain nor a police brain. This chair – it could be the sort they had in decent London clubs. He knew because he had been taken to lunch once or twice in White's by Turkey Latimer. Inviting a black to White's was Turkey's kind of joke. But London? Had Abelard been freighted back unconscious?

There was a real moment of terror: he opened his eyes and could see nothing except a hopelessly faint blur of blue tinged light. Christ, the head blows had done for his sight. He almost cried out again. Then he grew aware that his wrists were hand-cuffed in front of him. A second later he realised that a blue cloth bag was over his head. Cigarette smoke reached his nose, so he still had smell as well as sight. He closed his mouth but otherwise stayed motionless. He wanted a bit more time for guesswork. His head hurt badly, a deep, interior pain spreading down his neck and touching his shoulders. The rest of him seemed intact and he felt certain he would be able to stand and walk, if they let him. The bag was only loosely laced at his neck and despite the cuffs he could have pulled it off. But he remained still. The longer he looked helpless the longer he would be safe. Brain, after all, then.

He sensed the room was large. Maybe this as well as the chair made him think of a club. He also sensed there was more than one other person present. How had he decided this? Density of the smoke?

Perhaps he slid back into unconsciousness. When next he registered anything a woman was speaking in English and from very near him, the accent educated Scottish, its tone wheedling. His head was still bagged. She seemed to be concluding a question. He had missed the start: '…expected to find at the Chandon works so late? Did you wish to get some printing done? You see my difficulty.'

He saw fuck all but left this unsaid. She took a couple of paces. He heard them faintly and saw a momentary change in the dim spread of light through the bag as she crossed in front of him. Further off a man spoke, probably also in English, though Abelard caught no words.

'Naturally we know who you are,' she said. When she moved her footsteps were quiet. From that, and from the feel under his own shoes, he knew it was a thick carpet. If they were not in a club – how could they be? – if not, this must be some expensively furnished house or office. It astonished Abelard that the result of a couple of routine skull blows could last long enough for him to be shipped from that miserable street to somewhere so different. But perhaps these head bangs he had been collecting lately did things cumulatively, like punches to boxers. Abelard closed his eyes and let his mouth gape again in case the bag was suddenly tugged off. The woman seemed to stroll away and for a moment there was silence. Once more his nerves strained to chart what was happening. Then, suddenly, he heard his own voice. It boomed out, anxious, urgent. 'Julian. Stop, will you? It's Simon.' God, such mouth: not just his own name, but a colleague's, in terrain Abelard knew next to nothing about, except it was not friendly. Had he really come so far out of the old, beautifully wise constraints? Someone reversed the tape and it was played again, louder. 'Why did you imagine Julian Bowling to be there?' the woman asked.

Abelard knew his body had jerked uncontrollably in the chair when his words first reached him. Maybe they had noticed, maybe not. Oh, Christ, of course they noticed. This was their game – to frighten him into a response. They were hot at it. They would watch him like something in a lab. The idea grew that they were professional interrogators, possibly that other search team he had read of. Did he know any Scottish women in the Outfit or across the quadrangle? That was no real test, though. All sorts of Whitehall's security and Defence people would be interested in Bowling, defector, with $9,000,000 to his dishonoured name. This woman, and whoever was with her, could have come from any one of ten different offices with staffs unknown to him.

They reversed the tape again, but further this time. He heard it rush back. Then came the raw, banging beat of heavy rock music, some number he did not recognise or want to, the kind of junk his mother adored and upset the neighbours with. How was she getting on with the new next-doors? He sensed rhythmical movement in the room. What the hell was this? He had the idea the Scottish woman might be dancing, perhaps other people, too. If these folk wanted to mess up his thinking they were doing nicely. Maybe they served their apprenticeship in Northern Ireland. Had they written him off, forgotten him, while they had a knees-up?

One of those terrible cold sweats that had not come his way for years suddenly started. Last time it had been on a bus when Anita announced she was leaving him. Now he knew he would begin to shake as his temperature dropped, and his feet would twitch because his nerves were stretched. They'd think he wanted to get in on the dancing. Already he could feel moisture creeping down his arms and forming reservoirs against the handcuffs. God, wasn't the body a miserable give-away?

He had to do something to hit back. 'You lot, you're after the treasure, are you – Jules's hi-jacked takings? You had a trap for him at Chandon's, and he was too smart?' How did you make yourself sound unbeaten through a cloth bag and despite a tripe concert? He was not good anyway because of the shivers. He sounded like a frantic schoolteacher. 'If you know who I am, why the fuck treat me like this?'

In an effort to gauge what was going on at the other end of the room he sat straight, then leaned forward. He felt sweat from his head roll down his face and neck and legs, soaking his socks. The bag was wet and clung to him like a cloth on a boiled pudding. Thank God his ma would not hear about this. It would convince her for ever he picked up scrag end jobs.

Was this France? You bopped someone then slipped a needle in. It might be next week. He could be anywhere. Why not Washington or Jerusalem?

'This has been a real eye-opener for me,' he yelled out of his utter blindness in the bag.

The music blared on. He thought he heard a pistol cocked. Yes, these people had learned their techniques around Belfast: the bag on the head, the disorientating din, the scare tricks. No wonder he did not recognise the voice: even in these days of the new openness, people working Northern Ireland stayed apart, distrusted everybody except one another, and no wonder.

The tape ran into his call to Julian again and was switched off. Someone approached and seemed to sit very close. He caught the whiff of alcohol. It must be on their breath, smug bastards.

'What about a dram?' the woman said.

'As a matter of fact I *am* a little dry,' he replied. He tried not to scream the words and sound as frantic as he felt. That's what training – those invaluable self curbs – was all about: how to hide collapse. She undid the lace at the bottom of the hood and lifted the material enough to expose his lips. She put a glass to them. It was good whisky and tasted like a remission. Looking down he could see her feet and ankles, nice small feet in suede slippers, and slim ankles. He gulped and then gulped again. She poured it in as though feeding an oil lamp. Despite everything he had thought about her earlier, this woman might be all right. She had kindness and decency and a fine lavishness with drink. 'Why did you imagine Bowling was at Chandon's?' she asked. She took the glass from his mouth, laced the bag again, then seemed to go and sit down.

'You were hoping for a business meeting with him there, were you?' Abelard replied. 'This would be home ground for him, I suppose from way back. Where he used to buy. Where he could deal now. You were on the recent big-time trafficking with him, were you? You're another one he owes?'

'Simon, were you part of the network? Does he owe you?'

'Christ, no. I'm the kosher search. I'm the law now. Simple-minded. Principles. You've heard of those?' Abelard said. 'You don't believe me? That's why I'm trussed?'

'We're eager to know what you know.'

'Nothing.'

'But you were in Paris, and at Chandon's,' she replied.

'Everyone knows about Chandon's.'

'But you knew to turn up tonight.'

'So Bowling was there,' Abelard said.

'Don't piss us about, there's a sweetie.' She suddenly unlaced the hood again and with one quick movement pulled it off.

He had expected to be concerned above all with the sight of her. Hadn't she been the only one to speak directly to him, and wasn't her voice a youngish voice? Didn't what he had seen of her legs and feet suggest someone neat, slim? And he saw now that she was in fact neat and slim, but not youngish: not oldish, but not youngish, say early fifties. Her face was tough, wily, unsentimental, a management face like several he had seen around the Outfit or in the quadrangle, but not one he recognised. Even after the tedium of the hood it was no great treat to look at her.

In any case, his attention had to go to the man last seen dead at the print works. He was now laid out on the floor very near Abelard's chair. To protect the excellent carpet they had put a sheet of plastic under him. There seemed to be three deep wounds to his head. Abelard had decided earlier that the suit was splendid and most likely British, and he saw now that the shoes must have cost, too – probably custom-made. Was it a stunt, this sudden revelation of the body?

'We had to bring him out,' she said. 'One hell of a job, you can imagine. A corpse could tell too many tales, though. We might still be in trouble. Did anyone see us shifting him?' She took a few paces to stand near the body. 'Were you close when this happened?'

They thought he had killed their boy. He saw now why they had given him the rough. 'I found him dead,' Abelard replied.

'Yes?'

'Why would I kill him?'

'Why were you *there*?' she asked.

Nothing had been said about removing the manacles. 'We can give him a respectable burial, not leave him to…' She did not finish the thought. 'You saw someone you thought was Julian.'

'I hoped.'

'We think you've got it wrong.'

'Who do?'

'Colleagues were here,' she said.

'I take it this guy was carrying a pocket recorder.'

'Nothing else on the tape except the sound of blows, before you shouted – presumably what killed him, if you say you didn't, and I'm half inclined to believe that.'

'Great.'

'Appalling sounds, so I wiped it with the music. We danced just now, did you hear, just to get the other noises from my head.'

'I wondered. Some scene – discoing while there's a corpse in the room and another man with his head in a bag. Not the Hunt Ball.'

'May I?' she asked abruptly. Taking a key from a shelf she undid the handcuffs. 'Frankly, I can still hear those blows.'

Abelard's mother had taught him to be especially on guard when people said 'frankly.'

'Did you know this man personally?' he replied.

'I put him into the Chandon works so it's hit me a bit, yes. Tell me, did he speak?'

'Put him in the works for what? To meet Jules – a supposed deal, actually an ambush? You'd done some research and knew he was familiar with Chandon's and might feel at ease coming there, even if it was apparently a wreck now?

'If he said anything it might make matters less of a waste.' She took Abelard's hands and began to massage his chafed wrists, as though wanting to show a womanly side. Yet there was nothing warm or intimate to it, certainly nothing sexual. She might have been a physio. All the same, maybe it did humanise her a little.

As he had guessed from the quality of the chair and carpet, the room was richly furnished. Venetian blinds covered the windows and he could see nothing outside, but he had the impression it was night and that they were several floors up: traffic noise seemed distant. He could just make out a table with drinks on it and the tape recorder at the unlit end of a long, low-ceilinged room. More heavy armchairs stood there, some facing away from him, but as far as he could tell nobody else was present now. He stood.

'You'll want to stretch,' she said. 'My name's Judith Stewart. You work for Verdun, the celebrated Carmarthen dandy.' With the slippers she had on a blue and white silk suit which had seen some service and a spruce, cream blouse. She wore no rings and her only jewellery was what looked like real pearls in a heavy necklace: a weird mixture of styles. As he stood, she moved away to a spot near the record player. For her age she seemed nimble, full of purpose.

'You gave me a little sleeping shot?' he asked.

'We had so much to do because of the death. It would have been a nuisance if you'd come round. You've been out only a couple of hours.'

'It's still France?'

'*Certainement*. We had no idea how you fitted into things, nor who you were. Please forgive, but we were very frightened, in direst panic, to be blunt. We had a cheeky operation set up there on a foreign government's soil and suddenly we find an extra man in the middle.'

She had begun to speak the cowardly slang of officialdom.

'I thought everything was supposed to be transparent these

days, especially with allies,' Abelard said.

'Absolutely. Now and then.'

'Did I hear someone try the action of a pistol.'

'I wouldn't think so, Simon.' She was still fiddling with his wrists. 'Are you telling me fluke put you at Chandon's? OK, you get the address from a Jules contact, but how is it you're there for our little game? Colleagues will not believe you.' She stood and went to the other end of the room. 'Let's have another drink. I'd like to level with you.'

These words, like "frankly" lit a fuse of distrust. Levelling with someone meant telling the least you could and hoping they would cough the lot in gratitude. Here's a sprat, so where's the mackerel? He'd done it himself. They took chairs near the recorder and she placed hers to face away from the body on the floor, as though finding the sight unbearable again, a delicate touch. He would have liked to believe in it.

'Nine million dollars is a hell of a lot to run with,' Abelard said. 'I mean, the bulk.'

'Not like that. He did some clever stuff with numbered bank accounts in Zurich and customers thought they were paying into the syndicate, but really it was going to just Jules.'

'Slack.'

'Those Swiss bankers: too busy re-counting holocaust money to notice. Here's the possible scenario – but stop me if you can see it for yourself: Julian began to hear all the hints that drugs might be legalised. New millennium thinking. Where's his undercover trade role then? This is a man used to gauging trends, measuring political temperatures, planning against bad eventualities. He decides on a big personal coup while that's still possible, and then a disappearance. Lay not up for yourself treasures in heaven but in Zurich where it's more accessible. All these people you've been having trouble with want a route to Jules and his private retirement funds.'

'You?' he asked.

She laughed. 'Simon, you know fuck all, I'd say.'

'So why the bag and cuffs?'

'You were a puzzle. I've placed you now. You can't help us.'

'I can go?' he said.

'Simon, I'm here alone. Could I stop you?'

'And you'll have someone on my tail for the short-cut to Bowling?'

'No tail. You're a colleague. Have you thought why Verdun might be so intent on this one, apart from the possible chances of debriefing you, that is?'

'He has a staff member who might have skipped off. He wants him back. This is a routine reaction for someone at the head of a Department.'

'Skipped off with some formidable trove. Some say nine, some say seventeen.'

'Verdun wouldn't—'

'Verdun has a lovely country place to keep up in Italy, you know. Sucks money. A family spot, from early in the century. He feels responsible. His job could be on the slope, couldn't it?'

'Verdun wouldn't ever—'

'Is it one of your things not to carry a piece?' she asked in her gentle little Morningside Crescent tone.

'I can take it or leave it alone.'

'We think things could get combative. We must lend you something.'

'That would be remarkably white of you.'

'And there's a car waiting to take you to your hotel,' she said. 'Where is it?'

He told her the place in Monmartre, deciding to book out tomorrow, or sooner.

'Christ, Verdun's still saving the pennies.'

'That sort of area I can lose myself, I thought.' Or possibly discover himself, the new himself, if there really was one.

8

HE SAT ALONE and watched a girl of about twenty-six or seven weeping silently. She was pretty in her slight, sharp-featured way. A man held her hand and talked endlessly, his mouth almost touching her ear. She gazed out with unfocused eyes or occasionally let her head sink forward so she was staring at the table. Perhaps she heard some of the words, but her face showed little. Although she would stop crying for a few moments she always resumed. Abelard felt sure these changes did not relate to what was being said. The girl had her thoughts and griefs and dreads, and they were out of reach. Was she on something, at least alcohol but possibly something heavier? To Abelard she looked in need of help. And he could persuade himself, if he worked on it, that she needed his help. He did work on it. He would have liked to walk over to their table, sit down and say: 'Here am I, send me, use me. I am, despite all appearances, law and order, perhaps especially order. I am values, cleanness, solidity.' No, he would not actually have liked to say that because it would have sounded lunatic, as if he were on something stronger even than she was, and who wanted a crazed junky to help them? He wouldn't have said it, but it was what he felt.

This had to be the right place. Things were starting to go his way, weren't they? Were they? If so, he must keep them like that. It was definitely a step up from breathing someone else's cigarette smoke with your head in a bag. Here you could breathe others' cigarette smoke with your head out of a bag. This club, off the Place du Pont-Neuf was the second of two addresses from the Oxford don. Or not exactly. He had gone to that address but found it was now a very smart restaurant, certainly no knockabout drugs trading centre for students.

Perhaps a lot of people called there these days, recalling past comforts. At any rate, its *maître-d'* seemed to sense pretty quickly what Abelard was looking for and directed him to this place. Some time during the last dozen or so years it must have taken over the traffic. The girl seemed to have recovered, or had exhausted herself. At any rate, she no longer wept but sat now with her hands clasped on the table, still not appearing to see much of what went on around and doing nothing to repair her looks. The idea grew more and more solid in Abelard's mind that this was Lucy Mary McIver and the man Peter Glass/Graff, those twin stars of the Pimlico fireplace. There had been some signs, but Abelard would have admitted it was mostly guess and instinct. Glass/Graff: Abelard suddenly recalled Veronica Rombarde's hint of a German tentacle to all this.

The man continued talking, in short spasms now, not non-stop. Unlike the girl he watched everything around them in this club without relaxing and even while he spoke his eyes all the time probed the couple of smoky rooms. Abelard was not sure whether he had been noticed and was not sure either whether the Scots woman had someone on his heels: these would be accomplished people, perhaps his own kind of people. More than perhaps.

Although he had taken off his tie and undone a couple of shirt buttons he would still stand out among the jeans and bright shirts and blouses here. Thank God there were plenty of other blacks. He did what he could to hide his interest in the two and pretended to be thrilled by a creaky trio of jazz veterans playing terrible old plantation slop from the 1920s and '30s. He kept a half-baked groupie grin in place and did some finger drumming on the table cloth to the foul *Big Fat Ma And Skinny Pa* number. It might work. He must confront the two of them head-on shortly.

The club was in a quite decent street on the Ile de la Cité. There would be tolerable hotels around here, and he might make a move this way once he felt absolutely sure he was not watched. He had hung on in Monmartre despite his promise to himself.

At their table now the two had started to behave as if they did not know each other, or as if they had been married for ever and had said it all fifty times. The man no longer spoke to her, not even in bursts. Maybe something had been decided making more conversation superfluous. When he could, Abelard studied him. He was small and slim with shoulder-length fair hair and would be around thirty-five. Abelard tried to sort out how he had become so certain of this man's identity. After all, he had no description of Glass. Knowing it could scare him off, Abelard had not asked questions at this place, but on two earlier visits had watched and listened. The possible Glass had been present each night. Although he dressed like all the rest he spoke English, and once Abelard had heard someone call him Peter. Many customers knew him and until tonight he seemed to move a lot among the clientele and frequently disappeared with one or two into rooms behind the bar. A bit of business would be under way. Perhaps the girl had turned out to be a pain tonight, keeping him from his vocation. Abelard was here to dismantle his vocation, or at least to rescue Julian Theobald Bowling from it. God, what a notion, though, Simon Abelard sent to save the endlessly favoured one from his little naughtinesses, his little naughtinesses having apparently cost some slack colleagues $9 million. Perhaps Abelard could rescue Lucy Mary McIver from it, too. He fancied himself as a rescuer. That was a proper police role.

Glass had the kind of style that Abelard was used to and thought he might have himself, hoped so. There was a social ease and alertness to Glass that made you sure he could excel in any sort of business setting, any sort of business setting that depended on quickness of brain and the ability to get potential customers relaxed. At the same time, Abelard felt a good degree of physical power on tap there, despite Glass's slightness. The Outfit was full of men who relayed similar qualities, though most would be bigger: in some ways the Outfit was very trite and kept a reverence for big slabs of brawn, such as the Guards – although the Outfit had let Verdun Cadwallader in, the Celtic midget, and allowed him to climb.

The girl stood and made for stairs to a basement lavatory. After a moment Abelard followed, feeling like Jan Creemer in that famous novel, *I, Jan Creemer*. Creemer used to tail any fuckable woman to the wc for the small but select pleasure of sitting on the warm seat after her and communing thus. Here, too, the cubicle was for men and women and could accommodate only one person. He waited near the curtained glass door, taking care to face towards the stairs. He could have done with the armament promised by Judith Stewart but, of course, it never came. Did she and the dead man, and whoever had danced with her, make up that alternative search group from somewhere in the Whitehall emporium? One reason he stayed at his hotel was in case she did send weaponry. But she might fear it would be used on one of her own people, and especially one of her gum-shoes.

When the girl reappeared he said: 'Excuse me, you British, by any chance?'

'American,' she said, thank God. She seemed a bit scared of him, but not too bad.

'Same thing. I mean, the lingo. I'm a bit lost in this place.'

'Well, this is the john.'

'No, I mean generally.'

'This a pick-up? Look, I'm with a guy upstairs.'

'I'm looking for somebody.'

'Yea, I bet.'

'No, I mean for somebody.'

'Not for me.' She seemed suddenly very nervy, but made no effort to pass him and return upstairs. In his travels he had seen plenty of faces like this, tense and mobile because they were on the way down from a high, or dreaming of the next.

'I can see you need help,' he said abruptly, changing tone.

'How's that? Look, who—?'

'You can count on me.'

'We met before?' She meant, have I bumped into you some-time when I was fixed and with no memory? 'Hey, you're not a kindly medic, are you? Yea, someone like you at the clinic, big, not white, I guess I do recall. Well, thanks for all your help then, but as you see... Well, these things take time, don't they, doc?' There was no hesitation when she referred to his colour. She regarded it as a matter of description, like buck teeth. He liked that.

'I saw Peter Glass upstairs, trying to comfort you.'

'Graff,' she muttered. 'Graff this week. You can identify Pete? You in the business, then?' She squinted harder at him. 'That how I know you? Sure, sure, I remember now.'

'I—'

But before he could reply her mood suddenly switched. She gave what was almost the delighted, surprised kind of grin you might see on a child's face. Astonishing. 'I understand what it is,' she whispered. She reached out and touched his cheek. 'You have news – a message. Oh, I know who sent you. And I was sure you'd come. Look, what's your name? I think it would be safer in here.'

Swiftly she retreated into the cubicle. He followed and closed the door, told her his name. As French plumbing went it was fair and the flush obviously worked and had been work-ing all day. There was a pedestal, not a hole in the ground, and they stood each side of the seat facing each other. She was still smiling. It had nothing to do with the setting. She smiled hope. He understood.

'I suppose I could be wrong and just crazy,' she said. 'I mean, you could be – well, Jesus Christ, you could be from Her British Majesty's Intelligence and Security Services. I hear things change even there.' This time she seemed sensitive about referring to his colour, but nothing phoney or squeamish. She was saying without saying it that previously his colour would have barred him from a top Intelligence job, even in the enlightened nineties. 'No,' she said, 'you couldn't be, could you?'

He thought she would touch his cheek again, a sort of confirmation his skin was black and therefore an eternal career handicap, regardless of liberalising. She drew back, though. His pleasure in her nose-dived. So what did he look like in her eyes, some drug pusher's aide-de-campe, the traitor Bowling's pigeon post? This souped-up, know-all infant thought she had second sight.

But then he recovered and smiled in reply. It always shook him that even now, just occasionally, and at times when he expected it least, he could be so vulnerable, so bloody raw.

'You've actually seen him?' she said. Her voice soared, like asking about Michael Jackson or a vision of St Francis. Her eyes shone, some of it from feelings and longing, some from recent snow, or stronger.

Had she wept in the club for fear Jules had ditched her permanently? 'Can you leave here at once?' he asked. 'I'll go ahead and wait in the street, Lucy.'

'Is he near? In Paris? Has he collected?'

'Wait three or four minutes. Come alone,' he replied.

'Who would I bring?'

'Me you can trust.'

'Your Mr Blair said that, didn't he? Oh, I'd trust anyone. No choice.'

Ceremonially they clasped hands over the pan. Her smile had gone and he thought she might start crying once more, or even grow helpless. When he left she closed the door and locked herself in again. A big young woman waiting outside tapped the glass angrily and glared after Abelard.

'Courage, ma petite,' he said.

Upstairs he saw Graff/Glass still at the same table and walked swiftly out. He searched for a taxi and scanned the street hard for any shadow. He would need to look just as hard when she came out, *if* she did, to make sure she was alone. Already more than four minutes had gone.

A taxi pulled up and he waited near it. Five more minutes went. Then she appeared from a side street where the club must have another entrance. Graff was with her, walking close, talking, talking, as if to bulldoze some decision she'd made. Spotting Abelard she immediately raised a hand and pointed. For a moment he feared a trap. Could all that sweet childlike pleasure in the lav have been show? Perhaps he was getting soft and dim and trusting, in time for the millennium change. A woman touched his cheek so he thought he had her lifetime devotion.

But now she suddenly broke from Graff and ran towards Abelard, weeping again and trying to call out something, though breathlessness and her sobbing stopped the words.

Abelard pulled open the rear door of the taxi, ready. The driver looked sorry he had waited. This *bâtard* might drive off without them.

Abelard hurried forward to meet her, his arms open like a favourite aunty. Graff turned and yelled back down the side street, then sprinted after Lucy. In a moment Abelard had her by the arm and shoved her towards the taxi. He pushed Lucy in but before he could join her Graff caught him by the shoulder, a fierce, strong grip for such a miniature turd. Abelard had been right about his power. Glass pulled him back. 'Who the hell are you?' he screamed. Yes, the accent might be more German than French. 'You're not from Julian, you bloody snoop.'

That's it a snoop, no longer a spook, and snooping in the cause of… in the cause of right? Close behind Graff a couple of men were crossing the street at a trot, one carrying a length of metal pipe. Abelard suffered a gleaming flash of doubt. Was he playing this right? He so often played tactics wrong. It was probably on his Outfit dossier. The girl did not know where Bowling was. She wanted Abelard to take her to him. But Graff – he might know, and it could be squeezed out of him, maybe, given time. Questioned out of him, that is – nothing violent and throwback. Too late to do anything about that, though. This was a street full of people and cars, but if he stayed and tried to discuss things he could be in rough trouble. These three would not worry about witnesses. Straightening and turning, Abelard grabbed Graff's bomber jacket with two hands, jerked him forward and cracked down with his head, a passable piece of nutting. Graff grunted and put two hands to his nose for comfort. Blood ran into both his sleeves. It was like Paddington again. Abelard fell heavily into the taxi and slammed the door.

'He wouldn't let me come alone,' Lucy said. 'You *can* find Jules, can't you?'

The car sped forward. Abelard saw the man with the piping raise a hand and hurl it like a lance. It crashed through the front passenger's window, hit the dashboard then fell to the floor. The taxi swerved, struck a parked Mercedes, bounced off and kept going. The driver howled intricate Euro curses and waved his hand now and then to itemise damage.

'Are we going to Jules at once?' she asked, her voice alight with joy again.

How long would it take that crew at the club to find a car and follow? At least Graff would not be up to any driving.

'Are we?' she said.

'We wait for him to contact us.'

Lucy was silent for a while, except that the sobbing occasionally broke through. 'Peter said you were someone who used to work with Jules. Or maybe Stewart's outfit.'

'Julian will be in touch.' Abelard looked behind but saw nothing grave.

'Days? A week? A year?'

'When he thinks it's best. Not a year.'

She folded down into the corner, grew very small and child-like: 'You know nothing. OK, so you're grubbing for dollars, like all the rest. You, Judith Stewart, God knows how many others. I can't help.'

He felt he needed a different hotel more urgently than ever now. Years ago, as a doomed peace offering after one of their most internecine internecine times, he had brought Anita to Paris and showed he could spend on her by picking the Rembrandt towards Montparnasse. Actually, Anita did not care much about money or spending but Abelard had been told by his mother that a man was twice the man with a twenty- pound note in his pocket, and he had reasoned that a man not just with a twenty pound note in his pocket but who took his wife to the Rembrandt must be six times the man. But later he thought that if Anita had gone off him she wouldn't want him multiplied by six. Paris with her had been all right. Nothing restorative.

Now, he told the driver to take them there and searched in his wallet for something sizeable for the car damage. He wanted no Comédie Française show outside the hotel, no delays in getting to cover. In case the taxi driver did turn out difficult, Abelard practised the French in his head for, 'Look, Jock, don't try to tell me you've never had a fucking iron spear through your window in anger before. This is Paris we're talking about.'

'Don't you realise I'm sort of important?' Lucy said. 'You can't just snatch me. I don't mind you should snatch me if it's to see Jules, but it's no good at all if you just snatch me. Either way, powerful people will come looking – not just Peter, he's nothing.'

'I thought he was into big work.'

'What big work? she asked.

'Political.'

'Peter?'

'German political.'

'These rumours – they won't leave him alone.'

'Who?'

'The rumours.'

'They're all enraged with Jules, aren't they?' Abelard replied.

'Who?'

'All of them.'

'Who?'

'All of them. He must be terrified. I've never seen him really frightened. But now it—'

'That's because Jules doesn't get terrified,' she said. 'Do you really know him? I mean, if you can say terrified.'

'People coming at him from all points.'

'You,' she said. 'What's your point? You're the hunt? You're the police? You could be the police. You have that way.'

'Which?'

'Like pleased to get someone into a cell. Like confident, because you've got a whole barrel of laws to back you and to rely on.'

'No, I'm not confident.'

'They've turned you into a cop?'

'Why fight it?'

'Oh, best to fight it.'

At the Rembrandt he asked for a room looking down to the street. He left it a while before going to the window to watch. He did not want to scare her or get her hot with hope. She would probably imagine he was looking for Jules. He saw nothing to alarm him in the street. He had told the taxi driver to get away fast or he might run into people asking where he took his fares, and asking for their metal piping back. Abelard turned to examine the accommodation. The door was flush and flimsy with a lock and bolt a decently fed child of six could burst. Lucy ignored his worries. 'Does Julian know you'd book in here? This is a kind of drill? The place is a rendezvous? He can contact us? He'll really show?' Her voice sang at the start, then came down into a clamorous splutter. 'It's – well, Christ, it's never going to happen, is it?'

He returned to the window but the street remained unthreatening.

She changed tack. 'Picking me up – it's to do with what I heard happened at Chandon's the other night, is it?' She was seated on a hard little blue chair near a gaudy, padded dressing table which had made her wince when they first entered the room. 'You people feel mad about Chandon's. I understand.'

'Which people?'

'Was the guy killed a colleague, a friend?'

'Somebody's.'

'You're not trying to tell me you work alone?'

'Lucy, I'm—'

'OK, I ask questions. I'm having a flounder around, I guess.'

'Be my guest.' Years ago Abelard had promised himself he would never speak these words, so stress must be reaching him.

'You do work for the Scotch dame, yes? Judith Stewart? They say she swallowed a pin when she was three and never felt a prick yet. But maybe you know different.'

'I love those Max Miller jokes.'

'Who? Is that what's called a put down? Merciless. You must have been to a top class English school. Really? And now I guess you've got kids and want to give them the same chance. Big school fees, ponies and all that. You need a share. And Stewart wants hers and all the others want theirs. She's got no kids, though, has she?'

'Ever think she could be stalking Julian because he's a security risk, a defector?' He spoke over his shoulder, watching the street again.

She sighed and he turned to look at her. Straightening her white Leonard Cohen T-shirt she said: 'That's a great idea but you know it's very hard for people – some people – it's hard for them to worry, really worry, about a security risk. That's a big floating notion… kind of mushy? And especially these days. I mean, what security, what risk? But nine or maybe seventeen million dollars split only a few ways is not like that at all. See the difference? When Judith Stewart thinks about her share she can feel all those fat zeros and can go out and touch things at Balmain she'll buy just as soon as they get the bank to cough. Sure, the security of Western Europe and the US is quite a thing. Who'd say no? But they're doing OK, aren't they?'

If they put the two beds end to end across the room from the wall they would reach the door and jam it shut.

Lucy sighed, like an old lady, but an old lady with sharper

vision than his. 'Security risk? Oh, sure some would like to find Jules for that. A few do care about the professional angle. It's fun and promotion's nice, too, if you bring him in. Some live for it. That your thing? I'm not sure.'

'I thought you'd decided I needed the school fees.'

'Or it's police-type doggedness. Can't make up my mind.'

'What are you in it for?' Abelard replied.

'Am I in it?'

'You're here,' Abelard said.

'I was brought.'

'Are you in it because you want Jules?'

'Well, I do want Jules, yes, and not in a cop way.'

'No, I didn't think so.'

'You consider him sort of… sort of lightweight?' she asked.

'In what way?'

'The only way – concerned for himself and nobody else.'

'There's some of that,' Abelard said.

'How much?'

'Some. Some or quite a bit.'

'Yea, that's about right.'

'It makes no difference?' Abelard asked.

'Some. Some or quite a bit,' she said.

'But not enough to—'

'Not enough to kill it? Oh, of course not.'

'Of course not.' Abelard tried to recall what it was like to love in that fierce way. Fiercely stupid and uncomfortable, he thought. No, he didn't. He envied her. He envied Jules.

Her mind had gone back to motives and ambitions. 'Sure, some mean to clean up the cosmos, so they chase villains like Jules. Whereas nearly everybody cares about big gains not far off: dirty money nobody can go to the police about when it's stolen again. That's a retirement fund for anyone who's had enough of work. What we call Bermuda funds. Where is it the Brits go when they've had enough – Jersey, Majorca, that place like Turkey?'

'Not much. Torquay.'

'A lady with looks like Judith Stewart wants more than a government pension for her last years. Think what your Winston Churchill said: "Nice to have money when you're young, but vital when you're old".' She shifted and glanced at herself in the mirror of the foul dressing table, winced again, but made no attempt to do anything to her face. 'God, I guess you know all this. You're fooling when you play the integrity game. You really tell me a Brit black is the one guy who still believes in land of hope and glory and struggles to keep it clean? I mean … say, if you don't work for Stewart it could be the other Celt. Little half faggot Julian used to talk about – not that Jules was too consistent sexually, of course.' She sounded suddenly very miserable. Then she began expounding again. 'Isn't he called Cadwallader? I've heard some say he's on the level. Yea, honestly. It's true?'

This bloody kid, aged T-shirt, jeans, filthy desert boots, talked to him as if he'd just been let out by nuns. He began moving the beds. They fitted as he'd hoped and the door could not be opened. A couple of blows would break it down, of course, and it would not keep out bullets. But all that would involve noise, bring the hotel staff and the police. Possibly.

Lucy watched uneasily and he knew she would see the arrangement not just for keeping people out but for blocking her in. Someone short of a fix might find this unnerving. He said: 'Just for an hour or two, Lucy.' He had begun by wanting to help this girl and still wanted to, even if she did treat him like some *innocent*. 'I'll sleep nearest the door.'

In a moment she walked to the little bathroom with her handbag. Again he stood at the window: plenty of street activity, but nothing to disturb him. Lucy came back with her head wrapped in a hand towel and her face more serene and prettier. She had taken some of her favoured magic aboard and it was doing the trick. This troubled him, as it always troubled him to see anyone hooked. Childhood memories of dockland street scenes. For the moment, though, he would let her bask in escape. She rubbed her hair for a few minutes, then removed her jeans and swung into bed wearing briefs and the T-shirt.

Abelard undressed and lay under the coverlet. They were scalp to scalp, separated by the slatted headboards. The whole occasion was drably sexless, a matter of two people running from an enemy, pushed together in an expensive dug-out and making the best of it, a separate best. Abelard soon slept. After a couple of hours he awoke and found they were clinging to each other's hand through the slats, like prisoners in segregated cells. Enjoying the full coma of someone able to hit her dosage right, she snored steadily. Abelard thought about going through her handbag and jeans but rejected the idea as uncomradely. When he awoke again an hour later because her snoring had grown more shrill he could not understand that squeamishness, carefully unhooked his hand and started searching her things.

In her bag was a neat packet of downers, which should mean no trauma for a couple of days at least. She had plenty of money in francs and dollars – something like £600 at a quick count – and a lot of cosmetics, though he could not see that she used much. There was her supply of the pill and a picture of an unprosperous looking, slab-faced couple who might be her parents. They stood in what seemed a sunny American street. A US Embassy pass described her as 'senior clerk-stenographer' and gave her full name and her birthday, August 2nd. 1971. In the ID pic she was laughing, not just smiling, and looked happier than Abelard had ever seen her. She could not have been all that much younger then, but by comparison this was a carefree youngster, perhaps excited at landing Paris. It must have been taken in the States before all the pain set in with Julian.

He found a small, cheap cardboard covered French diary, which seemed virtually empty. Here and there a day was distinguished with an exclamation mark, sometimes two, once three. What had she been counting? Starch-free meals? Orgasms? Trips? Pats on the back or somewhere from her Section head?

When he came to the Name and Address pages he had the sudden, senseless terrifying conviction he would find his own particulars there as in that carrier bag, and his fingers shook so much he dropped the diary. Lucy grunted at the slight noise, then flung an arm out, like an accusation, but did not wake up. Recovering the book he studied the names listed and found them of no consequence with addresses mostly in Des Moines. There were three entries under A, none Abelard. Once the first dread had passed he felt disappointment at the omission. How come she hadn't heard of him when she knew so much about the Outfit? Didn't he rate?

The jeans had a hip pocket only and in it he found an airmail letter addressed to her at the Rue Erquy, Paris 8. The postmark was Des Moines and the date ten days earlier. He read it quickly.

My dear Lucy,
Your father and I are worried about you, dear, and please write as soon as you get this. Is everything all right? A strange thing happened. As you know your uncle Ed and aunt Astrid were in Paris three weeks ago on vacation on account of always being fond of Europe. I gave them your address and phone number so they could call on you. Well, it seems they did telephone and visit by taxi, but you were not there, Lucy. They are back home here now and told us that when they visited two men came from somewhere nearby, trying to find out who they were and what they wanted and how they knew you. They were American not French Ed says and he did not like it, you know what he's like.
Well, Lucy, next day he and Astrid went back to your apartment in the evening but you were still not there – as you know, of course!!! – so Ed called on the caretaker, known as a concierge. She did not want to help but Ed persuaded her and she came and opened the door with a pass key in case of tragedy, which thank God was not

so. But imagine their shock when they found that everything inside had been wrecked, things thrown everywhere, your uncle Ed says like a search not robbery. He always seems to know a lot and was an officer in the army. The caretaker also was shocked.

The three of them looked right through the apartment and then called the police. They brought somebody who could speak English and Ed told them about the two American men. This is the last he and Astrid heard. Afterwards Ed wrote down the questions the two men asked. They might help you decide who they could be.

1. When did you last see Lucy Mary McIver – it was your full name they had?

2. Is she expecting to meet you here?

3. Do you know her social habits?

4. Do you know her friends in Paris?

5. Do you know a man called Julian, an Englishman?

6. Have you heard anything to suggest she has recently come into possession of a large sum of money?

Well, Lucy, if you are reading this, I guess you must be at the apartment and all's OK. I'm sure it must have been a terrible shock to find such a mess. Have you been able to clear it up? Your father and I are still worried. A large sum of money? This that lottery over there? You've had good luck? We did not like the way the men used your full name, like police or a school list. We have tried to call you at the apartment and at the Embassy. There was no answer at the apartment and the Embassy said you were on leave, they did not know where. They sounded strange when we asked about you, like there was something they did not want to tell us, and they asked when we spoke to you last and said get in touch if we heard from you. It sounded like the kind of questions the men asked Astrid and Ed.

Wire or call, please. We would hate for you to be mixed up in anything, we read such terrible things about

Europe and other parts of the world in the papers. You were always a girl to go your own way. But I expect everything is fine really and we should not worry.
Your loving Mother.

Oh, yes, you should worry, Mrs McIver. Abelard replaced the letter, folded the jeans and put them under his pillow in case she tried to get out, despite the barrier, while he slept. Besides, there was something intimate about having a girl's trousers under your head. He lay down and took her hand again.

When he awoke it was daylight. In his first moments of awareness, even before he grew accustomed to the light, he realised her hand was no longer in his. She was at the side of the window surveying the street, as he had so frequently done last night.

'Something?' he asked, rolling from bed.

'Not that I can see, but I'm no professional.'

'No?'

'My jeans?'

He dressed quickly and took her the trousers. 'You had a good read of the letter?' she asked.

'The Embassy are on to you.'

'Sure. How not? At the beginning they were interested in me just as a possible drugging security failure in touch with a foreign body, a foreign body with a spy rating.'

'Like yours?' Abelard replied.

'Julian's from a "friendly country", but they still didn't like it. Now, I guess they smell big fat money around me and it's not much to do with security any more. It's like I said – that much loot concentrates minds. Traitors used to be ten a penny. Not Julian's kind. They know I'm close to him – was – yes, was – and they know what he does on the side, except it's not on the side now, it's everything.'

'You can't go back to your place.'

'I haven't been there for… well, you read the letter.'

'How did you get it then?'

'Ways.'

'You should be lying damn low,' Abelard said.

'I thought I was.'

'In a club with Graff?'

'I had things to try there,' she replied.

'Does he know where Julian is?'

'He says no.'

'You don't believe him? Is that why you were crying? Are they very close?' Julian's fireside notes had said AC/DC. Perhaps they were right, though Abelard had never seen bi-sex signs. She herself had suggested his sexuality was not simple.

'Close? Well, close enough I might have been crying because of that, too.

'Did Graff refuse to help you because he's jealous?'

She did not answer, but it seemed like a yes.

'Some German political people have their eye on Julian for a possible contribution to some slush fund?'

'I've heard the whisper,' she said.

'Does it sound sensible?'

'Not my area.'

'So, is Graff/Glass interested in Jules as Jules or Jules as heavy cash?'

'We distinguish?' she replied.

'Love or loot?'

'Tell me, where does your information about the money come from?' she asked.

Abelard longed to answer that he was not interested in the fucking money, that he had a simple, law and order job to do, recovery of a body, preferably alive and with a few honest beliefs still intact. Who could talk about $9,000,000 like that and still sound sane? And it might be $17,000,000. As Lucy had said, some people were hooked on principles and some on promotion; but everyone felt a bit of awe and excitement when faced with such plenty. Everyone. Abelard liked the sound of $9,000,000 – the exactitude: no rounding up to the neater ten, though some vague indications that it might be seventeen.

'Julian's private snowdrift,' she muttered. 'And you've come to scoop some out for yourself, yes?'

It was as if she had to cut him down to size, see him as a newly launched pirate like a lot of others, so she'd understand him. How could she, when he did not understand himself? He was here following orders from Verdun Cadwallader, a man he wanted to believe was honourable: a man who still recognised the offences of defection and treason. Maybe that was obsolete and quaint, but Abelard recognised them, too. Half recognised them, at any rate. Oh, of course his mother and people like Field might be right and 'the current GB' had nothing left worth making a song about. But on 'the current GB' his father had his word in first and it stuck.

And the money? It did interest him, as an amount to be talked of with wonder and possibly recovered. Recovered who for? Did he want a slice? Had Lucy spotted more about him that he realised himself? Perhaps she observed another of those divisions in Abelard, easily identified by someone so sharp. Or was Lucy drowning in cynicism after her time with Jules? Nothing looked pure or clear to her any longer? Abelard could recall feeling a bit like that himself after conversations with Julian, and with some others in the Outfit.

Whenever she spoke Julian's name there was a deep wistfulness in her voice, and this might have nothing to do with the dollars, or not much, at any rate. How did they do it, operators like Jules? Abelard felt that if he and Lucy were shut in this room for another month he'd get no further with her than he did last night: hand contact and head-to-head. As positions went, head-to-head was probably the least practical for sex. He had begun to feel very fond of the small, sharp features and drug-sad eyes. The way her moods moved, snort-aided or not, intrigued him. How could Julian Bowling let such a girl hang around Paris alone, badgered by creatures like Graff? And like Abelard?

Two church clocks struck 10am. 'I must go,' she said. 'Please. Please.'

The intensity shook him. 'Where? You can't go back to the apartment.'

'No. I'll be OK.'

'Words for a gravestone.'

'Which?'

'"I'll be OK." People may be waiting for you to appear.'

'Which people?' she asked.

'I thought at least another twenty four hours here.'

'What would we do for twenty four hours?'

Yes. 'This is part of that lying low I spoke about. Real lying low.'

'I can't.'

'Can't why?' But it dawned on him slowly – the way dawning ideas did sometimes come to Abelard – that to let her leave, to get her out of this hideaway, might be his best chance. He more or less accepted that she did not know where Julian was. Instead, she hoped he would come back and find her. But, of course, she knew he would not find her *here*. Watching Lucy respond so sharply to the clock chimes he wondered whether she and Jules did, after all, have some sort of arrangement. It would be the kind called in the trade 'a some day soon' rendezvous. She would go to a named spot at a set time every day or every other day or every week until he turned up and collected her. Don't call us, we'll call you, and maybe one day he would. Yes, maybe. Even before her place was smashed up Julian would never have risked visiting it. They might have some agreed meeting point, though: a station, a street corner, a church, a bar.

'But how do we keep in touch, Lucy?'

'I can leave a letter at the *poste restante* in your Embassy.'

'You can. Will you?'

'Sure.'

More don't call me. 'All right,' he said. 'I'll take a look in the street first.'

He went into the corridor, closed the door and walked towards the lifts but did not enter one. Instead, he moved fast up the corridor until he came to a junction, turned into it and from there watched the room door. In a moment Lucy came out and took a lift. Abelard found the stairs and went quickly down. From the back of the foyer he saw her gingerly approach the hotel's front door, obviously afraid she might bump into him. She turned right and started walking. He went after her.

Abelard was not a bad tail but there were the usual urban frets: she might call a taxi or disappear into the Métro: he had been taught skills for the Underground, but they did not work against anyone quick and determined, like that Italian waiter at Paddington. On the other hand, if Lucy was what he thought she was, she would have been taught to take herself fast somehow, anyhow, into the noisy warren when she wanted to shake a tail.

It looked now, though, as if Lucy might not be going far. They passed a couple of Métro stations. She stayed on the inside of the pavement showing no interest in taxis and walking fast. At just before 10.30 she began to run, and for a second he thought she had seen something. They were in a wide street off Rue de Rennes among groups of shoppers and tourists and as he ran, too, he scanned faces and tried to imagine how Jules would look behind sunglasses or a beard. Still running, Lucy turned off into another street, where there were fewer people and less cover for Abelard. Perhaps this was really her route. Or perhaps she had seen him and was leading away from some sensitive spot before disappearing. He had to drop back and tried to keep pace with her by walking quicker, his head bent forward to hide his face: at times being black was a right millstone.

To his surprise she had not looked around since they left the hotel. That did not mean she was unaware of him. She might be pretending she was unaware, so he would be wrong-footed by a sudden move to ditch him. There were shops, where the display windows would act as rear-view mirrors. Or, conceivably, she felt smug and believed she was totally solo. Perhaps she considered herself clever, slipping out like that. Might she be greener than he thought? Possibly the urgency of her flight gave no time to consider pursuit. She must be dazed with joy at the hope of meeting Julian, even if the hope was small. In a moment she slowed and Abelard assumed they had arrived. He made it 10.33. They were nearing a small roundabout at the junction of four very busy roads. *Remember the location, Simon, dear.* If Julian failed to show today she would be here again. She stopped.

Now he needed to get close. Things might happen swiftly if this were an anytime rendezvous point. He could be left floundering. Waiting, she seemed to him appallingly exposed. From the edge of the pavement Lucy stared excitedly at the traffic on the roundabout. If she had been attending here regularly she could have been spotted by any of those other charmers waiting for Jules, hunting for Jules, longing for Jules and his lovely funds. Lucy might be under watch as a route to him, that would be elementary. After all she was in the fireplace dossier. People had her located. All right, she had quit the Embassy and her flat it seemed, but might have been spotted before she withdrew from the Embassy and under surveillance ever since. In any case, she could have been seen drinking openly with Graff/Glass around Left Bank cafés. Abelard looked about. Were there pedestrians here who had waited for Lucy to turn up at the roundabout again and were watching her? In the white T-shirt and with few people nearby she could not be more obvious. She *wanted* to be obvious. She was desperate to be seen by Julian and taken back into his life and would have no thought for safety. What Abelard had to cater for, though, was that Jules himself might want her removed. Lucy's day could be over and she perhaps knew too much. All sorts might require her dead, including her own Embassy. What exactly was she, this girl who called herself no professional but who could spirit a letter out of an apartment watched by professionals?

Doorway by doorway he pushed a little nearer. She still

seemed unconcerned about what was behind her, too busy with other thoughts. He saw the car before she did and, at once abandoning secrecy, dashed towards Lucy. It was a left hand drive Daimler with Swiss number plates, which his mind fought to record and hold. From a distance of three hundred metres he had seen behind the wheel a head and face which was unmistakably Julian's, no beard, no moustache, no sunglasses. Abelard's first response was of joy and relief, nothing like the triumph of a successful tracker. Jules was safe. and Jules looked as he always did, in command, glossy, formidable. He was a friend, as well as what he had become. a new era villain. Abelard had read of bonds forming between a criminal and the detective chasing him. The bonds already existed with Jules, from years of career mongering together. They *still* existed. Just the same, Jules had to be brought in. Abelard raced across the road, set on reaching Lucy before the Daimler.

Now, she had seen the car and Bowling, too. Her body tensed and she crouched forward, head bobbing as she tried to peer between and around and over the traffic to confirm her hopes. Abelard was about thirty metres from her, his legs good, his breathing good so far, but his anxieties as heavy as a dud meal. He could lose them both. She wanted that. Of course she did. She'd see it as a matter of two into unspecified millions, not three. Or perhaps she just wanted Jules, with money or not.

The Daimler forced its way across lines of fast vehicles towards Lucy and she stepped off the pavement into the gutter, ready. Abelard wished he could see her face. Or, no, perhaps he didn't. It would be full of happiness now Jules had done what he said he would and come for her. Weeping with Graff at the club, she must have doubted that.

The car stopped and Bowling leaned across to push open the passenger door. He did not smile or speak a welcome, looked only calm and very capable, as ever. When Lucy started to get in Jules glanced up and for the first time saw Abelard a few metres behind, still sprinting. He yelled something and straightened behind the driving wheel, ready to go. As Abelard grabbed the rear door handle the car jumped forward, its front door still open. God, were the back ones locked? Had his store of luck gone when he forced the Rover boot?

But it did yield and he flung himself on to the seat then pulled his door to. It slammed at the same moment as Lucy's. Outsiders would probably think they were watching a nicely organised get-away for two. Bowling had to give some of his mind to the driving, thank Christ, but, keeping one hand on the wheel, he reached under his jacket at shoulder level with the other: just the sort of move Matson tried, but easier to deal with now since Jules had to manage the car. Again Abelard grabbed first and came out with the PPK. 'Highway code, Julian. Two hands.' He put the muzzle against Bowling's neck and covered it with a handkerchief.

'Is he with you, Lucy?

'You know him?' she asked.

'Black boy in search of gold.'

'How do you mean, with me?'

'A joint job. He's sweet-talked you into co-operation? Are there more, Simon? Cadwallader? Turkey?'

'Don't drive so fast,' Abelard replied. 'No need. You'll attract attention. Lucy didn't know I was there. It's no plot. She's all for you, as if you doubted it.'

'Julian, he knows plenty.'

'What's happened, Jules?' Abelard asked.

'You know what's happened.'

'I know how it seems.'

'How it seems is as it is,' Bowling replied. 'You don't want it to be, that's your trouble, Si.'

'Yes, that's my trouble.'

'I do appreciate it, you know.'

'Appreciate what?' Abelard asked.

'That you'd like to think the best of me.'

'But I'd also like to take you back.'

'Yes, I understand that.'

'What the fuck is this high tone conversation?' Lucy McIver asked.

'A high tone conversation,' Bowling replied, 'conducted with a gun at my neck.' He was staring into the mirror. 'You did bring friends then, Simon.'

'What?' Abelard was about to turn and look behind but resisted it, keeping his attention instead totally on Bowling and Lucy. 'Who's supposed to be there?'

'A VW van. They're a couple of vehicles away. But they seem fond of us. Two men. I can't see the faces properly. More in the back?'

9

BEFORE ABELARD LEFT London, Verdun Cadwallader had nominated a safe house near Orléans where Abelard should take Julian if he were ever found. Abelard told him to drive there now. Sometimes Abelard used to promise himself he would resign and write an autobiography, to be called *Safe Houses I Have Known*. There was no such thing as a safe house. He had scars on body and psyche to prove it, a few acquired even in these late enlightened days. So, what was he worried about. What were the dangers to *this* safe house? *Who* were the dangers? What, as Abelard saw it, was happening, for God's sake?

What was happening was that a one time respected agent of HMISS had decided that all the pre-millennium bullshit and Apocalypse Now stuff did, as a matter of fact, have some meaning for him. It said that the kind of work he had been doing was obsolete, played out, over. Spying was like the dead parrot in the *Monty Python* sketch. The new millennium approached and its message to Jules was that he should turn to something else in good time: use all his fine, duplicitous skills at something else. The something else turned out to be international drug dealing, and Jules seemed to have been good at it. Of course he was good at it: the kind of training he had been given could be quickly adapted to international crookedness. All the fundamentals were present already: the habit of secrecy, the habit of ruthlessness, the disregard for opposition. Some would even argue that spying was a kind of international crookedness, and that next to no adaptation was necessary. In the tense course of this business, Julian had naturally met some dubious and potentially very rough dealers, say like Matson and Field. There might turn out to be others. Oh, sure there would turn out to be others.

Jules had done his trading, taken his split of the profits but eventually decided he could get richer quicker by adjusting the machinery of the business so that a whole slab of takings was paid not to the syndicate he belonged to but to his personal bank account in Switzerland. This slab could be $9 million or $17 million, or something nice in between. Associates would be very pissed off at this and come looking for him, hoping to recover the funds as well as administer a little reproach. Peter Glass/Graff might be an associate, too, possibly with links to some political group in Germany, who had previously been able to draw on some of the syndicate's income for its slush fund. He and they would likewise be offended by Julian's sudden selfishness.

Then there were people such as Judith Stewart and her colleagues. They might be just another search unit from somewhere in the Ministry of Defence, honourably and secretly devoted, like Abelard, to nailing Jules as a defector, the old estimable game. Or, they, more like Jules, might have seen the chance of making a pleasant fortune for themselves, and meant to squeeze Bowling for it, if they could find him: a hijacking. Along the way, there were the women. Along the way there had *generally* been women in Julian Bowling's case. Abelard was not sure yet how Barbara Francis and Lucy Mary McIver were involved, except that they were probably both sexually drawn to Jules, damn it. How far were they also into the trade, and into Julian's accomplished double-cross of the trade? Matson seemed to believe Barbara Francis was – had been – important. Perhaps Glass/Graff thought Lucy Mary McIver was. Abelard wondered about both of them, but especially about Lucy Mary McIver, because she was alive, here, and possibly keen to help Julian get clear of Abelard, taking her with him to some private haven where the dollars would buy an idyll. She might be a hazard. Barbara Francis was never going to be that.

The Orléans house turned out to be a very pretty and nicely secluded old villa, but Abelard did not feel at ease. There might be trouble from inside and out. He took Jules and Lucy to a charming rear garden room, keeping the PPK in his hand while he telephoned and told Cadwallader the hunt was over. Verdun sounded genuinely pleased and excited and said he and Turkey Latimer, with Roger Link-Mite, would come to France at once. If Roger was invited very devilish interrogations must be due.

Abelard still did not know whether there really had been anything on their tail from Paris. It was certainly possible. Matson, Field, Stewart – any of them might have had Lucy Mary McIver under watch. Abelard had not noticed people on the lurk, but these might be gifted folk. He and Lucy could have been located at the Rembrandt and followed. All Glass/Graff had to do to trace the hotel after that small street battle was find a spectacularly damaged taxi and ask the driver where he went. Jules himself might have been spotted in Switzerland, or wherever he had driven from.

On the way here, Abelard had simply told him to take the autoroute towards Orléans and put his foot down. Not much could have kept up with the Daimler and once they were clear of Paris Abelard had risked a look back but saw no VW. With Cadwallader's hand drawn map he guided Jules to the safe house and told him to park two hundred metres away among trees. They waited an hour to see if any vehicle turned up. None did.

It would be part of Bowling's most elementary training to get himself out of a situation like this. Perhaps it was part of Lucy Mary McIver's training, as well. But it was also part of Abelard's most elementary training to make sure Bowling and Lucy couldn't, and Abelard had a gun. He felt fifty per cent confident that Julian did not, not another one. Of course, Abelard was aware of Jules continually measuring distances from himself to Abelard, from himself to the door, from himself to the window – and all the time estimating Abelard's readiness with the pistol. This, too, was basic stuff. Given any chance at all, Bowling would go for him. That was part of his elementary training, too, and $17,000,000, or even a mere nine, added zest. It would also cancel any scruples about attacking a colleague. Jules had never been famous for scruples, anyway. To him, Abelard would look a true grief who had to be dealt with before back-up arrived from the Outfit. Abelard felt confused. His job was not to put bullets into Bowling, not even in self-defence, but to hold him for a tête-`à-tête, establish he was not all modish greed – that there was still some British, HM soul to him. It could come to bullets, though.

'Did Verdun pick this place?' Jules asked.

'It's on the books.'

'But he selected it from the rest?'

'Why not?' Abelard asked.

'But you don't like it?'

'It's fine. Out of the way, not difficult to defend. Changes of occupancy will be unnoticed.'

'On the books since when?'

'Not long.'

'These addresses – they get around.'

'What are you worried about, Jules? You'll be away soon.'

'It wouldn't take long. Do you realise how many people are looking for me?

'I know some.'

'Which?'

'Verdun says few know about the house,' Abelard replied.

'But the few include Verdun. Turkey?'

'What's your message, Jules?'

Bowling grimaced then shrugged. 'Only that I'm a sitting duck. You could be a sitting duck.'

'Just you. Anyway, they'd want you alive. You've got things to tell them and do for them, haven't you? They'd need your signature on a cash authorisation. They'll want your bank code number.'

'At first they'll want me alive. Are you sure of Verdun's motives in all this, Si?'

'People don't call me Si, and especially people like you, Bowling.'

Lucy groaned. God, the pomp. 'They call me *Mr* Tibbs. You're one-time friends, aren't you?'

'One time,' Abelard said.

'This is life and death you know, Simon. Julian's trying to help you.'

'Julian's trying to make me feel like a dim exploited minion.' He turned to Bowling again. 'Are you saying Cadwallader was in on the trade with you? He's gone rotten, too? It's smear time?'

'What trade is that, Simon?' Julian replied.

Without raising her voice or changing position in the chair Lucy said: 'Someone. In the garden.' She was looking through the glass doors behind Abelard, peering into the dark outside.

'A man? More than one?' Julian asked. He, too, remained still and spoke normally. It ought to look like a relaxed conversation. The Walther PPK on Abelard's lap would be hidden by his body.

'I've seen only one,' Lucy replied.

She kept her voice low but Abelard read fear. All the same, he refused to turn and look where she was staring, just as in the car. Instead, he watched the two of them more closely. His grip tightened on the pistol. So, they *had* been tailed from Paris? He had heard no car, but it would be basic tactics to do the final approach on foot.

'Simon, I'm defenceless,' Bowling said. 'This might turn out to be you on your own against God knows what.'

'Never mind about God – *you* tell me what, who?'

'All sorts are looking for me.'

Lucy said: 'They move well, very quick, very low. Yes, definitely more than one.'

'Abelard, please. Is there other armament in the house?'

'Please, Simon.'

They prompted and fed each other beautifully and it sounded like a script. Or perhaps they were so in tune it came automatically. Either way, Abelard felt excluded.

'Julian, I'm scared.' Lucy turned to him and he raised an arm and put it gently around her shoulders. Perhaps, then, they were linked by something real, something Julian contributed to as well as her. Abelard saw terror in her face. It might be true after all that she was just a clerk. It could even be true she had seen people in the garden. Although Jules tried to comfort Lucy, all her composure seemed gone. Abelard listened hard again but for a while still heard nothing. And then from somewhere near the house, possibly inside, he thought he did catch a sound: short, slight, not repeated, unexplainable.

'Is there staff here?' Bowling asked. 'Guards?'

'No. People look after themselves,' Abelard said. 'It's so remote they've never anticipated trouble.'

'Oh, boy,' Lucy replied.

Abelard's back was to a window and the garden. He knew he could not be more expendable, an obstacle to everyone. He took the set of house keys from his pocket and tossed them to Julian: 'A Smith and Wesson in the safe. Behind the Duffy print in the other room.'

Bowling stood at once. 'Good stuff,' he said, like a Battle of Britain movie. He went swiftly from the room. When he returned he was not carrying the gun but gave a brief nod. 'What do you say, Simon – stay in here and let them make the running?'

Now they were comrades in arms, not prisoner and jailer. Abelard would fight to protect Bowling, because that was the job, but would Bowling do the same for him? What was in it for Jules?

Already Abelard had listed in his mind the pieces of furniture that might give cover, though they did not add up to much: a couple of big old farmhouse cabinets and presses and a brown mock leather chesterfield. People could come from three directions at once: front and rear windows of the room, and the door.

'We run for it?' Jules asked.

'They'll have blocked our car in or immobilised it.' Abelard's orders said stay until Verdun arrived.

'Yes. We'll let them come to us,' Jules replied.

To hear Bowling accept his leadership wrong-footed Abelard. But why the hell should it? He was in charge, wasn't he?

Then, not far off, a car approached at a gentle, innocent pace and stopped. Abelard waited to count how many doors slammed and when he heard none decided these extra visitors were too experienced for such mistakes. Walking to the front window Bowling closed the curtains, turned and went the length of the room and drew the others. 'I saw nothing.'

Abelard had almost forgotten his earlier fears of Jules but still tried to face him when he could. The two of them set chairs against the wall so they would have their backs to it, making all they could of cover from the furniture as they moved about the room. From where he sat Abelard could take one window and the door. Julian covered the other window and could help with the door. Lucy sat with Julian, still looking pretty bad and shaking.

Abelard grew convinced he was on a loser. If the attack from outside worked he would be killed, either during the onslaught or after. If it failed he was left with a messy situation now Julian had the pistol.

Lucy said: 'We ought to chat, for naturalness. They might be close, listening.'

Neither man took any notice. They wanted silence so *they* could listen, and count. Training said, Know your enemy and above all know numbers. There had been a couple more faint sounds, perhaps a footstep at the back of the house, perhaps a few words whispered near the front window. Abelard had put the PPK in his pocket for a time but now brought it out again. Jules sat with arms folded, no gun in sight, Lucy near him. Abelard still wondered what to make of them. He could have been fond of the girl, but, in these barren days, that went for almost any girl young, attractive, friendly. He ought to regard Jules as the degenerate of degenerates : a defector, a trafficker, a grab-all thief, maybe a nut. Yet Abelard found it hard to loathe him, and hard to fear him, though that might be stupid, suicidal. Sometimes hate was a good shield. Fear almost always was.

The first Molotov cocktail shattered the front window nearly an hour later, struck the curtains then dropped close to the wall and exploded with that fat, fuzzy, popping noise special to Molotovs, even when they fall on tarmac or concrete. Abelard thought then that perhaps he really was a cop after all. Police got fire bombed all the time, all countries. Here, muffled by a carpet, the missile sounded harmless, almost jokey. The broken bottle lay out of sight inside the curtains and for half a second the sense of harmlessness went on. There came the sudden smell of petrol, and that was it. Then a perfect horseshoe of flame began to eat fast up the draperies, torching prettily and reminding Abelard of a helpful column of fire his father used to read to him about from the Bible. Soon this shapeliness disintegrated, though, and wide, jagged lumps of blazing material floated down and curled lazily into an armchair. None of them shifted from their bits of cover to deal with the flames.

After a minute another bomb hurtled in, this time arcing to the centre of the room and now not slowed by glass or curtains because they had gone. Fragments of this bottle cracked against plaster and splintered a long wall mirror near the door. It tumbled in bits like melting ice. Fire flew all ways. Abelard heard Jules grunt and saw a blue-yellow line of flame jumping high along his jacket sleeve, on course for his neck and face. Now, Abelard and Lucy did move and helped him beat out the burning with their hands. No sound came from Lucy, as if she had shelved her terrors, or, as if once things began, the routines of training took over: *How to save a burning colleague, if he's not a colleague you want to burn.* More furniture and an open suitcase full of clothes blazed in the room and black smoke reached Abelard, hotting up his throat and the inside of his nose. Fumes from soft furniture alight would kill. Get out soon. It was not just the fire and smoke. The three would now be visible from outside, lovely illuminated targets. In minutes the fire between them and the door would be too much.

'You and me first, Jules. Together. Lucy behind. We try for any car. The Daimler if possible. Give me the keys.' Bowling handed them over. Abelard had to make sure Jules did not abandon Lucy and him.

Lucy said: 'Julian, stay together. Please.'

'Of course.'

'Please.'

'Of course.'

The three of them got up, skirted the flames and reached the hall. The outside door was solid wood and before opening it Bowling waited a second. 'Put the lights out. They'll have it easy enough without that.'

Abelard did. 'Haven't we decided they won't shoot you, Jules? What point?'

'I'm thinking of Lucy. And you,' Bowling replied.

'Really?' Abelard said.

'More or less,' Bowling said.

He threw open the door, firing twice into the darkness, scare shots only, no proper targets. Thinking about his ammunition, Abelard did not fire, though the PPK was in his hand. He could always – almost always – find a reason not to shoot. They probably had it on his dossier somewhere: 'psychological blockage re firearms'. Perhaps he had always been destined for a truncheon, instead. They charged out. Abelard was conscious of Lucy very close behind, while ahead he saw movement to left and right, men running, perhaps four, possibly more, and there must be others at the rear of the house. God, but $17 million was a lot of bait. Or even nine. Plus general vengefulness. Jules fired again. It would be just as useless at that distance: shifting targets and the marksman at a gallop.

Above all, the car interested Abelard. They had not blocked it in. He ran hard towards the Daimler, calling the others to follow. Pulling open the driver's door he tumbled aboard. He opened a rear door for Lucy. She stood staring about outside. 'Where's Julian?' she said.

'Get in.'

'Must find him.'

Abelard leaned across and pulled her into the car by the wrist, though she tugged away. He started the engine and switched on the headlights. As the car thrust forward she was attempting to bale out, the rear door still open. How had his life become such a series of hellish scrambled episodes with moving vehicles?

The lights picked up two men ahead, running crouched from the house and towards open country. One made good speed, the other laboured, more heavily built. They might have been Richard Field and Paul Matson. The Daimler's lights held them for only a second. He could not see whether they carried weapons. The car and its occupants did not interest them. They must know Bowling was not in it, and they wanted him, nothing and nobody else. A gorgeous price was on Jules. In his way Abelard wanted him, too, and in another way Lucy wanted him as well.

In a paved yard at the rear of the house he turned the car and brought it back down the drive. When he glanced behind he saw she must have left when his speed was down for the turn. God, he could come out of this with nothing. He stopped the car and jumped out. Fire had raced through the whole building and the glow lit up a huge circle of land around. He glimpsed Lucy hurrying after the two men and while he watched she passed out of the area of light and into blackness beyond. For a second more he could follow the slight glow from her T-shirt, and then nothing. Abelard sprinted after her, the PPK in his pocket now and thudding against his thigh. As much as he could he kept out of the light. Although these people might be willing enough to let him drive away untroubled – a complication removed – things would be different if they saw he might foul up the hunt for Julian and the profits.

At the edge of a small wood he paused and listened. Far off the siren of a fire engine sounded. Not long afterwards he heard two rapid shots and tried to pinpoint them, then moved in that direction, very slowly and carefully. They had seemed to come from a couple of hundred metres away, through the trees. To his right a man shouted, possibly giving an order, though too indistinct for Abelard even to be certain of the language used.

All along Lucy must have feared Jules would go his own way. 'Julian, stay together.' At the time the words had seemed about nothing more than tactics. Now, though, he saw she had known he might ditch her again – because she had brought Abelard, and with Abelard the London team. Julian's impulse to make contact with Lucy in Paris must now appear a bad error, and he had taken the chance to go solo once more, car or not.

Abelard heard more shouting. He would have liked to shout himself, calling both Jules and Lucy, letting them know he had not chickened out and done a car flit. Instead he tried for complete silence, treading carefully through the trees, fighting to suppress the sound of his breathing.

But it was the sound of someone else's terribly laboured breathing nearby that made him stop a few minutes later. At first he thought a man was approaching and he drew the Walther. Again he wanted to yell, a warning this time, an order to keep still. Once more he stayed silent, though, the gun out ahead in a stiff arm double grip. Abelard had heard no footsteps. It puzzled him that somebody careless about the din his lungs made seemed able to tread so quietly.

Then he realised why. The noise came no nearer. For another minute Abelard listened while the breathing grew louder and more agonised. He edged forward, the gun still in his hand, but pointed to the ground. In a moment he made out the shape of someone lying on his side and facing towards him.

It was too dark to see the features properly but thank God the clothes did not look like Julian's. This man wore a combat jacket, flannels and a woollen navy blue hat. He lay motionless. One fist seemed pressed into his body near the navel, as if to staunch a wound.

God, the speed of things and the intensity. No time ago he was holed up quietly in a hotel room, clasping hands with a girl through the lattice work of a couple of bed heads. Now... now a fire war, a gun war – serious gun war – with at least one serious casualty, and there could have been others, if they hadn't got out of the house faster. Was the situation breaking up around him? Until now, he had been able to impose simplicity. Find Julian's contacts and, with luck, one or more would show the way to him. It had happened like that. The old methodology stood the test. By basic track-following, he'd located Lucy Mary McIver, and she lead to Jules. But it looked now as if Lucy had lead others to Jules, also. Abelard did not know how many and not knowing how many meant he did not know if he could cope. This was no time to have a psychological blockage on firearms. In any case, what did 'cope' signify? It signified, recapturing Julian intact and holding him until Verdun and the magicians arrived. But Verdun? Was he all right? Were the troupe who would come with him all right? That is, were they acting for HMISS or for themselves, as Jules had almost said? Yes, break-up.

Covering the man on the ground with his pistol, Abelard went closer and crouched down. Now he recognised Paul Matson, could see under his open combat jacket the same rest-home pink cardigan. You could understand why seventeen million, or even nine, might be important to someone who had to dress like this. Or a cut of seventeen or nine. Blood streamed out over Matson's hand forming a little square pool on the soil before it soaked in. Abelard quickly made a pad from his handkerchief and put it gently into Matson's curled fingers against the wound. With leaves Abelard cleared the blood from his own hand. Whispering close to Matson's ear he said:

'I'm going to get help. Do you hear?'

There was no sign that he did, and although his eyes were open he seemed to see nothing, nor to know anything much. It looked as though Julian had moved on from random shooting. He might still be near. There was, in fact, nothing to do for Matson, and no time to do it if there had been. Then, as Abelard was about to start his slow advance again, a small rustling sound made him look back quickly, swinging the PPK as he turned. The man had raised himself on to an elbow and was staring at Abelard, his lips trying to form words, though no sound came yet. The arm supporting him shook and almost gave way as Abelard stepped back and put his head down again near the gasping figure on the soil. 'What can you tell me, Paul?'

Blood bubbled in Matson's mouth and when he spoke the words were thick and blurred. Abelard almost drew away to avoid a spattering, but resisted. That blood had been important to Matson. Respect it.

'Cadwallader's black boy? You can't help your skin.'

'Don't waste breath on tolerance.'

Matson paused, gathering strength and words. 'I ask you, is it fair, is it decent? Julian's a damn rotter. All I wanted was my portion.' His arm collapsed under him and he fell back silent, his hand no longer enough in his control to find the wound.

Quaint language about drug running: fair, decent, rotter, portion. Portions were what maidens used to take with them on marriage. Abelard moved away. He had worked out a method for progress in very small stages, taking a pause whenever he came to a tree stout enough to give cover. Perhaps the caution was unnecessary. The rest of them might be through the wood and clear a long time ago. Just the same, he stuck to the routine. He had to keep himself continuously aware that he lacked allies. Jules was at least as likely as the others to take a shot at him, and not even Lucy was all reliable friendship.

Passing through the wood he reached a field which sloped

gently down. A herd of Jerseys lumbered about uneasily, possibly just disturbed. Before committing himself to the open space Abelard took another pause and carefully scanned the landscape. Although light from the blazing house did not reach this far there was a half moon and little cloud, and a couple of metres off he could see what seemed to be a main road into Orléans. Possibly Julian was on his way there, looking for a lift.

At the far edge of the field something moved, something that gleamed a bit in the moonlight, almost certainly Lucy's T-shirt, still white enough after a couple of days to stand out. She walked very slowly across the bottom of the slope and towards more fields further on. At first he assumed she must simply be tired. There was an agricultural plod and weariness to it. But after a couple of seconds he decided she had lost Julian and was in despair. She might not be used to rural stress. Abelard wasn't. Her shoulders seemed hunched forward, her head hanging in misery. Then, suddenly, Abelard thought he detected two men a few hundred metres behind her moving quickly though half crouched. Occasionally they took cover and remained out of sight for so long he wondered if he had been wrong. They reappeared, though. Abelard knew it was stupid at such a distance and in darkness but did he recognise them from the motorway services when he was the genie in the Rover boot, and out?

He started to run down the field, making for a point between the pair and Lucy. When he was about half way, among the cavorting Jerseys, he heard more shots, so rapid he could not be sure how many, but at least four. At once he stopped and went low, the pistol in a two-handed grip again and moving left to right in a slow arc.

There was no more gunplay. He heard Lucy shouting and sobbing – not the sounds of someone who had been physically hurt but of a woman pleading, arguing hopelessly. It was a tone he had heard from her before and he still loathed it, because it was kept for Julian. Perhaps she could see him, or maybe she had located the pistol flashes and was talking blind to that spot. Abelard cantered again, on his way towards the sound of her voice now. He blamed himself. Hadn't he brought her to the house and been slack enough to let this crew tail them and attack?

In a moment he picked out her T-shirt very close and saw Lucy sitting on the ground, huddled like the charity picture of an autistic child. She had fallen into the same pose in the taxi. Kneeling beside her he turned the pistol towards where the two men ought to be.

'He fired at me,' she whispered.

'Julian? He wouldn't.'

'Do you know him? Know him as now?'

Abelard had wondered about that. Could people become someone else? Spies became someone else by trade. Actors become someone else by trade. Born-agains became someone else by conversion and conviction. Abelard wished there was a psychologist around to ask about Julian. He said: 'He's drifted off a bit because the job collapsed.'

'Yes, the job collapsed, didn't it?' she replied.

'For you as well?'

'I'm a clerk.'

'Yes?'

'There'll always be clerks.'

'How did you get to meet him in the first place?' Abelard asked.

'Just now I saw him and he fired,' she replied. Then she repeated this message slowly. 'He lifted the gun two handed, aimed and fired. This was serious, but I had the idea he was smiling. It was dark but that's the idea I had.'

'There were men behind you. He fired at them.' Abelard meant that if Jules wanted to shoot her he would not have missed. Perhaps he was telling her to come no further, and put a couple of bullets past her for emphasis.

'He was there.' Lifting her arm wearily she pointed at a gate. 'I spoke to him.'

'What did he say?'

'I didn't say he spoke.'

'What did you say, then?'

'I said, Please.'

'I've heard you say that before. Please what?'

'Please don't go without me. Please take me with you. Please.' She imitated her own odiously plaintive voice.

'He was protecting you.'

'Why?'

That threw him. 'You're his girl.'

'Yes?'

'Of course.'

'Me, I don't understand how you get to be so sure. Men behind me?'

'I'll look.'

'Can you get me out of here?' she said. 'He's gone. He doesn't care.'

'You shine like the Declaration of Independence. Rub some mud on your shirt.' He held a lump of soil towards her.

'You do it.' She turned to face him, waiting. It was one of those wholly dead, unsexual moments that flocked to Abelard.

'No, you. Don't move from here.' Almost double he made his way back along the edge of the field expecting to come across two more bodies. He found nothing. They could have been scared off by the sound of firing, or by the sight of him running. Or more likely they had spotted Jules and gone after him. Jules was irresistible.

He returned to Lucy. She had smeared herself and the resemblance to a blighted child was even more powerful. 'We'll look for him,' he said. She remained sitting on the ground. Taking her hand he tried to draw her up.

'Why?' she asked.

'Oh, it's the job.'

'But why do you have to stick to it? Who else does these days? You've tried to nail him. Give up. Find something for yourself. The new *faut de mieux* philosophy. Or perhaps Jules and the booty are something for yourself?' She waited a bit for an answer, which he did not give. 'Simon, he'll kill you. He told me in the house.' She still sat there. 'Listen, you're never going to get your hands on the gains, you know.'

Abelard said: 'Someone in the States called JJ Ovalle. Heard of him?'

'Julian's too far in now.'

'Ovalle. A trader but CIA links.'

'Even Julian's parents want a cut. My God.'

He tugged and she stood up. He said: 'If they've lost him they'll hunt us as second best. Or hunt *you*, anyway. I lead nowhere.'

She said nothing else but when he started down towards the distant road she followed. The stalkers might have found Julian and taken him away. Would that be the easiest answer? No need for Abelard to deal with him then because others would in their own extreme fashion. And Abelard could shelve the doubts about Cadwallader's motives in the search, and the doubts about his own. Now and then he found himself thinking fondly of all those dollars and all the freedom and indifference they could buy. Lucy seemed to sense this, smart cow.

The ground flattened out and he was among trees again, this time the corner of what seemed a full-scale forest. Once through here they would be at the road. If they failed to find Julian soon they never would. He waited for Lucy to catch up. She was standing about fifteen metres behind him, her head hanging down over the soiled T-shirt, as if fatigue and despair had once more destroyed all her strength. But when he started walking back towards her she suddenly lifted a hand and signalled him to wait. At first he thought she had seen something and stared towards where her hand seemed to point. Then he realised that she was listening. Her head was slumped forward to make that easier, not because her spirits had collapsed. The noise of his footsteps had been a distraction.

Now from somewhere deep among the trees he himself caught the sound of what could be someone at arduous violent work. Or of someone taking a hammering. Or both. Occasionally came men's voices, curt, sharp, impatient. Lucy held up an arm again, this time showing the direction they must take. They left at once, she in the lead and moving swiftly, no trace of tiredness.

More cloud had massed and for a time the moon was covered. Lucy had camouflaged only the front of herself and moving ahead of him she appeared a ghostly floating oblong of white, and a soft target. Dry thick undergrowth crackled as they walked. In a moment the voice or voices grew louder. Before Abelard could make out the words he noticed they were spoken as though with huge effort and accompanied by panting.

And then he did understand what was being said. There were two voices, both British, though neither Julian's. The words were interspersed with the sounds of punching or blows with a weapon, and he knew why the speakers seemed breathless.

'Come on, Jules, give us a break. Give yourself a break, yes?'

'Where, Jules?'

'How do we make the withdrawal?'

'Tell us, Jules, love.'

'You know we hate doing this. We're of a decent business background, like your good self.'

'We heard a Zurich bank. Not too original, but you'll take us there and sign it out?'

'Won't you, Jules?'

'Won't you, you sod? Oh, yes, you fucking will.'

There was the sound of a single blow and then a brief groan, really not much more than a bored sigh.

'It's *our* money, Jules.'

'But Jules can still have his slice.'

'Naturally.'

'Just we've got to be paid. That's only decent.'

Silence followed and then a series of heavy thuds. The panting grew.

'Julian, look at it from our point of view. This could kill you. Nobody comes out smiling.'

'Your pile is 150,000. Pounds. You could do plenty with that. Tax free. Our word. Where's business without integrity?'

'We're not the only ones looking for you. This black berk – he's not around to swap fishing yarns. Abelard. We got a dossier on him. Perhaps he wants his hand in the pot. This lad's from a nothing background and has a mother to support. Or perhaps he's turned cop and is on a cleansing mission. Some people get obsessed about cleansing, believe me. Either way, he's committed, Jules. But you know him, don't you? You know the way he'd go, but it don't matter which way he'd go, he's still after you. Then the little Welsh guy from the Outfit and Latimer. I don't know – they might be full of integrity and that and just hate you for what you done, or they could be looking for a share, like we're all looking for a share. Again, dangerous, whichever, especially the little one. Well, do I need to tell you? Time to disappear, Jules. South Africa. Brazil. Do a Lucan. You've got the breeding. Plus that other Ministry crew Paul and Richard Field heard a whisper of, getting close – I mean the Stewart bitch.'

'If they reach you, Jules, none of these others are going to cut you in. They'll cut your throat or lock you up, but they won't cut you in. Paul Matson, God rest his soul most probably, said from the start that if we found you we ought to treat you reasonably correct, Jule. He had a thing about correctness, no matter how he looked, such as a cardigan. All right, he died and you killed him, but we think he would still like you given the proper articles of war handling. This is unique to us, this old-time gallantry. You ought to grab it, Jules.'

'You've done them, Jules, the rest of them. They'll do you back. First lesson at the Harvard Business School.'

Lucy seemed to be feeling for Abelard's hand. He thought she needed comforting, as when they slept with fingers hooked together. But she released her hold on him immediately and he knew she had been seeking the pistol, still in his pocket. She might be right.

Abelard edged forward and after a few steps could see the

shapes of two men ahead. They stood talking quietly in a clearing, one of them holding a long barrelled pistol at his side, ideal for whipping. They could be the stalkers from the field. Abelard scanned the ground in case the beating and conversation had felled Julian, but could not see him. The smaller man, the one with the pistol, walked towards what looked from this distance in the dark simply a tree.

Then Abelard saw that a third man was standing with his back to it, very upright, head jaunty, gazing out into the night. This was Jules, arms stretched back on either side of the trunk, obviously tied, and his feet lashed together with what seemed to be a trousers belt. He was naked. His face, chest and legs were marked and blood ran from a head wound down his cheek and on to his shoulder. To stand straight must be costing him.

The small man stood in front of Bowling, swinging the pistol back and forth amiably across his own body. 'No rush, Jules. Four or five hours to dawn. Before that we must leave because there'll be unhelpful activity re the fire.' Abelard had heard rougher cockney but not much. 'As it is, one of our boys is very missing, as I've said, but let it go. Anyway, Jules, we decided to carry on parleying like for quite a while yet. But I got to tell you that Alec here don't think you'll ever cough. You've impressed him – strength of character. I told him it's breeding and training, plus a greedy fucking determination to hang on to all you've fucking pinched, Jules. That right, you sod? Alec's nerve's gone, that's the truth of it. He'd finish you and get clear. Forget the treasure. But you tell me, Jules, how do I forget that much? Revenge is so primitive, blood-simple. I keep telling Alec patience don't I?'

He raised his arm, still swinging the pistol, and let the barrel crack against Bowling's jaw, forcing him to tug his face away fast and try to ride the blow. For a few seconds he sagged as if dazed, but then straightened and glared directly forward, ignoring the man with the gun.

'So come on, Jules, fucking decorum, please, and a sense of

what's decent and in line with nice business practice. No system can run without that, you got to admit. This whole enterprise—it's only something on the side for you. Oh, something big on the side, yes, but not your whole life, like for us. You got an important government career, pension. Index linked. If you don't flit you could still go back to that. Well, perhaps. You *have* been a bit naughty. Do we want to do you harm? You got to be able to talk clear and sign, so them Swiss don't get hesitant, like they did for quite a while with all that Jewish money. Can we travel to Zurich or wherever with somebody who looks like he's been caught in the fucking mangle?'

The other man had kept out of the way but now took position in front of Bowling, too. More beating was due. Abelard feared Lucy would scream or rush forward. Abelard brought out the PPK. He did loath firearms, but once in a while it had to be done, and he had schooled himself. Christ, of course. Even in these peaceful times what sort of operator got through his career a gun virgin? And he still was an operator, still HMISS. He made Lucy crouch, then crouched himself and took two-handed aim at the man holding the pistol. Alec might be armed, as well, but the short one had the weapon in view, ready.

Before any more blows could fall on Jules, Abelard yelled: 'Both of you, freeze! I'm armed. Throw down the pistol.' It was stuff he'd learned from American cop drama on TV, not what he'd been instructed in, and as he spoke he knew they would not obey. Maybe he should have fired, not talked at all – what Lucy had wanted when she felt for the gun. His mission was police-like and he had come to think half like a police officer, but he was not a police officer, not bound by all the heavy rigmarole of shouted warnings. He had been trained as for war. Do it.

Obviously sensing he was the target, the little man hurled himself to the side, falling, turning and firing as he did. He'd read the Jungle Warrior's Survival Manual.

A bullet dug into the soil between Abelard and Lucy, throwing up dust and twigs. He recalled the exercise range at Dartford. The notion pleased him: made Abelard think of the job he was still supposed to be part of, and also made him remember how then he had believed entirely in it. Possibly even Julian did at that time. Lucy bellowed at Abelard: 'Shoot, for Christ's sake. What the fuck are you waiting for?' This was not like the exercise range at Dartford: you were supposed to shoot without any further prompting, and in those days he did. At dummies. The small man would have fired again, guided by her voice, but his head and face were square in Abelard's sights and he shot first, shot twice. So, those reactions instilled at Dartford did still work, eventually, and after a bit of screaming from Lucy. And because of an anxiety about what would happen to her if he did not shoot.

Although he saw no hit marks, Abelard watched the man's head sink towards the soil and the gun tumble from his grip. He did not move. Abelard kept the PPK pointed at him and only switched when it had become almost too late: Alec now was running towards Lucy and him, feet flailing, fists ready. He seemed to have no gun.

More rigmarole: 'Stop or I fire,' Abelard shouted, but Alec came on, burly, silent, obviously fit. Abelard threw the PPK to Lucy. Himself, he would not shoot an unarmed man, and no amount of training could have changed that in him. No, but if things turned bad he hoped Lucy or Julian might do that piece of rough stuff for him. *Fine moral point, Simon, so fine it doesn't fucking exist.* In the moment before Abelard grappled with the charging figure he saw Lucy dash to help Julian now the way was open. Her priorities were always obvious, the daft bitch. Abelard took in a store of oxygen. This kind of fighting he preferred. Wasn't he built for it, wasn't he bred to it? At home around Cardiff docks, hadn't there been dirty street fights and dirty pub fights over girls or cards or bugger all, and dirty rugby games?

Alec, this rushing well-tuned thug, could be a failed boxer.

Traces of his worked-on physique were there and the big marked face looked like an often over-matched pro's. Abelard felt almost a kind of sympathy for him, despite what he had just seen happening to Julian. In fact, on all accounts sympathy for Alec was stupid. He could do without it. Abelard was still straightening from his sniper's position and nowhere near properly balanced when Alec reached him. An intelligent fist caught Abelard square in the eye and on the side of his nose, half spinning him. There was timing in that fist and economy. Abelard nearly fell. Briefly, the punch shadowed his senses. He knew he had to keep on his feet or he was finished. And somehow he did right himself and swung out an arm in a wild karate chop which hit nothing. One eye was beginning to close fast and the other had lost focus after the crack on the nose. He peered for Alec as another punch caught him in the stomach, but nothing too fatal.

Momentarily he got a glimpse of Alec very close and this time lashed out with a foot at his legs, trying to sweep them away. It failed. The man was too strong and too ready for Abelard's standard issue Dartford ploys. Alec had seen a lot of street action, too. Although Abelard struggled for vision, the next two punches reached him out of nowhere, one to the side of the jaw, one over the heart. He was right – this boy had boxed and knew how to land. Why the hell wouldn't Lucy or Julian shoot the sod? Didn't he, Abelard, rate any longer now those two were reunited? Couldn't they realise who'd made the reunion possible?

Alec had hurt his fist and for a second was bent over, nursing injured fingers. Perhaps he had forgotten that central boxer's rule, Protect yourself at all times. With everything he had left Abelard aimed a kick at his chin, a toe cap uppercut. Thank God for brogues, not trainers. There came that fine, fourteen carat feel of enemy bone against real leather, and of bone giving, spreading out and disintegrating. Alec was jerked up straight, stunned, wide open. Abelard could still not see him properly, but well enough, and he had time now. It was like that encounter near the Rover. Jumping forward he chopped twice at Alec's neck with the right and put a left on the spot where the kick had caught him. A bit of a scream came before he folded slowly downwards, and the moment Alec hit the ground he began the profound, unnatural snores of the concussed. Abelard stepped away, craving a moment to find his breath and pamper his wounds. At once Bowling came forward quickly, still naked, and stood straddling Alec, the PPK pointed down at his head. Lucy had given him the gun. Naturally.

'Christ, no, we need to talk to him!' Abelard bellowed and, as the gun went off, struck Julian with a shoulder charge, knocking him into the undergrowth. It was too late. The snoring became gasping and then gargling, like Matson, and then there was no sound at all. Julian righted himself and Abelard took the PPK from him without a fight. Going quickly to the body, Abelard picked up the long barrelled pistol, emptied the chamber and put the gun in his pocket. That left Julian's .38 to be accounted for.

'Where are your clothes?' Abelard asked.

'I was clobbered,' Julian said. 'When I came to they were tying me to the tree.'

The three of them scoured the clearing and some woodland but found nothing. It would have to be one of the dead men's gear. 'Too big or too small, Jules?' Abelard asked.

They searched both bodies and piled up what they found alongside each: bits and pieces any man might have in his pockets – money, condoms, cigarettes, cough sweets, pens. No identification. These boys had known what they were doing, until they got shot. Abelard undressed Alec: 'Everything?'

'Except the underclothes, I think. That's a quote. *The Military Philosophers*. Anthony Powell.'

'You read *and* thieve? But I forgot you're literary. I traced you through Oxford – saw your poem.'

'Poem?'

'*Going Straight*? The lecturer was very keen on that.'

'Plagiarised it from a collection of jail poems I nicked at a stall.'

'Not going straight, then.'

'Who does? These days, who does?'

Bowling had begun to shiver – part cold, part shock, and hurriedly pulled on the shirt, suit and raincoat. All of it hung loose. Abelard said: 'And yet your class shines through. I take it the little fellow matters and Alec is hired knuckles.'

'Both mattered. Both in the trade. I wouldn't have knocked him off if he was nobody would I, Simon? That would be bloody evil. Am I into that sort of game, for God's sake?'

But Abelard left it.

'You'll stay with me, with us this time, Julian?' Lucy asked. It was that sickening, imploring voice again. Jesus, the life long devotion.

'What else would I want, Lucy?' Julian held her hand while he walked a few steps, trying his legs. But the speed when he moved in to kill had showed not much was wrong. And his mind seemed fine – dirty but fine. Jules had steel, or at least pig iron.

They could not go back to the house for the Daimler, but somehow they must put distance between themselves and the police search. At first light it would intensify. They might have found Matson by now, dying or dead, and there were the two men here. Abelard would hate the job of explaining to French police how the pair had been killed, and why. These deaths could look like murders. Perhaps they were. Verdun Cadwallader would go mad if the Outfit were implicated. Mad dwarfs could be dismaying.

'Down to the main road, then hire a car,' he said. 'No bugger will give us a lift, looking like this.' Scarred and engulfed in his borrowed suit Julian might have been part of a 1939 refugee march. Lucy's clothes were covered with disguise mud and Abelard knew he had the marks of the fight still on him. He was struck again by a thought that came earlier, one he still disliked: his own safety seemed more and more bound up with Julian's, as if he had ceased to be the hunter and become Bowling's and Lucy's partner. Perhaps in the new scheme of things there were no hunters, only business and all the bits and pieces of business, such as partnerships.

It took them more than an hour to pass through the forest and then they paused in fields bordering the road. There had been no pursuit. After a rest they followed the road, keeping to the fields when they could. On the edge of a small town they waited until 8am and then Abelard asked Lucy to go in and try to hire a car. In place of her murky shirt he gave Lucy his own and they cleaned up her shoes. A woman alone and reasonably spruce should not cause too much interest. Bowling wanted to go instead, but neither she nor Abelard agreed. 'You might forget your way back, Jules,' Abelard told him. 'You and I will talk about the dead.' As long as Abelard was with Julian, Lucy would return.

Carrying some of the money they had taken from the corpses she left, walking vigorously, as if on her way to work. To see her in his shirt warmed Abelard. This was another of those little intimacies, and with Lucy little intimacies were the only sort he got.

On the ground between Jules and him he placed the two heaps of possessions from the men's clothes, but before they could start picking through he heard the harsh, bustling chunter of a helicopter, not far off and very low. Lucy had obviously heard it, too, and he saw her falter and glance up and back at the din. For a second he thought she might stop altogether, the strength suddenly taken from her legs by fear. Then she got control again and walked doggedly on.

Quickly Abelard and Bowling slid into a dried-up drainage ditch, lying flat, faces down. Of course, police would have top-notch spotting equipment up there and if the helicopter came any closer he and Jules would be detected. But it passed on towards the town and towards Lucy. Abelard lifted his head and watched it hang for a while above her before continuing. Bluffing things out she looked up and waved. It might work.

He and Bowling stayed in the ditch, lying head to head, just as he had with Lucy in the hotel, but no hand holding. For a time the helicopter disappeared and when it came back began a patterned search far off, very slowly covering squares of landscape on the edge of the town.

'Let's hope she doesn't roll up in a car until they've gone,' Abelard said. But perhaps the chopper had already made a radio call about her, so she might not arrive at all.

'Don't fret about Lucy. She wouldn't about you.'

'And you don't give a shit about anyone, anything, do you, including her?'

'You want her?' Bowling replied. He was half up, watching the helicopter. 'I don't care about the blobs who died last night, obviously. They were asking to be taken. When it happens they bleat about fair's fair.' The helicopter came no closer. He lay back in the ditch again. 'Lucy? I went back to Paris for her, didn't I, put myself on toast for you?'

'You'd have finished her last night. She says you shot at her.'

'Near. I shot to put her off.'

'I did wonder.'

'Because I knew where she came you'd follow, Simon. Part that famous sense of responsibility of yours. Part sex. Which more? Can't tell. Something in you scares me. It's as though you've gone all lawman. Is that it, Simon? Some turn like me, maybe some turn that other way, the path of rectitude. Once in a while Cadwallader and the rest can be damn smart. They pick you to do the chase and you give it everything. It's become part of the fucking race war and the class war. You want to settle long-time old scores.'

'No, not like that. I need to prove things haven't rotted all the way through.'

'They have. Suddenly it's you with the jambok and me on the end of it. Even without the colour bit, it's the poor boy from the slums hitting back at the gilded team like me who still regard the Outfit as their preserve.'

'Fuck the sociology,' Abelard replied.

The helicopter seemed to be drifting away towards the burned house. They climbed from the ditch. Bowling bent down and stirred one of the heaps of possessions with his finger, then picked out a Parker ball-point pen.

'Who are they, Jules – Alec and the other?'

'Partners, obviously. You meet all sorts in this trade.'

'Your partners?'

'Once.'

'So they had a right to some of it.'

'Right? Fuck rights in this game. It's take. Does that sound like melodrama?'

'Yes.'

'Oh, there are some rules. They're made to be broken. Why ex-spies are good at the trade.'

'Then there's Glass/Graff,' Abelard said.

'Another partner, in several ways a partner, as you've guessed. He'd claim an entitlement. He has to claim an entitlement because some political louts are leaning on him for donations. He's frightened, poor Pete.'

'Matson, Field?'

'Business connections, naturally. You find you've got a lot of business connections if you take off with a tranche of the profits.' Staring up the road towards the town he said, 'Where's this bloody woman?'

'Matson and Field reached another girl of yours.'

'I heard. Poor Barbara Francis. She knew nothing. Just a girl.'

'Not how her sister saw it.'

'Sister?'

'Veronica Rombarde.'

'Oh, Ronnie. Not really her sister, Simon. She's called Ronnie for sound reasons.'

'She didn't seem like that?' Abelard said.

'How many have you known? She was even jealous of Barbara's hamster, you know. She'd want to make things between me and Barbara sound like business only.'

'Matson's probably dead,' Abelard replied.

'Only probably? I thought I'd done him right. This Lucy?' He moved towards the road as a small Renault with a woman driving seemed to pull in, but accelerated away. 'She's seen something?' He searched the sky for the helicopter and then looked across the fields to the woods. 'What's she playing at?'

'I trust her.'

Bowling shrugged, as though he found the word bizarre. Abelard began going through the possessions, making notes. Bowling unscrewed the body of the pen and took from it a rolled piece of paper which he glanced at, then handed to Abelard. It was a tiny picture of Julian, with the dossier material on the back.

'All this true, Jules?'

Bowling was shaking out the condoms from their packets on the ground. There were about two dozen and he started slitting them open with a penknife, still searching. They contained nothing. He took his biog back from Abelard and read it slowly. '"Schizo". Who wouldn't be, in this trade. And with my parents.'

Oh, God, potty-training psychology. 'You don't see them?' Abelard asked. 'Parents are important. Mine were. My mother is.'

'They liked the distance, until they heard about the funds,' Julian said. He stared towards the road again.

'Heard how?'

'I told them. I thought it would make an impression – show Julian could do things on his own. My father's very keen on that sort of thing – he's supreme self-made-man. Who else would make anything like him?'

'And it did impress them?'

'Yes, I've gone high in their rating. They wouldn't feel degraded to bleed me, now. Anything with six noughts on it they can respond to, even dollars. You must meet them.'

'I might.'

'Breaking the news I've snuffed it?'

'Are you going to snuff it?' Abelard asked.

'We're unprotected here.'

'Lucy wouldn't abandon us,' Abelard said.

'No, she can't,' Bowling replied.

'What's that mean?'

He did not answer.

'Because of her unbreakable loyalty to you?' Abelard said.

Bowling chuckled. 'Along those lines.' But he spoke as if he did not know why anyone should be loyal to anyone. Abelard had met traces of that palsy in the Outfit. This wasn't any longer a matter of disloyalty used calculatedly and ideologically as a weapon. Not Philby-type disloyalty. Today, people behaved as if so little deserved their fidelity that betrayal had grown negligible, like adultery with a tart. The great polarities were gone. Treachery came very various in the late 1990s, and the Outfit always expected a fresh form of it, which Bowling's probably was. He had adapted. He, too, was a version of the next millennium spy. As he'd said, some went one way, some the other, like Abelard. And if these inconstancies were now central to the job Abelard would expect them in love, too – except where people had become manacled together in some way, as Jules claimed he and Lucy were. Which way? It would bring her back now, would it, as it had brought him back to Paris?

'The dossier mentions NATO duties – the Middle East,' Abelard said.

'That was accurate, wasn't it? You'd know. You were Personnel. Still are?'

'But how did—?'

'How come the drugs business? You must have heard all this so many times, Simon. Anyone can see it. One helps the other. Overlap. People open private operations as a spin off from the career. All countries' agents moonlight now, including the Russians. Espionage isn't John Buchan any more or even John le Carré.' He glared towards the road again.

'She'll come. She adores you.' Abelard would have liked to spit the word.

'Not since she saw me in this suit.'

And maybe not since she decided he had tried to kill her. Abelard did not believe his denial. Perhaps Lucy didn't either. Did he hope she didn't? Of course. Abelard said: 'Does Lucy qualify for a cut of the takings? Or is she just a girl, like Barbara Francis?'

'You don't accept that about Barbara?'

'She had a tooth knocked out and then worse for being just a girl.'

'Here's that bloody Renault again,' Julian replied. It was approaching from the opposite direction. Even Abelard's single, clouded working eye could make out Lucy now. They scanned the countryside and the sky and saw nothing to worry them. The car pulled in and she beckoned urgently. Abelard and Bowling ran from near the ditch and up an embankment to the road. Was Jules still his prisoner?

Lucy said: 'I wanted to scout. You weren't anxious I hope.'

'Not a bit,' Bowling replied. 'I knew that was it.' He sat alongside her, with Abelard in the back.

'Main roads?' she asked.

'Yes,' Bowling said. 'Go where we can lose ourselves in traffic, or the chopper will get us.'

'They'll have blocks on the big roads,' Abelard said, only in part because he thought Bowling's tactics wrong. He had to show he was in command, especially show Lucy.

'Yes, possibly,' Bowling said.

'I turn off?' Lucy asked. They were nearing what might be the last side road before the town.

'OK,' Bowling said.

She went left and for the next fifteen minutes followed small roads taking them deeper into the countryside. She kept the speed respectably low. From the air they might look like the farmer's wife back from shopping. Abelard felt more comfortable but still listened for the chopper, imagined its shadow suddenly darkening the car.

They came to a village or something less. He saw no name. There was a café and a small store, a straggle of cottages, a gleaming steel and glass telephone booth, a farm giving on to the road. Dogs mildly savaged one another and Lucy let the speed drop even lower. It looked too bloody innocent, too French. 'Gently,' Abelard muttered, though by now they were crawling. There must be no accidents.

There weren't. They passed safely through. Abelard let himself relax again a bit. Ten kilometres later on a stretch of totally deserted minor road a single, elderly stout cop suddenly appeared from nowhere and stood in their way holding up a fat hand. As far as Abelard could see he had no vehicle, not even a bike. Perhaps all he wanted was a lift. 'Do I stop?' Lucy whispered. Her voice had deserted her.

'I don't think so,' Julian said.

'Yes,' Abelard said.

But this time she listened to Julian and when they were about twenty metres from the gendarme she pushed the accelerator down to the floor. Even before that the policeman sensed trouble and began pulling open his holster.

'Go through the bastard,' Julian yelled.

The little car jumped ahead. The officer had his pistol out and fired as they reached him. But maybe he had orders not to kill. He shot at the front tyres. The car shuddered three times, first as one of the tyres went, then when it hit the cop, and lastly as a rear wheel passed over him.

'Hold straight,' Bowling shouted, but Lucy couldn't and the Renault lurched off the road to the left. Her foot seemed still jammed down on the accelerator and she took her hands from the wheel in despair. Bowling grabbed at it, too late. The Renault began sliding down a steep grass bank and Abelard was thrown hard against the side. He knew that in a moment they would turn over. This flimsy foreign box was likely to cave in and a man could get his neck broken or his skull crushed. His luck with cars might finally be about to close. He gripped the butt of the PPK. Even if the tumble did not do for him there was Julian to think about.

Or not. Abelard came to still huddled in the rear of the Renault, which seemed to have righted itself again. Pain jabbed at him in various areas – head, balls, both knees and a thumb, but nothing he could not cope with. He found he no longer had his fingers on the pistol, nor could he locate it when he urgently felt around.

Lucy said: 'Si, I think you're OK – but you don't like being called Si, especially during recuperation.'

'From some it's all right.'

'I ran my hand around a few of your most vulnerable spots while you slumbered. The areas I could reach from here.'

'I thought I was dreaming.'

'I guess nothing's broken.' She was outside the car, speaking to him through a shattered rear window. A bruise like a charcoal biscuit had come up on her cheek and blood coated her teeth. When Abelard gingerly moved his head to look for Bowling she said: 'Julian's gone – again. We came to a sort of agreement.'

'Oh, yes?'

'He wanted to kill you.'

'Love-hate. It's hate this month.'

'This calmness – is that what's called phlegm, the thing all you English have?'

'I'm Welsh,' Abelard said. 'We call it bronchitis. It's the damp.'

'Jules decided you knew too much, obviously: the takings, this Ovalle in the States, the other contacts.'

'So how did you stop him.'

'From killing you? He was knocked cold, too. I took your PPK, reloaded it and frisked him while he was out. I've been doing tours of inert male physiques. He was clean. That Smith and Wesson must be lost. When he woke up I told him we all stayed together or he could split. I had the Walther in my hand when I said it. He split.' She took a gaze over the car roof at the terrain and then at the sky. 'Could I let him finish you, for God's sake? Look, Si, we more or less slept together.'

'Less.'

'These things can take time. Anyway, I wouldn't stand by and see… I mean, I always knew Julian could be a shit, but that would have been super shit.'

Abelard stirred. Some pains grew, though still nothing beyond. 'Thanks.'

'I pulled the cop off the road and out of sight. The car's under trees here so we've got a chance. We need to make a move soon.' She tugged at the buckled door and managed to open it a couple of feet. 'Give me your hand.' She helped him out.

'Move where?'

'In due course, the UK, I guess. Would you take me?'

He tried a few steps. A little while ago he had watched Julian do the same after injuries. There was a lurch element and the small pain element but he did not fall. Not far away he saw the policeman's elbow sticking out from bushes.

Approaching slowly, he covered it. 'Why to Britain?'

'Where else? You have to return, yes? We're boxed together again. I need some protection. Just till we get there. I won't be a nuisance. I mean, I don't know your set-up at home. You married or something like that?'

'I have a very nice mother.'

'I'll go my own way once we get there, if that's what you want.'

No, that was not what he wanted. 'You said protection.'

'Only *en route*.'

'You think Julian will come looking again? Others?'

She fingered her bruised cheek, seemed to be deciding whether she could tell him the next bit. Then she said: 'It takes two signatures to get the loot out, his and mine. We fixed that in happier, trusting times, though being Julian he was never really in favour. For that much money we have actually to turn up together, sign in their presence.'

He saw now why Julian said she had to return to him, understood what the manacles were that kept them together. 'Why he came back to Paris for you?'

'I want to think there was more to it. I don't.'

'So you'll have to join up again eventually,' Abelard said.

'Eventually will do.'

'You told him you'd be findable through me?'

'It was obvious, wasn't it?'

Could he leave for home? Was he entitled? Cadwallader and party were on their way to what had once been called the safe house and Abelard's job in France was to find and hold Julian Bowling, not find and let go. 'Would you have shot him?' Abelard asked.

'If?'

'If he'd tried to take the gun back to kill me,' Abelard replied.

'I couldn't see killing you was necessary.'

'No, but would you have shot him?'

'I couldn't see killing you was necessary,' she said.

'Jules isn't always too rational.'

'Right.'

In a while, Abelard said: 'Best walk back to Orléans. We'll be less conspicuous there.'

'Oh?'

She had a point. How did a couple make themselves unnoticeable when the girl looked as if she had been kicked in the face with a Doc Marten's, and the man had a both-legs limp and wore a damn good suit over a filthy, too small, Leonard Cohen T-shirt? All the same, they began to walk and for the first time since the Rembrandt he felt cheerful. But he said: 'If you're needed to co-sign you must have known he didn't try to kill you in the field last night.'

'Oh, no, I know he did try. Jules isn't always too rational.'

'I'd heard that, as a matter of fact.'

'In some ways it can be attractive,' she said. 'Only some. How did a psychotic stay ahead of the Outfit's medicos, for

God's sake? Remember that would-be agent in Harris's *Red Dragon* who's kept out of the FBI by "procedures designed to detect instability"? You people don't have procedures?'

'We're Brits. Jules is from a rich family, proper education. Those used to rate above stability. Anyway, think of who did get into the FBI, starting with Hoover and his frocks. If Jules had shot you in the field it would be impossible to get the money, and if you'd shot him because he wanted to kill me it would be impossible to get the money.'

'We're all alive.'

'You're a clerk and can reload a PPK?'

10

'I KNOW YOU'VE met Judith Stewart, Simon. She's going to sit in with us today,' Cadwallader said warmly.

'Grand to see you again, Simon. We seemed to lose track in France.' She grinned, with total friendliness. He still thought of her voice as coming to him through a bag.

'Nice to have female company occasionally,' Cadwallader declared. 'And especially from another Section. We mustn't lead narrow little lives.'

'Honoured to be asked,' she replied.

'And here come drinks,' Cadwallader trumpeted: Tio Pepe on that tray, g&t's on this one.' Turkey Latimer took his jacket off and undid the buttons of his waistcoat. Informality was the thing. Around the Outfit everyone knew that whenever Cadwallader wanted to do some off-the-record interrogating – and especially some off-the-record interrogating of *staff* – he organised it over dinner in this private room above the lounge bar of The Blade. Heavy rock from a juke box would occasionally boom up through the floor and drown out a question or answer, but Cadwallader kept coming back. It suited because the scruffiness and din and absence of security all proclaimed these sessions casual. If Verdun staged the gathering in the Outfit they might have copped official status and anyone under questioning could then demand a lawyer. He would have found that a procedural pain.

Abelard took a gin. Cadwallader would note whether he acted normally. Abelard promised himself it would be only one. Keep the brain unswamped.

'And how's your mother, Simon?' Roger Link-Mite asked. 'Settled into the new digs all right? A bore for her. She has to suffer because of our foolish job.'

Link-Mite had on his Prince of Wales grey suit and a white spotted maroon bow tie. He was almost small, very lean, bony faced, with thick fair hair and a small moustache. The story said he had his job as the only man in the Outfit who did not make Cadwallader feel short. There were other reasons.

As they stood around with drinks, Link-Mite said: 'Simon, nobody's blaming you for that imbroglio at the safe house. Verdun and Turkey and I fortunately had an early tip something was wrong, so we didn't travel. You did damn well to get the people out of there alive.' He nodded emphatically.

'It's their brilliant shepherd's pie,' Cadwallader cried.

Anyone sat anywhere. It could have looked bad and threatening if the questioners were on one side of the table and the victim on the other. Just the same, Abelard knew he was the victim. He had Judith Stewart on his right and Turkey to his left. Link-Mite sat opposite, so perhaps things were not so very random.

Cadwallader said: 'Of course, we've had the bloody Frog police creating and the Minister doing his tender nut: corpses, a burned-out house, the wrecked hire car. The Foreign Office are very bothered about compo for the Renault.'

'I've been saying to Simon that regardless of these snags, Verdun, he did well at Orléans,' Link-Mite remarked.

'Leave the French and the fucking Minister, to me,' Cadwallader replied.

'And so clever of Simon to bring the girl back,' Link-Mite added. 'One doesn't wish to sound heavy but she is the best possible bait. Bowling *must* try to reach her. We wait.'

'Are you fond of her, Simon?' Judith Stewart asked. She was in denim and tall boots today, a brave attempt to lop off a decade.

Abelard said: 'I didn't want to see her hurt.'

'Quite,' Judith Stewart said, 'but I meant more. We hear you spent a night with her at the Rembrandt.'

'A hideaway,' Abelard replied.

'But she went willingly with you?' Link-Mite asked.

'We know quite a bit about this girl, Verdun,' Judith said.

'Perhaps I should have invited her,' Cadwallader replied.

'She wouldn't have come,' Abelard said. He was labouring through pie. He wondered, as people always wondered at these meals, how many of the people investigating his loyalty had much of it themselves, and who and what to. Above all he watched Cadwallader. If Verdun regarded the dollars as what really mattered it would probably mean all the rest of them did, too, and were helping him try to corner it. Or were working to corner it themselves, independently. That would seem to be Judith Stewart's category. Whichever way you looked at it there was a lot of menace about, too much for easy digestion.

Abelard had, of course, sat in at a hundred meetings and umpteen meals in The Blade where he was the only black present, and it had never seemed especially relevant. Today was different. He felt targeted, pinpointed. When he looked around this table he recalled a question of his mother's: how could any of these people really understand him? He added another: why should they want to? Downstairs in the bar there was always a good sprinkling of blacks and he might have felt more comfortable there, less exposed. But this was the late 1990s and he had climbed, was up there with the big and dangerous and grasping folk, his chosen colleagues, and exactly the kind of people his father had warned against. 'Straight as a butcher's hook,' his dad used to say about West Walians like Cadwallader. Could Abelard manage?

Link-Mite said: 'It's likely the girl is on a double signature with Bowling. Have you anything about that, Simon?'

'Not to date.'

'But does the relationship with Jules go beyond this?' Link-Mite banged his fork down as he finished the dish and looked for more. He licked his moustache.

'They were fond of each other,' Abelard replied.

'I find it hard to think of Jules as *fond* of anyone,' Judith said. 'In and out of beds, yes, men and women's, but fond? That's a human word.'

'Did the girl object to his bisexuality, Simon?' Link-Mite asked. 'Could be seen as mucky.'

'Not that I saw,' Abelard said.

'You said *were* fond,' Turkey said. 'What turned it off?'

'I'm not sure,' Abelard replied.

'Whatever it was it gave you a kind of entrée to her, if you'll accept that term, yes?' Turkey asked. 'I mean the Rembrandt and coming back to GB with you.'

'I'm safety. She knew I worked for the government,' Abelard replied.

'Too modest,' Judith said.

From next to her on the other side Turkey Latimer began his heart-of-the-matter, let's-get-to-basics-and-cut-the-bullshit turn. He was leaning back in his chair, a fork with some sort of meat on it held pointing upwards in his left hand. 'I've seen the paper work on the Renault and I still don't understand why they let you live, Simon.'

'Yes, I was surprised,' Abelard said. 'And grateful. Is that OK?'

'I like it,' Cadwallader chortled. Turkey said: 'Does it seem likely that, even if the girl was armed and Julian wasn't, he would just walk away because she told him to? This is a man trained to take a weapon from a Stasi sentry.'

Link-Mite said: 'What we're getting at, I suppose, Simon, is that factors indicate a compact between you and them, certainly between you and the girl – which could be cock-based – a powerful element, and nobody here would dispute it – but also between you and Bowling. You were, are, partners, that's one possibility. So, of course he didn't see you off after the accident.'

'We have your account of the crash and then the French police version done later, and largely from ignorance it's true,' Turkey said. 'We don't really know that things happened as you report, Simon. Faked car prangs – oldest ploy in the *Teach Yourself Spying* handbook. It might all have been manufactured by the three of you to provide conditions for Julian's disappearance. The dead cop's genuine enough, yes, but you could have run him down and then seen the chance to concoct a tableau. You're both trained to spot opportunities.'

Link-Mite said: 'You see, Simon, the damage report puts the main impact near the driver's seat. You tell us the girl was driving, yet she's the only one not knocked out, and not just not knocked out but fit and bright enough to search both of you, move the policeman's body into cover, and for all I know play a game of Patience while she's waiting for you to come round.'

'Were you in with Julian from the start or simply able to force a deal on him in Orléans?' Judith asked.

'What deal?' Abelard replied.

'He goes free at Orléans and eventually you get a cut in recompense. You'd trust him to honour an agreement like that?'

'No Orléans deal,' Abelard said.

'No. My feeling is that you were in it together from the start,' Stewart replied. 'You were always so bloody well briefed. You get to the Chandon works at spot on the crux time. You know where to pick up the girl when she's with Glass. You're at the rendezvous when he joins Lucy in Paris.'

Cadwallader said: 'We're all very upset about the death of Judith's lad, Rex Laver, at Chandon's, Simon. We'd be glad to hear your considered account of what went on.'

'You were alone with the body,' Link-Mite said. 'Were you acting as Bowling's bodyguard? Did you kill Laver because he was getting too close to Julian?'

'That's to put it very, very bluntly,' Cadwallader said chattily through a mouthful. He made no attempt to withdraw the question, though, or rephrase it, but sat gazing at Abelard, chewing with system and waiting for the answer.

'I didn't know Laver was getting close to Julian,' Abelard said. 'As I understood it from Judith, Bowling was nowhere near Chandon's. Christ, I got that address from someone at Oxford. It was an official inquiry.'

'That's on record,' Link-Mite replied. 'But didn't it seem unlikely to you that Julian would still be interested in a place he'd used years ago as an undergraduate? Didn't it seem unlikely that the place would still be there, in fact, or be there in the capacity he remembered it for.'

'Certainly it did,' Abelard said.

'Yet you still went?' Link-Mite replied.

'It was one of only two possibles I had. And it turned out… it turned out as it turned out, didn't it?' Abelard said. 'It was unlikely, but it worked.'

'Worked?' Link-Mite asked.

'There were relevant people there.'

'Very relevant, oh, indeed,' Link-Mite said.

'What the fuck does that mean?' Abelard replied.

Link-Mite said: Of course, Verdun, we'd heard that Julian was to be at Chandon's that night for some sort of transaction. Laver established this and gave a call, but was dead by the time back-up arrived.'

'The big Peugeot team,' Abelard said.

'Perhaps we should have been on the spot, not hanging back for a summons,' Judith Stewart said. 'The small delay became crucial.'

Latimer was going at what remained of his food in the gobble-gobble style that had brought his nickname. He summoned some benignness. 'Disaffection would be quite understandable in you, Simon,' he said, 'as would determination to get among big private funds – not leave them all to some despicable self-seeker, despicable white self-seeker, from a very comfortable family, like Julian.'

Abelard said: 'He thinks that's why you put me on his tail.'

Turkey ignored this. 'Why the hell should you be loyal? Why the devil should you be happy to spy for a fourth-rate country, which has no secrets of its own and which can't profit from the secrets of others should we manage to pinch a few, because every damn thing has to be referred to Brussels – or Bonn? Why, more to the point, should you wish to act the

policeman for this fourth-rate country – because that's the kind
of role this is, isn't it? Oh, I feel so. We were asking you to go
and feel someone's collar. I think that's the slang term for an
arrest, isn't it? Not just feel someone's collar, but the collar of a
friend and colleague. And what has this fourth-rate country
done for you, or for admirable but underprivileged people like
your mother? Sod all. Even in these advanced Blairite times
you and your fellows are tolerated here merely as a political
sop and come up against people like Jules – like most of us here.
And now you look around at us and wonder how far we are
into the rackets, too. Are we quizzing you as upright officers
from HMISS or as moonlighters like Julian, but not so bright
or rich? You're wholly entitled to ask.'

Abelard wondered if he was being led on. Of course he did.
It was a piece of interrogation technique.

'All for pudding?' Cadwallader trilled. 'I'm never sure how
I fit into these social analyses: a Welshman from a farming
family – chapel, no spoken English until I was six. In a sense
Simon and I are both Welsh outsiders.'

Turkey said: 'Verdun, you've stayed about as Welsh as
Richard Burton did.'

'Bread and butter pudding,' Cadwallader cried out.
'Heaven!'

'The girl's with your mother now?' Link-Mite asked.

'And some of our people watching in case Jules turns up,'
Abelard said.

'It becomes a question of what your relationship is with the
girl, Lucy Mary McIver, doesn't it, Simon?' Judith Stewart
said. 'Have you got a nice little threesome going, you looking
after her when Jules is away or on a gay kick? Or have you
somehow managed to cut Julian out? She's in your house,
enjoying full domesticity. Do you and she hope to locate Julian
and do a deal for the takings? He can't touch the cash without
her signature, and she's going to insist you're counted in, that
it? Lucky Simon. You must be providing something she was
short of.'

'She's a nice kid,' Abelard replied.

'Where's the money?' Link-Mite asked.

'Switzerland. No originality.'

'That much we know. Which bank? Account number?' Link-Mite said.

'She doesn't tell me.'

'You give her accommodation, bring her to safety, yet she holds out on you? We're supposed to believe that?' Link-Mite said.

'She might think I'm not interested,' Abelard replied.

Turkey said: 'Simon's certainly going to get the notion we're in this for the money, Verdun, if Roger continues that approach.'

'Does it fucking matter what he thinks?' Link-Mite replied. 'We know where we are. We want to know where he is.'

Turkey said: 'I still feel that—'

Link-Mite said: 'In every interrogation—'

'Interrogation?' Turkey asked. 'We are all friends here, surely.'

Link-Mite said: 'In every interrogation there are questions that ultimately have to be put direct. Listen, Turkey – you and your bogus sympathy – all that mush about understanding him because he's black and back-street and his bloody prole mother being so noble – don't you think he can see through that? He's as well trained as you and I. He's done the three months' question and answer course. You make with the brotherly love bit and Simon just switches over to maximum resistance – and to maximum contempt for your crudity. "Disaffection would be quite understandable in you." My God, that's a lift, word for word, from HW Sampler's Interrogation Procedures. Don't you think he recognises the smarmy self-deprecation line and the suffering buddies talk – let's hate Brussels and Bonn together.'

Abelard supposed this come-clean outburst would also be part of an act, rehearsed before by Turkey and Link-Mite, and designed to draw him to Roger Link-Mite as the one who

respected his brain and experience. Another famed interrogation route. There was ploy within ploy here.

'Forgive me, Simon, if I spoke disparagingly about your
mother,' Link-Mite said.

Abelard shrugged. 'She says much worse about you.
Nothing that comes out of your mouth I take at face value,
Roger. You'd be hurt if I did. You'd hate to seem transparent.'

'Which bank?' Link-Mite replied. 'What the fuck do you
take us for?'

Cadwallader held up a hand with a milky spoon in it. 'Let's
keep things temperate. How did Bowling and this girl come
together in the first place?'

Turkey said: 'Oh, Julian was to look for US Paris Embassy
contacts. You recall the operation, Verdun – we wanted, still
want, between-the-lines stuff on US-French Mid-East policy.
He managed to get something nice going with McIver, offi-
cially a clerk in management services, though that's probably
a cover. There are big gaps in her career dossier, which might
indicate special training. In her turn, she could have been told
to get close to Jules, for the Americans' own purposes. Her
competence in handling matters after the Renault accident
would be fairly extraordinary for a female clerk.'

'*Any* bloody clerk, Turkey,' Judith said.

'*Supposed* accident,' Link-Mite said.

Abelard suddenly began to feel anxious about his mother
and Lucy. This meeting kept him away from the protector role.
And everyone in the room knew it. Were matters being spun
out for that reason – the jousting between Turkey and Link-
Mite, Cadwallader's call for information which he must
already know, Judith Stewart's dud questions about the sexual
state of things. The meals always went slowly but this one
seemed abnormally laboured.

Turkey said: 'We aren't sure whether the girl had a habit
before she met Julian. Inquiries in the States say no. At any
rate, not long after she and Julian made contact we began to
sense problems. A few sketchy bits of information came

through her – typical apéritif material that anyone trying to create a connection might use. Then, even that died and our contact with Julian became uncertain. He'd disappear for days and when he resurfaced it was with bugger all and a sheaf of wet excuses. It became damn difficult to explain ourselves to the Foreign Office. I think Beal started to find our attitude smelly.'

'He tried to poke into things about Julian when I saw him,' Abelard said.

'We deduce now that this was when Jules's trafficking began,' Turkey said. 'Who put who on to it, though, we don't know.'

'Does it matter?' Link-Mite asked. 'It exists. We're circling around the edge of things again.'

Turkey said: 'Look, Roger, why don't you just fuck off? Go play with your finger irons. You're not in charge here.'

Link-Mite said something Abelard did not hear because, as a break from rock, Randy Crawford's 'One Day I'll Fly Away' climbed up from below at full weight.

He wanted to fly away himself but perhaps it was still too soon for that. They were not even on the coffee. He said: 'So you put two people on to tracking him – me and Judith – and tell neither about the other. You trust nobody. Why the hell isn't Judith under scrutiny as well?'

'Perhaps she is, Simon,' Cadwallader replied gently.

'Abelard has a legit grievance here, I think,' Turkey said.

'Perfectly normal on a defector recovery operation of this type to do it double,' Link-Mite said. 'And especially when big boodle is involved. How the hell can anyone be sure where an agent's loyalties lie?'

'And I suppose the more so if the agent is a half-caste from Cardiff docks,' Turkey said.

'Oh, Christ, are we back to the Martin Luther King stuff?' Link-Mite replied.

'Yes, it does sound like a scenario,' Abelard said. 'I ought to go. This is where I came in.'

'You what?' Link-Mite said, and looked at his watch. 'This is an important meeting.'

'But informal,' Abelard said. 'No agenda, I think.'

'Of course not,' Link-Mite replied, 'but—'

'So I'm away,' Abelard said. 'I'll skip the rest, if you don't mind, Verdun. It's been as ever delightful.'

He took a cab. The Outfit had provided the temporary flat near playing fields and a park in a roughish corner of Lewisham and he had brought Lucy there on arrival from France. His mother disapproved but was slowly getting used to the idea. Lucy seemed to accept the arrangement and had said no more about going her own way.

A hundred yards from the flat he paid off the taxi and did the rest on foot. Although all the curtains were open he saw no lights, yet both women should have been there. Verdun had deputed a couple of men to watch in case Jules turned up but Abelard could not see them or their car. A gang of young white yobs lounged and talked and fooled not far from the flat, and he might have asked them whether they had seen anything. But he was new to the street, the wrong colour and with a nowhere accent. They would not help. As Abelard passed, one of them whistled the Laurel and Hardy signature tune in time to his footsteps. TV did open youth's mind to culture.

As soon as he turned the key Abelard knew he had been right to feel anxious. Something lay behind the door, preventing him from opening it. When he pushed, the obstruction gave a little but for a moment he lacked strength to push harder because fear of what he might find suddenly drained him. There had been no sharp impact when the door touched, so this could not be a piece of wooden furniture or anything metal. It seemed appallingly soft and yielding. He forced himself to keep pushing and tried to think of the blockage as impersonal, a thing, but his mind wouldn't have that, went its own panicky way for a time, telling him insistently it was a body. He tried to guess from the resistance if it was the hefty physique of his mother or Lucy's slight frame. He didn't know which would upset him more.

Using steady gradual pressure he forced the door back. To anyone watching he must look like a burglar. After a few minutes his alarm slackened. This was not a body after all. It lacked solidity. He shoved harder until he was able to step inside. Light from the street showed a double bed mattress. It must have been flung over the banister from upstairs. Closing the door behind him he stood still for a couple of seconds in the dark hall and listened.

If Link-Mite and Turkey had sent people they would be looking for anything of his or Lucy's that might say where Julian kept the funds. And they might still be here. Perhaps Abelard had upset the timetable by leaving early. Those two would be able to order the guards away for long enough. Or the guards might be in on it. This was big bucks.

Edging forward a few steps, he encountered all kinds of débris underfoot. There was a heavy smell. Glass fragments crackled, and when he switched on the hall light he saw the floor was strewn with wreckage of framed pictures and prints and chunks of some pleasant lion cub ornaments which had stood on a window sill. The mattress had been slashed three times from end to end and the cover stripped back for a search. In a rush and without any of the care he would normally have taken he began to go through the rest of the house looking for his mother and Lucy and for anyone else. Everything had been turned over, a gifted but unsubtle operation. They, too, had been hurrying. People coached personally by Link-Mite? Thank God it was all rented stuff.

He identified the smell suddenly. Chloroform or something close. He followed it to the smallest bedroom, moving fast, and found his mother and Lucy lying across the single bed there, both with their arms and legs expertly roped. Lucy's face was badly marked, as if she had taken a beating before being doped. Crazy. A scamper. If you chloroformed people you did not let them see you. Lucy must have a memory of her attacker, attackers.

Quickly he undid them. There had been some brandy in a

sideboard downstairs and he went for it but found the bottle smashed. When he returned to the bedroom his mother was beginning to come round. Lucy still snored, a sound he recognised, almost loved.

'On a bed?' his mother said. 'Have I been raped? I didn't feel anything. They say that can happen with age.'

'Who were they?'

'Not kids. Men in good suits.'

'How many?'

She frowned and tried to get her mind working. 'Three I saw. But they had eye masks. Aplomb. Definitely aplomb. Are these folk of your profession, Simon, not just vandals and burglars?' With an effort she half sat up and gazed at Lucy. 'Poor kid. All right, so she drugs. But to knock a young girl about – not on.'

'Did they say anything?'

She lay flat again. 'I don't think so. Not to me. When I say aplomb, I mean the way they moved, not conversation. Would trained heavies speak?'

'Ma, what the devil would you know about trained heavies?'

'I know you. I know Verdun Cadwallader. You should get a doc for Lucy. That snoring. Not healthy, even for a junky.'

No, she sounded like Alec in the French wood. 'See if you can remember any more about the three men. Take each at a time: height, weight, colour of hair, age.'

'What are you now, some sort of cop?' his mother replied. She struggled to her feet. 'I'll call a doctor myself.' She went unsteadily from the room.

Abelard soaked a flannel in the bathroom and bathed Lucy's face wounds. She opened her eyes: 'Jules and friends, Simon?'

'Have you been in touch with him? Would he know this address?'

'Been in touch? Of course I haven't,' she said weakly.

'Addresses leak.'

'Leak how?

'What are you now, some sort of cop?' Lucy replied.

'Rest,' he said. 'Later, check if anything's missing. Say papers to do with the bank. Did you tell them anything?'

She shook her head. 'But they did ask,' she said, and pointed at a couple of the bruises.

His mother had returned. 'Bank? Money? I thought this was an incident from your career, not burglars.'

'Some money could be involved this time.'

She nodded wearily. 'I should have guessed. When people do damage like this and like on Lucy it's got to be the funds, private funds, not ideas stuff. This flat's supposed to be safe and hidden away, yes? So who'd know to come here except the people who arranged it for us, Simon?'

'I've been asking Lucy.'

'You've been *blaming* Lucy? Don't take any notice of him, kid. He suddenly thinks he's some sort of cop, I think.'

'People keep telling me,' Abelard replied. 'In the same words. Were you talking about me before all this happened?'

'Your father always said when you took that job your biggest enemies would be your friends,' Mrs Abelard replied, 'and he didn't even know then there was the money side. He thought it was all invisible ink and patriotism and that.'

In half an hour the doctor arrived. Abelard prowled the house trying to discover any pattern or objective in the search. It was a tic, habit. He knew what they were after and had known it from the start: the funds, as his mother would call them, or the way to the funds. Even if they found the bank name and the codes, how would they manage about signatures? Perhaps they would leave that difficulty until it mattered. Now, they did what they could, and what they could was to break up a flat and knock a girl about, a girl who might know something. Yes, she might.

The dinner party would have dispersed so he rang Link-Mite at home but got no answer. He dialled the out-of-hours contact number for department heads, gave his identity code to the woman who answered and asked if she could find Link-Mite.

'He's not receiving calls. I'm authorised to take messages.'

'You're joking.'

'You can't speak to him direct, sir. If you give me a message he'll doubtless be in touch.'

'Oh, doubtless. I want to know who wrecked my fucking flat and abused two women who are close to me.'

'Excuse me, but would we know?'

'*He'll* know.'

'Please say again what you believe happened.'

'Not believe. I'm standing in the shambles now, up to my balls in rubble.'

'A police matter?'

'Did the sod give orders not to put calls through from me?'

'What is the exact address where this alleged break-in took place, sir?'

'He's got it. What about Turkey?'

'Sir?'

'Can you raise RCV Latimer?'

In a moment Turkey spoke: 'Simon, what's this I hear from the operator? Outrageous. Is your dear mother all right? I gather you think Roger Link-Mite is involved.'

'Is he with you now?'

There was a pause. 'Roger? Oh, certainly not. Why do you ask that? What makes you think Roger organised it?'

'Only the level of destruction.'

'I hardly think he would be implicated – though as you'll have gathered earlier we're not the best of friends.'

'No, I didn't gather that. Were you in on this, too, Turkey? Is Verdun? Is Stewart? Where were the minders?'

'Simon, you're upset. I don't blame you. Did your mother or Lucy see enough of the people for IDs?'

'I'll be showing them staff pix.'

'I wish you wouldn't talk like that. Is anything missing?'

'I don't know. Ask them. Aren't they back yet?'

That night he and Lucy really slept together. Now one mattress had been ruined sharing a bed made extra sense, but they could not have stayed away from each other, anyway. Suddenly and wonderfully it was as if she found the delay, the holding off, as incomprehensible as he did. He undressed her very carefully because they had beaten her about the body as well as on the face and head and she was still tender there – her stomach, her ribs, her neck. She had trouble holding her left arm up straight when he drew her shirt off. Her breasts, he saw now, were not marked. Some rules prevailed.

He said: 'If you like, we'll just lie alongside each other. That would be a real start – a definite move on from the Rembrandt. It would be enough for me now.'

'It wouldn't,' she said. 'Take a look at yourself.'

'That's containable.'

'Of course it is. By me.'

'Well, we can be gentle,' he said.

'Fuck gentle.'

'Exactly.'

'No, I mean *fuck* gentleness. That's *no* fuck.'

They were standing near the bed, both naked and she got her arms up around his neck with a bit of effort, pulled herself close to Abelard and kissed him briefly three or four times on his adam's apple. 'Few know this is an erogenous zone,' she said. Then she bent her head back so he could kiss her properly on the mouth. Her lower lip was swollen and now he would have begun to be restrained but she wouldn't have it, shoving her face into his with perky, unflinching strength, growling from somewhere way back in her throat as though she longed to say great things to him but refused to break her mouth from his to say them.

In the bed, too, Abelard tried for tenderness with her, but she would not wear it here, either. She demanded passion, demanded ferocity and gave them with flyweight violence. It it was silent passion, silent ferocity, because his mother slept in the next room. When he stroked her arms he could feel the rope marks. When he stared down at her, though, he made himself ignore the bruising of her face and fix on the beautiful line of Lucy's nose and the love in her eyes. It was that, wasn't it? Their faces banged together a couple of times as they shoved each other around the bed but she continued to ignore the pain. Her lip bled, messing him up, matting his chest hair and messing up the bed, too.

'I don't think your mother will imagine you deflowered me,' she muttered later. ' Some honeymoon suite.' She gazed around the wrecked bedroom. In a few minutes she climbed out and picked her way to her handbag on what was left of the glass-topped dressing table. She perched there and prepared herself a fix. 'As you'll know, Simon, this is usually better before sex, not after. Things can sing then.'

'I thought they sang just now.'

'OK, they sang. But with this even when two people are really used to each other it can be like the first time again.'

'So good?' Perhaps he sounded envious. Hadn't he seen a marriage die?

Her face went hard. 'But keep off it. I like you best without.' She fell back into bed and slept, an arm across Abelard's chest, as if his presence made her safe. Oh, yeah?

After a while he eased himself out, went to the window and surveyed the street from around the edge of the curtain, as she had at the Rembrandt. And also like her then he was looking for Julian. Perhaps his mother was right to say only those who arranged the accommodation knew Abelard's address. But the smell of large funds made men very clever and very determined, and Julian Bowling had been expensively trained to find people who went to ground.

Now and then the odour of fat funds still affected even Abelard himself. Of course. When you were in bed with a woman worth, in theory, half of $9,000,000 – or even $17 million, or even the whole lot of either nine or seventeen, if she could work it – when your bedmate was like that you felt something beyond the usual friendliness and warmth, though these rated, too. You felt like a custodian, a guardian of some precious bait, to use Link-Mite's word. Abelard went back to the bed and Lucy once more threw a possessive arm arm across him. He was happy to belong.

He awoke abruptly with someone tugging at his hair. There was light from the landing. His mother stood by the bed in her dressing gown and of course made a big production of noticing Lucy. 'Phone,' she said. 'What's the matter with your ears?' Abelard rolled clear of Lucy once more. 'Another woman,' his mother added, making her way back to her own room. '"So you're not hurt, Alice?" she said. 'How did she know my name? Oh, but your sort know everything.'

On the telephone Judith Stewart spoke in her most sympathetic and comradely voice. 'I've been making inquiries about what happened at your flat, Simon. An utter disgrace. Almost certainly a posse of freelances or people from the US Embassy. I'm told you thought the Outfit or we across the quadrangle had something to do with it. Hurtful. No, Simon, the Yanks. Don't ask me how they got round our watchers there.'

'How did they get round your watchers here?'

'They're upset about Lucy Mary McIver. And they've heard about the takings, of course. Is Lucy still with you? It's vital we should help each other, Simon.'

'What's that mean – you've got Julian and want to bring him and Lucy together for the pay-out signatures?'

'Got Julian?'

'Are you sitting on him somewhere, waiting for the moment?'

'Nobody sits on Julian – except when he's pleasuring that is.' She was silent for a while. 'We must talk together properly soon, without apes like Link-Mite present. I'm going out of town briefly. But when I get back.'

'Out of town where?'

'Some air.'

'Air where?' he said. She had rung off. On impulse, now he was at the phone, he rang Charlie Tate, his investigative journalist friend from postgraduate days in New York. A man answered at once, very quiet, very terse, as if to make the voice unidentifiable. 'Yes?'

'I'm trying to reach Mr Charles Tate.'

'Not a name I know. Who are you?'

'Abelard.'

'Simon!' The tone grew relaxed. 'This is Charlie.'

'What's wrong?'

'It's night here. And there are a few problems, anyway. But don't worry. I've been meaning to give you a call. Some progress. This boy Ovalle – not easy to reach. I'm in touch with someone who knows someone who... that kind of approach. It will take a little while. Ovalle – big-time coke, of course, and maybe smack and crack. Your phone clean? The cornucopia. You knew all this? A killer, some say. There are powerful British colleagues, freelances in the trade linked to him. Let's look at the notes. Matson? Richard Field – extensive womaniser? Matson could be dead.'

'He is.'

'Oh, well, I've got something right. Look, I'm in a bit of a shambles, here, Si. My room was given a going over.'

Abelard felt dazed for a moment.

'You there?' Tate asked.

'Something similar here.'

Tate said: 'Nothing stolen. Somebody wanted to check me out. It was nicely done.'

'What about the notes?'

'No, I had them on me. It looks like start asking about Ovalle and anything can happen.'

'Well, Jesus Christ, Charlie, I wouldn't want—'

'I've begun now. It kind of interests me. I'll push on a bit further. There might be a story in it. Big-time drugs, I mean, *really* big time, still rates in the papers. Ovalle-CIA? You hear of that, too? The Agency into the commerce? Maybe all the world's security departments have people who trade and courier. What a sweet idea, Simon. Almost unbelievable and brilliant newspaper stuff. I hear mutterings about you and some incidents in France.'

'Mutterings from where?'

'You don't ask a reporter that.'

'Is *your* phone OK, Charlie? Might it be an idea to move house. I did.'

'If someone's watching me here and I spot him that's a lead. And a full, substantive lead is what I'm short of. That's the big word in investigative journalism, you know – substantive.'

'It's exposed, Charlie.' Exposed: bloody feeble word, in investigative journalism or anything else. Charlie was sticking his head under the guillotine.

'Get exposed to expose,' Tate said. 'It's sometimes necessary.' He rang off and Abelard went back to bed. Lucy snored unreachably on. He climbed in and slept some more.

It was mid-morning when they awoke. He said: 'Judith Stewart seems to be offering me a partnership.'

'Yea? In?'

'Whatever she's got.'

'Which is?'

'I don't know.' He did some self-pity, a kind of sigh. 'I don't know what anybody's got, you included.'

'Does that mean you have to tie yourself to someone like Stewart?'

'It means she might have half and I've got half – like the divided pound note.'

'Jules is one half, I'm the other?' Lucy asked.

'How Stewart might see it.'

'How do you?'

'I see just you.'

'Nice. I half believe it.'

'He'll come back, won't he?' Abelard replied. 'Either via her or you. Lucy, I'm sure you and Jules must have an arrangement. I'm going to be dropped, aren't I?'

'No arrangement. When he left he was being pushed by a handgun, remember.' She leaned across and butterfly- kissed him on the nose and forehead. A small breast touched his arm. 'Things have begun to change, you know, Simon. He shot at me.'

'He'll make contact.'

'Sure. But no arrangement.' She flopped back and stared at the ceiling for a while.

Abelard said: 'I've always believed in Cadwallader.'

'Why?'

'I just do.'

'Slippery ground, Simon.'

'I need to believe in someone. How high does the rot go?'

'We all need to believe in someone,' she said. 'Pathetic. Me, I believe in you. Now.'

'Reciprocated. I'm going to talk to Cadwallader.'

'Don't jump too far too soon.'

11

ABELARD DECIDED HE would see Verdun away from the office and next evening went to a public park in the London suburb of Enfield, carrying under his arm a pair of bowling shoes bought that afternoon. Bowls obsessed Cadwallader. The game had so far failed to catch on with blacks, and Abelard felt conspicuous as he waited near the wooden changing room.

At a little after 7pm the slight figure of Cadwallader appeared. He wore a very old navy blazer with some huge, elaborate and desperately faded badge on the breast pocket, like a congealed dinner. He carried a round leather case containing his woods, this also very worn and tattered. Not much about him proclaimed a man of secret, dark and violent power.

Abelard was aware of Verdun's grey eyes passing quickly over him, but no sign of recognition came. For a while they both watched the players already out and then Abelard said: 'Excuse me, sir, are you looking for a game. I'm a novice but I'm—'

'Always nice to meet a new enthusiast.'

Abelard hired woods and they went to the green, choosing a rink far from other players.

Cadwallader said: 'Sometimes I think too many people know they can find me here, Simon.' He bowled and Abelard followed ineptly but very much in the general direction.

'What the hell's going on, Verdun? That dinner – Link-Mite, Judith, Turkey all playing their various games. The same game. You're in on it?'

'The question we all want to ask you. My game is bowls.' He sent a wood towards the jack. It nestled against it.

'I couldn't—'

'The other game? Simple. We have a colleague who is AWOL, possibly a defector, haven't we, Simon? It's traditional to try to bring such people back. We are all engaged in this, you especially. However, this defector is heavy with money. Some folk in HMISS are more interested in recovering this for their own use than in recovering a defector. Also, some of the folk the defector has worked with and against in his new trade want to trace him and recover the money. Some are Brits, some not. *Their* motives are clear and criminal. The motives of people within HMISS are less clear. This one might be concerned with Julian as a traitor, that one with Jules as a money bags.'

'Which one?'

'This one, that one,' Cadwallader replied.

'Yours?'

'What?' Cadwallader asked.

'Motives.'

'Yours?' Cadwallader replied. 'Bowl.' Abelard did and knocked Cadwallader's wood clear of the jack. Verdun snarled: 'Two-timing bastard, you've played this game before.'

'Which?' Abelard replied.

'Bowls.'

'Have you heard anything of Julian?' Abelard asked.

'You want to see him? Why?'

'It was my job to find him.'

'You did, and let him go,' Cadwallader replied.

For twenty minutes they played more or less in silence, Abelard getting worse at it after that first freak shot, inclined to over-power his wood. Cadwallader had left his blazer in the changing room and displayed a short sleeved shirt and skimpy tanned arms. His trousers belt was thick enough to hold a prisoner in the electric chair. 'Judith phoned me before questioning you under the bag in Paris,' he said. 'It was touch and go.'

'What was?'

'She had a mind to knock you off. We didn't know what you

were up to – I mean, the corpse at Chandon's. She thought you might have lost it – your mind. There was some talk of a multi-stabbed hamster thrown from a flat she knew you'd searched.'

'What the fuck are you saying, Verdun? Of course you knew what I was up to. You sent me.'

'The Chandon killing confused us. Were you, are you, playing your own game? Or your own and Julian's game?'

'She'd have shot me for carrying out your orders?'

'She wasn't fully in the picture,' Cadwallader replied.

'Who the fuck *is*?'

It had begun to grow dark. They gathered the woods and walked back. 'Judith is due for a DBE at least. Sexually null, I gather, but a noble worker.'

'For?' Abelard asked.

'The realm in all its devolved fucking fragments.'

Jesus, could Cadwallader be in on it, after all? Was it credible that someone as clever and informed and worldly really did not know which prized members of HMISS staff spent their time trawling for Jules's dirty millions?

'I've enjoyed our conversation, Simon. It's nice to talk informally with someone from my own patch, South Wales.' Abelard thought Verdun was about to reach and stroke his arm, but Cadwallader drew back.

'Judith's probably a villain, you simpering twat,' Abelard blurted. 'I think all she's interested in is Julian's fortune. Why did you put her on the search with me? What in God's name will you do about her, Verdun?'

He did not answer because his attention appeared suddenly focused elsewhere, outside the park in the street.

Abelard hammered on. 'Are you content to be running a—'

'I hear you.' Before they reached the park gates Cadwallader stopped and seemed to study a rose, handling it sensitively. 'All right, Abelard, you've brought a mate with you, maybe mates. About thirty-three or four, shoulder-length fair hair, my build – that's to say, dwarf emaciated.'

'Where?' Abelard said, but did not look about yet.

'Don't be a tease. This slob's with you? There are others? You all think I know where Julian is?'

'Which slob?' Abelard replied. It sounded like a description of Peter Glass/Graff.

'Stand still, will you. Completely still.' He seemed to examine the undercarriage of the rose, its stalk and base. 'This man is not with you? Well, you could have been followed. Maybe they think you know where Jules is. Have people got your new address?'

'Of course some have my new address. Didn't they hit the be-Jesus out of the place? I thought they were friends of yours, or friends of your friends.'

Cadwallader said: 'Abelard, I can take care of this, deal comfortably with both of you if you're some sort of hunting party.' He ambled towards the park gates, like the most wanked-out competitor in a Senior Citizens' Olympics. He seemed hardly strong enough to carry his bowls case. The park keeper waited for them, ready to lock up and Cadwallader chatted graciously with him about cricket and roses and bees, showing no fret.

Abelard saw now in the street outside a man with long fair hair who might be Glass. Keeping close to the park railings, head lowered to make identification difficult, this figure approached them swiftly through the dusk. Abelard could not see whether his face was marked after that street jostle in Paris, but remembered from then the jerky, slightly awkward style of moving and the wide, bony shoulders.

The park keeper fixed the gates behind them. They were in a small ill-lit street separating the park from an open recreation field. In parked cars lovers waited for full darkness.

'Well, look at this,' Cadwallader said.

At about ten metres from them, Glass had suddenly produced a Luger pistol and pointing it at Abelard, said confidingly: 'There's a car around the corner. Keep walking in the same direction as now. I'm going to follow. Piss about, you lose the back of your head.'

'Who are you, sir?' Verdun asked. 'My name is Cadwallader, a long-time member of the bowls club and perturbed about the rising incidence of street violence near the park.'

'Keep clear of this, Outfit runt,' Glass replied. 'Go home. Think yourself a lucky lad with a long future in bowls.'

If a car waited there would be somebody in it, perhaps more than one. A kind of panic struck Abelard. When they realised he could not put them on a sure road to the golden store the only move left would be to get rid of him. And, God, what might happen before that? His mother had it right: he did always cop the shittiest assignments.

'I said get lost, friend,' Glass told Cadwallader, as the three of them walked towards the corner. In a way it might be consoling. Did Glass believe everything was going to work out sweetly and that there would be no need for violence? He would not have let a witness go, otherwise.

'I'm no use to you,' Abelard said. He stopped and turned to face Glass. 'The money's on a double signature.'

'Liar. Lucy can get it. That's my information.'

'Information from where?' Abelard replied.

'Let's go to her now.'

'Go to her where?'

'Wherever she is. Come on, you're hiding her.' He began to whine. 'Listen, I've got pressure. I'm expected to produce.'

'Tough.' So, Glass did not know where she was. He had not been involved in breaking up the flat. Perhaps Judith Stewart was right and it had been people from the US Embassy. Or possibly it had been people from Judith Stewart or from Roger Link-Mite or from Turkey or from Cadwallader or from Richard Field. Abelard had come to the bowling green via the office. Glass must have watched the Outfit building and followed. Talented gumshoeing. Abelard had seen nothing, and he was alert these days.

'They both have to be present at the bank,' Abelard said. 'You've got to assemble Julian and Lucy even to start.'

'Who says?' Glass replied.

'Lucy says.'

'She's lying to you, in case you want a cut. She's a good liar. She's trained.' But Glass's body seemed for a moment to wilt, as if Abelard's words about the signatures had reached him, part convinced him. This small breakdown of morale and concentration must have been instantly spotted by Cadwallader. Despite the warnings, he had continued to walk with them. Now he seemed to lurch and spin, and for a second Abelard thought Glass had lost patience and struck him with his free hand. Cadwallader gave what seemed at first to be a shout of pain and Abelard turned towards him instinctively, arms out in protection. Wasn't he schooled to get his skin between that of chosen others and any danger? Verdun was a chosen other until shown not to be, and nobody had shown that yet, nor anywhere near.

As he touched Verdun, though, Abelard was conscious not of someone slumping under a blow but of frenetic physical power bursting from the small frame. Cadwallader swung the case of woods violently up, knocking the pistol from Glass's hand. It fell to the ground near the railings. Abelard realised that the cry had been a yell of battle, not a scream of anguish. Darting forward, Cadwallader grabbed at Glass's jacket, unbalancing him in a primitive judo ploy, and then kicked his legs away.

Glass fell heavily and as soon as he was on the floor Verdun once more swung the bowls case, swung it four times alto-gether with the same hammering force. The end of it struck the side of Glass's head like a battering ram. Abelard heard hellish structural sounds.

He stretched out and touched Cadwallader's arm. 'That's enough, Verdun.'

'Is it?

'Yes, I think so.'

'Well, yes, possibly.' Cadwallader's breathing seemed hardly disturbed. His words could mean that further blows would be cruel, or that he considered Glass neutralised.

Neither of them had time to look at him closely. Verdun collected the Luger. 'He said a car. Possibly a crew.' For a moment he looked as if he wanted to take on whatever might be around the corner, gun in one hand, woods in the other. There was a terrible, minute eagerness to him.

'We should beat it,' Abelard said.

Cadwallader's head twitched in mighty surprise and he glared at Abelard. 'You can't mean we should leave this tiny-talented lout here. He'll tell me buckets about all sorts when he wakes up. I want him back in the Outfit. He'll come round in a couple of hours. We'll do a Spenlow and Jorkins.'

'A what?'

'Hard and soft interview. Didn't they cover *David Copperfield* at Eton when you were there, Simon? Or was it Cemetery Road Comprehensive you went to?'

'How shift him? You've got a vehicle? There are people watching, you know. They might call the police or make trouble.'

'Lovers. They can't do much with the pants down. We find an empty vehicle. Watch him, would you? Jab your foot on his throat if he stirs.' He handed Abelard the Luger and put his case of woods on the ground near Glass. Briskly, Verdun walked off and tried the door of what looked like an unoccupied Vauxhall, but a man and woman sat up startled and riotously dishevelled from the back seat and Abelard heard Verdun say in an exaggerated South Walian accent: 'So sorry, I was looking for my mam and her friend.' He moved away and reached an old locked Citroen. Taking keys from his pocket he worked briefly, entered and started it. He drew up alongside Abelard and they loaded Glass into the back. Before they could move off, Cadwallader glanced in the mirror and said: 'This looks like them.'

Abelard turned and saw a big Toyota estate car slowly nosing its way down the road, as if searching. In the darkness he could not tell how many people it contained, but the car looked heavily laden, like that Rover in Paddington.

'Give us a nice kiss, will you, Si?' With extravagant languor Verdun leaned across from the driving seat and embraced Abelard, bringing their lips together and vigorously fondling his hair. The Toyota passed. Verdun's mouth seemed a bit keen and Abelard felt a sharp little Welsh-English bilingual tongue doing its best to get into his mouth. Besides the hand in his hair Abelard was aware of another placed lightly on his knee, waiting for a signal. On the floor in the back Glass groaned loudly once, a bad, throaty noise lasting half a minute. Abelard gently disengaged himself from the clinch and with the pistol barrel shoved Cadwallader's hand away. 'Whenever I'm male groped I reach for my Luger, Verdun.'

The Toyota continued along the road, disappearing left around a corner. Swiftly Cadwallader turned their car and they drove out of the opposite end of the road. 'Simon, I come to believe some of the things you've tried to tell me. Obviously I knew Julian had taken us for the ride of rides and that we weren't looking for a mere defector. But you say Judith Stewart as well? Possibly Link-Mite? Even Turkey?'

This Abelard recognised as a sideways affirmation that Verdun personally had no part in the dirty trading, nor in any debasement of duty. Well, maybe.

'Nailing Julian should be easy, Si. The girl will draw him and he must get out of France. They don't care to have their police killed. Jules will show.'

They drove in no rush to the back of the Outfit where Cadwallader unlocked steel doors and they entered the yard. Between them they lifted Glass out and placed him on the ground. Then Cadwallader rang a bell in another inner steel door. It was opened by a porter who sniffed angrily when he saw the unconscious man, as if they had brought home a drunk friend. Perhaps he really thought it was a drunk friend and was meant to: after all, even Cadwallader could have trouble explaining why he brought a skulled enemy to the office. Cadwallader and Abelard carried Glass in and upstairs to Verdun's suite where they laid him on the carpet. Verdun rated several rooms, with offices adjoining his for secretaries and conferences, and a large safe-vault. On the walls hung a few bright abstract prints and a foul rural scene in oils which Abelard had always assumed was Verdun's own and displayed to unnerve people. Cadwallader crouched beside Glass, about to begin a search, but said: 'God, I think this jerk's snuffoo, Simon.'

'You were clubbing the temple. The bone's thin there.'

'Yes, doctor.' For the second time that evening Cadwallader pressed his lips to a man's, working hard and expertly at the kiss of life. Again Abelard was aware above all of Verdun's energy and strength as for minutes he fought to get Glass breathing again, never pausing except to glance occasionally for signs of a flutter in his chest.

When the little man gave up he remained on hands and knees and went through Glass's clothes. He found only a handful of shells for the Luger. 'I'll have him dumped somewhere and the car dropped in the river. Might this be Glass/Graff, AC/DC like Jules himself, not to mention another nearer home? I do wish men would commit themselves, don't you?'

'Not to me.'

'Glass came looking for the spouse's portion, I take it.'

'Plus he was squeezed for contributions to some German political fund.'

'Election fund?'

'Probably.'

'We don't want to get too close to that.'

'You've heard of it?' Abelard asked.

'It will get very public-domained soon. I'd say a revelation for the very start of the new millennium, but not a religious one. He must have been keen to come from Paris.'

'Pressured,' Abelard said.

'Locates you somehow, then a trail to my holy bowling green. I do object to that kind of infringement. Odd – Bowling, bowling.' He unlocked the huge wall safe, went back to Glass and, gripping him by the long fair hair, began to drag the body across the room. Abelard took hold of a shoulder and helped. Together they jammed and folded him somehow into the vault.

Verdun locked up.

'I thought things were supposed to be open these days,' Abelard said.

'This *will* be opened in a day or so. Nobody's going to do much about disposal at this time of night. The porters have girls in and won't want to be disturbed. He'll be fine in there till morning. I've got a new lad starting tomorrow, Lancing and Cambridge, just like the pre-dumbing down days. Starred first, English. A fine, devious gloss on him, the kind Julian used to have. I'll make getting rid of Glass this recruit's first job. Let him know early that life here's not all fucking *Tristram Shandy* and Derrida.'

12

ABELARD TOOK a taxi to his car at Enfield then drove home. As was his habit he parked some way from the flat and walked the last stretch: a vehicle outside a house did more identifying than a name plate. When he first turned into the street he thought it deserted. At this hour the kids who normally hung about would be where the action was livelier. Then, from somewhere very near the flat, a car suddenly revved up and drew away. He was too far off to read the registration or notice much else about it. He thought it must be pretty old because the engine sounded rough and a rear light was on the blink. When he reached the house Lucy and his mother were in dressing gowns watching television. 'Did we have more visitors?' he asked.

'Like who?' Lucy said.

'Jules?'

'Here?' Lucy replied. 'How?'

'We thought maybe someone was loitering in the garden just now,' his mother said. 'Lucy went out to look but she didn't find anyone, did you, love?'

'Thank God, no,' Lucy replied.

'Good,' Abelard said.

Lucy took his hand. 'You don't trust me to tell you if he's been here, do you, Simon?'

'She went out very brave by herself and was looking around for ages and didn't find a soul,' Mrs Abelard said.

'Simon, you don't believe in anyone, do you?'

'It's his work,' Mrs Abelard said.

'Yes, I believe you, Lucy.'

She shook her head. 'Think I was liaising with Jules?'

When his mother went to the kitchen to make tea Abelard

told Lucy about Glass. 'Always he asked for trouble,' she said. 'I never understood what Julian found in him. But I guess that would be simple old jealousy.' She laughed at herself as if all this were long ago now and impossible to fathom.

Mrs Abelard came back. 'Oh, a call from New York, Simon.'

'Charlie Tate?'

'A name like that. He's doing a bit for you out there? You must be into really big stuff, Stateside inquiries.'

'Ma, what did he say?'

'He's got through to some big timer. He'll be seeing him soon for you. He wouldn't give me a name – said you'd know.'

'Is this JJ Ovalle?' Lucy asked.

'He's dangerous, Simon? But do you know anybody who's not?' She had a ponder. 'Ever think of this boy's poor mother?'

'Which boy?' Abelard replied.

'Don't play stupid. The boy you're hunting.'

'She's not poor,' he said.

'How would I feel if it was happening to you – chased all round Europe by a well-dressed rough-house gang like yours, college boy muscle? You should go and see her.'

'They won't know where he is, Alice,' Lucy said.

'But wouldn't it be a *kind* thing to do, a decent thing, or have you forgotten such words, Simon? Show her even this job has a human face. Do something none of your mates in the Outfit ever would. No, it takes a black.'

Abelard had intended seeing Julian's parents some time, anyway. It would please his mother if she thought it her idea, so next morning he did go to the Bowling flat near Marble Arch and asked a security man in the sealed reception hall to ring through and say one of their son's colleagues wanted to see them. The guard looked at him carefully: boardroom suit, tie and shirt, Rome shoes, non-white skin, heavyweight shoulders, intriguing face scars. 'Would's't have some ID, sir?'

'Just get on the intercom,' Abelard suggested.

The guard looked at the scars and shoulders again and then

called the flat. In a moment an elderly woman of impressive jutting beauty – nose, chin, cheek-bones – appeared from a lift and they went up together. 'It happens that we are concerned about Julian,' she said as they entered the flat. 'Quite a time since he was in touch. Of course, we understand the demands of his work, but all the same…'

It was a huge high-ceilinged place, full of insurable oddments: china, silver, gadgetry. The décor looked professionally schemed, tasteful and costly. There were modern paintings which Abelard would bet were not bad. He had looked up the Bowlings in the library and knew they owned a place in Wiltshire and a flat in the Vendée, also. Had they checked those bolt holes for Jules? Perhaps Abelard would.

He and Mrs Bowling sat down in a large room full of the sound of traffic, reaching them through open windows. 'One of your colleagues has already called some days ago,' she said, 'a Mr Link-Mite. Delightful man. But what is the problem with Julian, Mr Abelard?'

Just fucking greed, Mrs Bowling. And possibly the same with Roger. Possibly the same with everyone.

But Abelard did not say this or even think of saying it. Before he could say anything at all, Philip Bowling entered the room, pushing a loaded, ancient drinks trolley and beaming a welcome. He was tall,thin, steaming with leadership qualities and the healthy joy of possessions. He wore jeans and a Manchester United football shirt. His neck looked powerful. Although the teeth were not his own, a fine job had been done, much better than approximate. These were teeth that would get him through even the most meat-based menu. Both the Bowlings were in their seventies, but hellishly spry. It struck Abelard they could have taken by storm one of those homes for the retired wealthy in Florida.

Abelard felt he would never last so well, and probably not so long. Philip Bowling poured drinks, hefty, rich man's drinks, the kind for folk who didn't have to get up in the morning or work a chain-saw.

Abelard said: 'Could I ask how long since Julian was in touch and how he communicated?'

'The very questions Mr Link-Mite put!' Pamela Bowling cried.

'I haven't seen Roger's notes,' Abelard replied. And never would.

'About two months ago,' Mrs Bowling said. 'He rang from Paris.'

Philip Bowling said: 'Link-Mite told us Julian was fine. That's still so, I trust.'

'I saw him myself a week or so ago and he was in cracking form,' Abelard replied.

'Why this interest in him, then?' Pamela asked.

'We have the same trouble as you. He hasn't been in touch.'

'But you said you were with him.'

'That was a kind of accident – bumping into, you know,' Abelard replied. 'He hasn't made contact through standard procedures. And of course at the Outfit they're fussy about standard procedures.'

'Some unusual difficulty in his work?' Philip asked.

'The most likely explanation,' Abelard said. 'There are often instances when people in the field go silent for a while – sometimes for much, much longer than in this case. But after a set period of "contact lost", as it's rather melodramatically known, certain precautionary measures come into play. This is one of them – and Roger's visit. Routine.'

Pamela brought the brandy over and put another torrent into Abelard's glass. 'I gather inquiries have been made in Julian's London haunts,' she said.

'People asking questions in such spots are fed lies as a matter of course, I should think,' Philip said.

Worse than that happened to them. Abelard said: 'I heard of a woman he took regularly to the Bête Noire club. Did you meet her?'

'Excuse my asking this, Mr Abelard, in the circumstances,' Philip replied, 'but what colour?'

'Oh, quite whitish. About thirty. Not on the game. Now. She seems to have been really fond of Julian. He lived at her place in Paddington for a month, then took off. Barbara Francis or Roxana or Melanie. Possibly bisexual.'

Philip flexed his soccer shirt. 'This doesn't sound too good, does it, Mr Abelard? He might be diseased. A slapper? A girl who uses three names?'

'They can see to all that these days with a couple of pills,' Pamela grunted.

'Syphilis?' Philip pondered, fingering his strong nose. 'It can get through the whole body, Pam. Ask Mr Abelard. What I mean, he meets all sorts in his work, BBC people, journalists, barristers.'

'There's a degree of rottenness in Julian, obviously,' his mother said, 'but he *is* blood.'

'And the kind of work he chose – it was exactly right for him,' Philip said. 'He's resourceful, brave and, you won't mind my mentioning this, Mr Abelard, well able to handle the duplicity so central to your business. Julian has a way with lies like a priest with the litany.'

'You should have taken him aboard as a salesman,' Abelard said.

'Never interested in my business,' Philip replied. He seemed hurt and his head dropped for a moment. He folded his arms defensively, obscuring the Manchester United logo. According to the library dossier Philip's principal finance came from carpet making in government-aided factories. Hard to tell how much of his operation was hand-out: not clear how secure the wealth might be. Jules had said they were sniffing around his little nest egg.

'Ever get the idea Julian might be into his own type of business on the side?' Abelard asked. The brandy had begun to buffet him and he had trouble with some words.

'Drugs?' Pamela asked. 'Link-Mite gave a hint.'

'Drugs!' Philip screamed, 'I'd prefer he—'

Pamela said: 'Deep down Julian is a chateau-bottled shit.'

'But a Bowling shit,' Philip said. 'Does this seem absurd to you, contemptible, Mr Abelard, the flourishing of a name? And not a name with lineage to it. A name we have given its distinction ourselves. I am not ashamed we have no glistening history. We are *now*, the Bowlings.'

'Julian is very now,' Abelard said.

'I don't know what we can do,' Pamela replied.

Philip stood and gazed from an open window towards Marble Arch. 'Mr Abelard, should you be in touch with him, even for a second, do ask him to scrutinise his person, will you, and seek medication if there is the slightest sign. Pamela is casual, but, well, one knows a little more about these matters, via reading. What one cannot trust to with pox and even Aids is luck. Perhaps I'll let you speak to a dear ruined friend of mine one day soon on this entire topic, Pamela. Now, if you'll both excuse me, I have some tiresome business calls to make.' He shook hands with a commanding, dry grip and strode from the room.

When they were alone, Pamela poured further drinks. 'I hear a figure of $9,000,000. US dollars. Or more. Julian has talent.'

'As I said, a now person. I liked him. Or I liked him before all these changes.'

'Mr Abelard, let me not sound grasping, but I do have to wonder if some of that money will come my way. Would you understand, I wonder?'

'It's certainly a talking point,' Abelard replied.

'Not to Philip. Me, personally.' She briefly touched the elegant line of her chin, drawing a finger slowly along the bone from just under her ear. Perhaps she needed some reassurance that the framework of her beauty was still there. 'Julian and I always had our close secrets, you know. He has never spoken of them to you, I imagine.'

'He thinks *so* highly of you.'

She sat forward, her face close to Abelard and wide open, confiding, untrustworthy. 'You comprehend about mothers, sons, I'm sure.'

'I live with mine,' Abelard replied.

'I expect you heard Julian was a little uncertain sexually, possibly still is. This is a genuine problem.'

'People can have difficulties,' Abelard replied.

'What is a mother for but to help?'

'There's all kind of help around these days, I'm glad to say,' Abelard replied.

'You don't mind my speaking of family matters?'

'These can often contribute towards what we call a profile.'

She shrugged and sat back. 'As a result Julian has always hated Phil, as he might hate a rival. A bit of *Sons and Lovers*?'

'We may never see this money or Julian.'

'As I heard it, you've cornered his girl and he can't do a thing without her. Sharp.'

'Are you in contact with him?' Abelard replied.

'Regrettably not. You must believe that.'

'Certainly,' Abelard said.

'All sorts have been badgering me, naturally. Link-Mite, the shite, that Scotch cow, Stewart, and Turkey Latimer.'

'Cadwallader?'

'Not so far. None of these gets a cut, surely?'

'They're very intense about it I expect,' Abelard replied.

'Stewart will be damned hard to deal with. She can pretend her interests are noble and patriotic. So can they all. So can you, come to that.' She glanced about. Her voice bristled with hope. 'I don't begrudge. But *my* share would be an exit from all this. One wouldn't stay with Phil, obviously, given certain private funds. Freedom costs, doesn't it, Mr Abelard? Please, release me from this place. You've seen and heard him. You know some of the picture. But think of the day in, day out dullness, the perfumed breath, his fatuous ward-room handsomeness on a Dinky Toy soul.'

She saw him out and said at the door: 'Will this girl McIver switch everything to you? I mean, emotionally she already has, clearly, and I can partially understand that. But does she intend you to have Julian's share of the gains? How the hell will you

manage that? You'd try forgery? My God, Abelard, despicable. You'd go with her and pretend to the Swiss you were
Julian? There are difficulties, surely. Not to stress the matter,
but skin? Abelard, you must help me get out of this place.'

'You have others.'

'Those, too. If you have any feeling for my boy – he would
want it.'

'Make my best adieux to your husband,' Abelard replied.

'Oh, Christ, the quiet rectitude of his eating. Have you ever
seen Philip carve a fried egg? But of course you haven't.'

'I might call one breakfast time.'

13

AT HOME NEXT morning Abelard's mother took another phone call. 'Someone asking for Lucy Mary McIver's live-in lover,' she said, handing him the receiver. 'Charming.'

The voice at the other aimed at Cockney as disguise, but it was a poor shot. 'Guv, here's a tip for you. I wants you to go straight away to 22 Kendall Street, Kings Cross. A house. You'll find it open at the rear. Go in and see what you will see.'

'How did you get this number?'

'It's the right one, ain't it, or why answer?'

'Julian, is that you, for God's sake? You want me out of the flat again?'

'Julian who? Get there quick. Within an hour or it's no good. Developments. Think of me like that Deep Throat in the TV film, you know.'

'I don't like calls out of fucking nowhere.'

'What else you got?'

Too right. He dialled a 1471 check and, of course, the number was 'withheld by caller'. Perhaps it could be discovered, but not quickly. Abelard left at once, a .38 Smith and Wesson Baby Barrel in his pocket.

For ten minutes he watched the house from a pub porch. The young middle classes had started to do an Islington here, moving in on the terrace of what had been workmen's cottages. Expensive restoration was under way, some of it suitable. Number 22 looked in as good nick as any of them, its plain beige curtains back, allowing Abelard a pretty thorough survey of the downstairs once he'd finished his spell of preliminary observation and decided to walk past.

Nothing told him whose the place was, but it looked tidy inside. If he hadn't been so rushed he could have consulted the voters' register and found the names. There was even a bit of good taste on show: he spotted a chaise longue, nicely done up in green velvet, an original tiled fireplace respectfully preserved and four or five water colours grouped on what could be William Morris wallpaper, or Laura Ashley.

He kept walking, turned at the corner and in this street found the entrance to a back lane that would take him to the rear of number 22. The telephone had promised easy entrance here, but the lane door was bolted and he had to climb the wall into a small, concreted garden: not even a daisy patch for cover. And so, here he was, coming in like a target on exactly the route nominated, in daylight and to the suggested timetable.

From the rear everything looked as serene as at the front. A room with french windows gave on to the garden, again with curtains pulled back. He saw no movement inside, nor heard anything. The back yards of the terrace were divided from one another by low brick walls, and anyone looking out from a neighbouring house might have spotted him, especially when climbing in. He moved forward quickly and checked a couple of outhouses. Then he pushed on towards the french windows, his hand on the pistol in his pocket.

Who would want to trap him? The list went on and on like the First Book of Chronicles. There was Julian, of course, then anyone who thought Abelard knew the way to that sweet handful of coin. The names crowded his mind and started a pain a bit too near his heart: Judith Stewart, Richard Field, Link-Mite, Turkey, possibly Cadwallader, associates of Glass/Graff and every survivor of that Orléans fracas.

As promised, the french windows were not locked and he stepped into the room, closing them behind him. Once more he paused and listened and watched. It was a more plainly furnished room than the one glimpsed from the front, again containing nothing to indicate the owner. Three at a time he went up the stairs, not too quietly, but sod that. The landing had four doors leading off, two open, allowing Abelard to see small bedrooms. Quickly he looked them over. More and more it was like a Pimlico re-run.

He approached the closed door at the front of the house, guessing this must be the main bedroom. Everything he had learned in training and from *Hill Street Blues* said that if you wanted to open a door not knowing who or what was on the other side you did it in one sudden full movement and stood back out of the line of fire. And once or twice he *had* done things that way, but today he found he couldn't. Instead, he turned the handle very gently, gradually easing open the door.

Before he saw much he smelled perfume, something quite classy and matching that refined taste downstairs, possibly *Rive Gauche*. As he pushed the door he grew convinced it was a woman's room, a woman living alone, despite the king-size double bed. He saw more Victorian pieces, not all of them pretty. But what interested him now was a collection of framed photographs on the dressing table and he crossed the room and studied them, as he had studied Barbara Francis's photographs in Paddington.

At first they meant nothing. Two were college pictures of students in gowns and tasselled hats, the kind of graduation souvenirs he had himself and which his mother used to keep on the wall of the flat in Loudoun Square as proof of something or other. Where were they now? The photographs here had grey, rather bleak buildings as background and he decided the setting was certainly not Oxbridge. Without recognising anyone he scanned the faces. The third picture was a wedding job, bride and groom flanked by a best man and two brides-maids. He stared hard at this beaming couple, but again failed to recognise them. It looked a run-of-the-mill do, men in High Street lounge suits, women without hats.

He had another go at the college photographs. The fash-ions seemed to say late 1960s, so these happy, gullible-looking kids would be into their fifties and he tried to imagine what thirty years of being chewed by events and complexes would have done. Because of the perfume and his certainty about this bedroom – even about the house – he concentrated on the women in all three pictures and then suddenly realised that what he ought to be doing first was to seek a face common to all.

Failing to find anybody in the college groups who looked like the bride, he spread his attention to the attendants and saw that one of the bridesmaids, a plain, thin, brainy looking girl did appear in both the student groups. At the same instant he realised he was staring at pictures of Judith Stewart, possibly always a bridesmaid and not a bride, and probably celebrating her degree in front of some venerable bit of granite at a Scottish university. Giving them a careful rub with his tie, he put the photographs down. He felt jumpy, confused. This was a woman who lived security, yet left her house open. Or someone had kindly fixed that.

The fear that he had been set up rocketed, and he gripped the pistol again. For a while he kept still, listening, but there seemed no sound in the house except water dripping somewhere. It seemed to come from a closed door not far from him, which must lead to the bathroom. He approached and tugged the door open.

Gazing in he heard himself produce a deep agonised groan again, as when he came across his own wedding photograph in Pimlico. The room was combined bathroom and lavatory and to guard the character of the place she had retained the old style overhead flush tank and chain. A man Abelard recognised first from his clothes had been jammed head down in the lavatory bowl and his feet lashed with rope to the tank above. His tie hung over his face and his trouser legs had slipped back up to his calves, revealing white sports socks. Abelard went closer and pulled the tie aside so he could look at that face, though he knew what he would see. The end of the tie was soaked. Glass/Graff's head rested against both walls of the bowl and his long fair locks floated in the water beneath. His lips were clenched but his eyes remained open, a lot of white, some blue. Abelard was looking down into his nostrils and saw they were full of water, as if after the corpse had been fixed in place someone had flushed the tank on him or worse. Some of his clothes were wet, too, and dripped on to the bathroom floor, the sound Abelard had heard. When he accidentally touched the body a 5p piece which must have lodged in the top of a pocket fell and rolled across the floor.

So it had been Verdun, not Jules, who sent him here?

Why? In Abelard's head was a picture of that tiny, raging, powerful, blazer-clad man dragging the body upstairs to the bathroom, then fitting it into place. But, of course, he might have people who would handle such a ploy for him. Was this how the Lancing and Cambridge novice had been told to manage his first delicate assignment? No. Somehow Abelard felt sure Cadwallader had done it personally, and alone. And he could do it. Abelard visualised him having a cheery smirk as he pulled the chain on Glass, or dowsed him personally. Could piss identify?

Abelard went on to the landing. Presumably Verdun wanted to incriminate Judith and dispose of the body at the same time. There must be easier ways of doing both, but none which would appeal so much to Cadwallader's merry mind. Abelard thought of the bowling woods crashing repeatedly against Glass's skull. Verdun had enjoyed that, too. Abelard feared his mother might be right and the trade bred a special kind of off-key mind. As Philip Bowling said, What could you expect?

Abelard left number 22 as he had entered and decided to stay near. Hadn't 'developments' been promised? He took up his pub doorway position again and watched. After about ten minutes a taxi arrived and Judith stepped out. The driver carried a couple of suitcases to the front door. She must have been away for a spell and, of course, Cadwallader would know that when preparing the welcome home. She went in. It might be a while before she visited the bathroom or noticed that somebody had magicked the lock on the french windows. When the pub opened Abelard transferred to the bar and took his drink to a window seat from which he could continue viewing.

To his amazement he found he felt sorry for her. Was he
getting a bit prosy for this work? All right, she had terrorised
him in Paris and seemed to have abandoned the proper interests of the job and turned trader. But that intelligent-looking,
cheerful kid in the photographs must have thought then that
the future would give her a reasonably decent run once she had
done her bit and landed a degree. Instead, she was facing this:
a body in the plumbing and a ferocious dwarf boss probably
planning something else for her soon – and not a DBE recom-
mendation. What had made Cadwallader change his rating of
her so decisively? And was he thinking of something similar
for Link-Mite and Turkey?

A big unmarked van arrived at the house as he watched and
men unloaded a tall, gleaming freezer cabinet and were
welcomed into the house with it by Judith. In a little while the
men brought out a long, low -style freezer showing some wear
and shoved it carelessly into the van, junk now. She must have
phoned somewhere as soon as she found Glass's body, and
friends had devised this smart exit. In the front garden she gave
each of them what appeared to be a few pound coins.

The details of the charade were important. She had to
assume someone was observing.

Judith Stewart watched them leave, looking as pleased as
any woman might who had just swapped a worn out piece of
kitchen equipment for a new, sleeker one. In a day or two
Glass's body might be washed ashore somewhere distant, and
the head damage could seem the result of a battering against
coastal rocks. Or if they had access to a furnace or disused
mine shaft Glass was gone for ever. He took the number of the
van and wrote descriptions of its crew. Should he one day
decide to chart the spread of rot and list the corrupt every little
would help, and this was very little.

He had begun to feel uneasy about Lucy and called home
on his mobile. 'She's gone for a walk, Simon,' his mother said.

'Where?'

'Just a walk.'

'When?'

'About an hour ago. I told her you wouldn't like it, but she went anyway.'

'By herself?'

'By herself as far as I know. Who would she go with, except me?'

Who? Only Jules. Had they bolted for the money, as Abelard had always feared, and as all the rest feared, too? When he returned to the bar Cadwallader was there, a white wine in front of him. 'I wondered if you'd be about, Simon. After what you said I decided to keep an eye on Judith. You're doing the same?' He walked to the window and gazed briefly at the house. Today he had on an unusually smart silk grey light-weight suit which screamed status but did nothing for stature. Abelard joined him.

'What was the idea of that fucking Cockney call, Verdun?'

'Which call would that be?'

'I was in time to see the sights.'

'I recall she keeps things very nice,' Cadwallader replied.

'The removers have been.'

'Really?' Cadwallader said. 'Judith's one who'd be constantly changing and renewing in there, I expect. Some Scots have taste, despite their bent for disorder and mad violence. What do you say we stroll over, doorstep her, ask her straight out.'

'Ask her what?'

'The matters you spoke of. Personal gain, private money.'

'Why pick on *her*,' Abelard replied. 'There are others.'

'She's the one I've become most sure of. Later we can move against the rest. We'll purge ourselves of all degenerates.'

They crossed the road. Judith must have seen them coming and the door was opened before they could knock. She tried a smile, which never had a chance. 'Are you working together on something?' she asked. She looked very frightened. 'Do I need my lawyer, Verdun?' It was half joke but a poor half.

'First thing *I* need is a pee,' Cadwallader said. 'I've been drinking since dawn. Don't trouble yourself, Judith – I remember my way upstairs.' At once he stepped towards the door and staircase.

And then she broke. 'Damn it, you sods did it, didn't you, did it between you?' she yelled. She went to the foot of the stairs and called after him. 'Didn't you?'

It was as if she couldn't stick with the scenario. Why scream when the body had gone? She had beaten Verdun, hadn't she? He took no notice and continued up. Abelard heard a door opened and then Cadwallader's footsteps abruptly stopped. They resumed as he came back out on to the landing and called: 'Could you come up, please. Both.'

'Some poisonous game you've cooked up between you, is it, Simon?' she hissed.

Following her up he found that in the bathroom almost everything was as it had been. Glass's body still hung there upside down, but now Cadwallader crouched near it, staring into his face. Echoes all the time in this operation: hadn't Abelard's first serious conversation with Lucy taken place over a lavatory bowl?

'Judith,' Cadwallader said, 'this would be Julian's gay butty, Glass/Graff, would it? To me it looks as though he died under questioning. Correct? This means a problem or two. My God, he drowned? All this floating hair, like Ophelia. An international pusher I think. One of the biggest.'

So Judith had changed her old freezer, had she, simply that? Or was she doing something cleverer than Abelard could understand?

'Wonderful theatre, Verdun,' she said.

Cadwallader was on hands and knees now. His voice echoed slightly around the pedestal : 'Judith, what purpose would I have in—? Look, as I see it, you and selected colleagues located Glass, and all credit to you. You bring him here for a session of quiet, off-the-record questioning – the kind of thing that does happen, though I disapprove. Then you overdo things. That can also happen. Someone with too many strong-arm techniques gets unduly firm. Result, snuffoo. Was Cedric here, for instance? He can become extreme. Almost always does. Glass had something we needed, did he? What? Is this related to the US pull-out from Europe thing? What does Turkey Latimer call it, Exeunt Hombres?'

'Oh, come on, Verdun, don't mess me about,' Judith snarled.

Cadwallader gave no answer right away, but remained on his knees in the rich suit between the pan and the cleaning brush in its tin holder. Abelard and Judith stood on each side of the hanging body. Then, with sadness in his tone, Cadwallader said: 'All right, Judith, dear, I won't play at ignorance with an old friend. I have to put it to you that this fortuitous discovery of Glass today only confirms reports I've already had of a link between you and trafficking.'

'Have I been stitched up or have I been stitched up?' she replied in her mild Miss Brodie accent. 'I suppose Julian and Simon and their woman are cutting you in, Verdun. God, I'm so dim. You and Simon work together, plant Glass here so you can put me out of the running for a share. Will you bring the police?'

Cadwallader stood, the glorious suit falling immaculately back into place. 'Now, Judith, I'm afraid Simon and I must take this as an admission that what I've heard about you is right.'

She said: 'Don't tell me you're not in on it yourself, Verdun. Or you want to be. Stupid I've been but not *that* stupid. You and Simon – you pose as the last white men in the West?'

Cadwallader said: 'A mark on his head, which could be the death blow. It's near the temple and I believe the skull is at its thinnest there. I'd say this was not a punch. Some sort of broad faced weapon has been employed, wouldn't you agree, Simon? Cedric tends to use anything to hand. The bottom of a full bottle? A log? Have you a wood burning stove, Judith? Handsome things. Cedric's a comfort to have on your side in an all-out rough house but isn't suitable for much else. One could say the same about the SS.'

He unzipped the fly of Glass's jeans, reached in and pulled the underpants down, or up on this inverted body, then peered earnestly inside for a while. 'Cedric also goes for the balls, as I remember. Did you have him with you in Paris, Judith, when you snared Abelard? No. You're a lucky man, Simon, live to fuck again.' He slipped a hand inside. 'Yes, Glass's feel pulpy. They've been given heavy attention. I suppose Julian would be au fait with this area.' He closed the zip, making a grave ceremony of it. 'A body does deserve our reverence,' he told them, 'even when it's rubbish.' He washed his hands. 'Well, Judith, obviously I ought to inform the constabulary. This is not a simple situation, something that can be kept within the confines of the Outfit, as I might normally arrange. Simon happens to be here and has witnessed all this. You think we're in cahoots, but really it's not like that. Simon's his own man, very much so, and I've no idea what his attitude might be to hushing things up. He is part of the admirable new openness. Obviously in other circumstances the Praepostor and Ivo could lose this wreckage without complications. Nobody's going to miss Glass.'

Judith looked at him, something like hope in her eyes. 'How do you mean, Verdun, handle it within the Outfit?'

Cadwallader held up tiny hands, like a child mobster's surrender in *Bugsy Malone*. 'I said it couldn't be handled like that, didn't I? Now, don't pressure me. Judith.'

'But if it *could*, Verdun?' She seemed to read a positive in his negatives. Perhaps he had only mentioned the impossibility of an Outfit cover-up to suggest the possibility. Judith would be even more familiar with his subtleties than Abelard.

Cadwallader answered at once: 'First, we'd get rid of Glass. Then I'd need a proper tête-à-tête with you in more suitable surroundings. Obviously I have to know who else is with you in the trade, besides Julian. One hears the most depressing whispers – Link-Mite, Turkey, God knows where it stops. My aim, naturally, would be to put the Outfit right again, cleanse it, if that's not too Old Testament a word. Of course, you'd be retired, Judith. I might be able to wangle a sickness pension for you. After all, I do not regard what I've seen today in this lav as the product of a normal mind. Forgive me, but I have to say it, and I feel Simon will share this view.' He waited but Abelard stayed impassive. 'Your exit, Judith, could probably be managed without publicity. We might even be able to arrange a security job somewhere. Porton Down?' He turned to Abelard, 'Perhaps everything depends on you, Simon. Upon your willingness or not to remain silent, for the sake of the name of the Outfit. Do you seek the kind of cleansing I mentioned?'

How did he answer? Yes, it was one of his aims. One of his *first* aims? He could not be sure. Judith had been nailed and perhaps Link-Mite and Turkey with her. Wasn't that good, even when it was achieved by Cadwallader's special juggling? 'Yes, I want things made clean, Verdun,' he said.

'Simon, let's be explicit. You would keep quiet about the body and Judith's sad implication in the death?' He stared unblinkingly at Abelard.

'No implication at all,' Judith said, 'but—'

'Yes, I'd keep quiet,' Abelard replied.

'Good man.' He shook Abelard's hand and signalled that Judith should do so as well. She took a fleeting grip on his fingers. 'Judith, we're lucky,' Cadwallader said. 'I speak as head of an organisation which dreads public scandal. I hate dealing with *Insight, Foresight, Private Eyesight, The New Stuttersman* and *The Absurder*. Where's the phone? I'll get this refuse collection in hand.'

Shortly afterwards he and Abelard left. 'My kingdom for a piss,' Verdun said. 'That was a genuine urge of mine in there, though *inter alia*, of course. One needed to know what developments there'd been. I could scarcely empty myself over a hanging man, could I?'

'I don't know. But good God, how did you get a body into the house on your own and hung up like a partridge?' Abelard replied. It seemed to him that even in the most secret and tooth-and-nail era of the Outfit, what had been happening now would have rated as extreme; might have rated as preposterous and impossible. Was it the dollar element that had resurrected the old shady violence, only more so? Abelard's mother had said something like that about the money motive, hadn't she? Love of country, love of money – no contest? Jesus.

'I thought things went fairly sweetly,' Cadwallader said. Judith might still kick a little, but last throes stuff. Undoubtedly she's got some dirty little cash-mad clique in the Outfit, or across the quadrangle, the usual English Home Counties assholes, but I can sort them. She's finished and they're finished. Beal and Labour would have liked to put her on top, you know. Their Up Women policy. They'd have blamed me for all the Jules Bowling disasters. Scapegoating. But I told you my family knows how to look after itself. You've done distinguished work, Simon, have helped purge a noble service. You might be the first black, well, blackish, deputy chief here. The situation's made for you, millennium lad. Labour will love that – if it can't be a woman, at least ethnic. Don't fret about your miserable ungayness. Ashton was almost totally straight and still ran the place admirably. In any case, gayness can develop late. You could, perhaps, let me know if you get urges – now, please. You might need guidance. Yes. Of course, we haven't finished with Jules yet. My God, have you met his mother? That explains so much.'

Cadwallader still talked like the ambassador of Integrity on earth, his only mission purity, regardless of what Judith had said. 'Doesn't Julian get in touch at all?' Abelard asked.

'Why should he? He knows I'll grab him by the ear and put him in the Tower till his teeth drop out.'

Was this right? Cadwallader remained genuine? Abelard went home. He felt this whole business, the spy business, the policing business – which was it, now, and did it matter? – the whole situation had shifted close to flashpoint, and he worried about leaving Lucy unprotected. He worried about his mother, too, but his mother was no stepping stone to a possible $17,000,000, and so perhaps safer.

She greeted him at the flat. Lucy seemed absent. He glanced around the room. 'She came back from her walk but has gone out again. If you're looking for a note there isn't one,' Mrs Abelard said. Then, speaking one of his own thoughts, she went on: 'Has she done a runner, like Anita? They tire, Simon.'

'I've just been talking to Cadwallader about men's mothers.'

'Lucy's got some new guy?' Mrs Abelard replied.

'Why do you say that?'

'Or some previous guy reclaiming?'

'Why do you say that?

'Your father always maintained no white woman would put up with you and your so-called job for long.'

'Only no *white* woman?'

'He knew about white women. Me.'

'Have you seen anyone near the flat, now or earlier?' He described Julian Bowling. Had Lucy been fixing up something on her 'walk', and perhaps before, in the garden?

'No. But that's how it happened with Anita, and it could happen again.'

'I don't think of Lucy like that.'

'Your trouble. They're all like that.'

'Who, white women? She came back looking OK?' he asked.

'Except for the standard scars. I went into the sitting room to watch the motorbike rally; I didn't know I was supposed to be guarding her. I'm not a Doberman.'

He and Lucy had given the flat a rough tidy up last night and he saw no new breakages in the hall or dining room. It could mean she had left willingly. Who kicked against going to pick up $9 million, maybe $17 million? Was that vicious? Now and then he did feel vicious. Quickly Abelard had a look at the rest of the place. In the kitchen he saw the glass door of a wall cabinet had been cracked right across, the kind of damage that could result if someone's head went hard against it in a struggle. Christ, was that fresh? His mother might not have heard a fight above the race bikes. Maybe Lucy had not simply left for her cut of the winnings after all.

Abelard went out and approached one of the layabout gangs in the street. There were five lads, three white, two not. 'Seen anything unusual near my place today?' he asked.

One of them did a fair take-off of his mixed Cardiff and Manchester and New York and Whitehall accent. 'Seen anything unusual near my place today?'

The rest of them gazed at Abelard, their faces dead. Then a small, mixed race lad in a blazer of brilliant clashing stripes asked: 'Unusual, Eminence? What's that mean?'

'Comings or goings.'

'Tricky.'

'Have you seen a woman, young, leave the house – alone or in company?'

A tall skinny white boy said: 'This don't sound like the kind of info that comes free or even cheap.'

Abelard said: 'If you've got anything I'll buy it.'

'We got to consider it could be dangerous,' the black boy said. 'People who talk to strangers in the street, even brothers – people who talk get problems.'

Abelard pulled out a five. It was back to the Paddington waiters.

'Oh, I was afraid of that,' the one in the blazer said.

'Meagre.'

But the black lad took the note. 'About 2.30 a man arrives at your place in a car, a Morris, old, a heap. He goes inside and a couple of minutes later comes out with the bird you're belting and they leave.'

'Was one of the tail lights gone?' The car he saw last night might have been casing.

'Tail light? This was afternoon. You wanna know what was the reg, did she go willing, what did he look like? We're right down here, where we are now, a long way from your place, not taking no interest at all because we see it's no law car, and we're all so busy talking about what careers we'll have, like poets, archbishops, stockbrokers, that sort of thing. What's your job then? Nice suit, regardless. He wasn't dragging her when they came out and she wasn't hurt but he's walking very close behind so he might have a shiv in his pocket or even a piece. Listen, what kind of people do you know, then? What is your job? Before you, this was a nice respectable street. I can tell you a bit about the visitor: older than you, sharper dresser, going grey, maybe, square face, not too big.'

Not Jules. 'Did he have on red and white trainers.'

'I said he was in a suit. Sharp.'

'Yes, but did you see trainers?' It could be Richard Field, survivor of that Pimlico pair. That is, if it wasn't someone from the US embassy, or from the Outfit, or across the quadrangle, or from almost anywhere else. For a second Abelard felt a kind of relief. It did look as though Lucy had not run from him to collect. But if she had not gone to Switzerland and the bank she was sure to be a prisoner somewhere. 'Any more you remember about him?'

'OK, he was getting old, but he could move. Soon as he had her in the car he was around to the driving seat like shit off a shovel.' He looked down at the five. 'This is some bargain you're getting.'

Abelard handed him a couple of pound coins, then returned to the house and ate with his mother. To go ahead with the meal was an admission he did not know when Lucy would return, or if she ever would. 'Yes, ma, she was taken from here forcibly. She didn't just ditch us. Me.'

'Anita did. How do you know this one hasn't?'

'It was seen. He must have used plastic on the front door lock.'

'So had the minders been pulled off again? Who by?'

Yes, who by?

'Your info comes from those young cruds in the street, does it? I bet you had to shell out good. You trust them? They'd tell you any yarn for cash.' Yet Abelard had the notion that she wanted to believe him. In a while she asked: 'So, you'll find her and bring her back? What we got to look for is clues, yes?'

'Right.'

What clues? He took the telephone directories and a pad and on the kitchen table began to list every Field in the London area with an R in his initials. It would take a time and was useless. People like Field stayed out of phone books. Abelard thought of trying the office library for a dossier but no longer felt sure about anyone in HMISS. Ah, the new openness.

And what would he do when he had finished his list – visit every R Field? Or should he ring up and ask each whether he wore trainers with a suit and had recently abducted an American girl junky and former Intelligence agent? Was Field a genuine name? Abelard had started something farcical, but stuck at it just the same.

After half an hour his mother appeared in the kitchen door carrying a bit of writing paper. She watched him for a while with pity or contempt then said: 'I've made a few inquiries, Simon.'

'Yes? You shouldn't bother, ma.'

'I just knocked some doors along the street in case anybody beside the youths saw what happened. They are *youths*, aren't they?'

'Any dangerous-looking male under twenty is a youth. These days a youth club is what they hit you with.'

'Well, a bit of luck. Some posh old dear who used to be a school teacher, I should think, saw a really ancient car pull up near her house, a black Morris, and she was afraid it was being dumped and would stay there for ever. This street has some wrecks. So she phones the local police and reports it. That's the sort she is, loud and tough. Half the time, cars she makes a fuss about are not abandoned, just parked, I bet. The police do a computer check and tell her the car's all right. I suppose she kept on and eventually to shut her up they say, crummy appearance or not, the car's registered with someone in a decent address.'

Abelard pushed the phone book aside. 'And?'

'She not satisfied and watches the car. After a while, Lucy comes out with a man from our flat and they leave in the Morris. She throws the name and address away then.'

'They gave her the name and address?'

'To get her off their backs. To prove the driver wasn't some nobody.'

'She threw it away?' Abelard whispered. 'Where?'

'I asked her could she find it.'

'And?'

His mother said: 'It could be good, it could be nothing at all' – a sentence she must have heard Abelard use now and then. Reading from the fragment of paper she said: 'Mr Abel Chandon, 26 Linklade Street, Knightsbridge, London W1. Simon, you know him? The car's deliberately old as a cover?'

'I know the name Chandon. It's French.'

'You don't say.'

'There was a works on the edge of Paris, a place called La Courneuve.'

She must have read darkness in Abelard's voice. 'Something bad happen there?'

'Not too good.'

'How bad is that?' She looked almost sorry now to have come up with the information, if that's what it was. 'You talk like them people in waistcoats and collars you work with, nothing clear, everything "not too bad" or "not too pleasant" or "a little difficult." They all mean the same – people getting killed and hell swallowing everything.'

He drove to Knightsbridge. This was a bit more like it – nicely up-market from the dreary spots he had spent so much time at lately: Paddington, a bloody suburban bowling green and King's Cross. His mother might be right about the ancient car as disguise. Under his raincoat he put on body armour and he took the .38. He would not have minded some help, but where was help he could trust?

Linklade street had small, select shops offering shoes or clothes or jewellery and high-priced oddments, a street probably burgled twice a week. Number 26 was Nino's Fashion Accessories and sold handbags, the kind of thin, elegant Italian things made for nothing smaller than £50 notes, and for getting snatched in Bond Street. Loitering at the window, he studied the interior. If they knew him – and didn't all the world? – this was dangerous, but he needed some idea of the layout. A woman in her thirties, and as smart as the stuff on show, stood at the back of the shop gazing out. She recognised him? He was decently dressed and possibly looked like a potential customer. Well, if all this worked out right he might get his mother a gift from Nino's. It was not a shop for presents for mothers, but she deserved something special. Of course, if things worked out right Nino's might be finished, anyway.

The woman moved suddenly and disappeared into a back room. Scared she was telephoning or alerting someone else inside Abelard entered the shop. As he opened the door a buzzer roared and he noticed watch-dog TV over the cash desk. A door slammed and the woman returned quickly. She smiled, welcoming him to the lovely wares: smiled until he was very close to her and still walking, and obviously not interested in handbags but in reaching the part of the building she had just come from. In an attempt to block his way, she shifted suddenly and the smile all at once took very sick and fell dead.

He did not stop but, gripping her as gently as he could by the shoulder, shoved her to the side. Silently she fought Abelard, trying to hold him back. A mixture of smells hit him: sweat and Arpège, a scent he knew from Anita, and much better on its own. 'Stay and watch the shop, dear,' he said. 'Think what types might walk in.'

Gingerly he opened a door and found a small empty kitchen. The woman had followed him into the corridor and tugged ferociously at his coat. He did his best to ignore her and tried the next door. It was locked. 'What's in here?' he yelled. Suddenly he had a panicky dread it would turn out as grim as Judith Stewart's bathroom. But surely nobody would kill Lucy. She had to go with them to the bank. 'What's inside?' he said, levelling his voice off a bit. From the shop the buzzer sounded twice. If she could leave all those fine items unwatched it was because her main worries lay here. Putting his shoulder to the locked door he shoved, swung back from foot to foot and shoved again and again, giving that steady pressure which might do the trick. He felt the socket shift, then burst, and the door flew back and cracked against a wall. Behind him the woman grew more frenzied, pulling at his hair and ears now, not his clothes, and he dropped good manners and with two hands threw her off, threw her so hard she fell and had to struggle to get up.

'Fool,' she muttered.

'Take a look at yourself.'

He switched on a light and found himself staring into a small, white-washed room containing a supermarket trolley. In it, slumped like a drunk, Lucy slept, her head and one arm hanging back over the end, mouth gaping. This was no self-induced dream-time, and someone with fair knowledge of such matters had put her under: perhaps the same skills as had been applied to Abelard in Paris, and to Lucy and his mother in Lewisham. Lucy wore the clothes she had been in an breakfast, and he saw no sign on them or on her skin that she had been knocked around this time. Abelard stepped towards the trolley and as he did became aware that the woman had picked herself up and was in the room.

She no longer grappled with him. Instead, as he touched Lucy's forehead and tried to arrange her more symmetrically, the woman said: 'In an hour she'll be completely right again, I swear. My God, Abelard, don't you think we're entitled?'

'So have you got Jules as well, whoever you are?' Abelard replied. 'A Swiss trip?'

'Those two, McIver and Bowling, can't keep it all, the grasping sods. There's years and years of work behind that money, a lot of risk, a lot of deaths, a lot of jail. Does Bowling really think he can just pick it up and keep it, like a child with shells from the beach? They've promised to cut you in? You believe it? They'll never beat us, let me assure you.'

'Who's us? Who's Abel Chandon?'

'We have a totally legitimate interest in these funds.'

'Sue then.'

'I mean from the point of view of natural justice. You act like a damn policeman and think only of the narrownesses of the law. But there is something above that, and we invoke it now.'

'Invoke? Really? What is it, decency?'

'We'll fight. Don't obstruct. This is a beautifully organised, beautifully regulated, international commercial complex. If you attempt to undo it, you'll go the same way as your reporter friend in New York, Charles Robert Tate.'

For a second Abelard was wrecked. 'Charlie?'

'You didn't know? It will be in his newspaper, whichever, tomorrow, I should think. Perhaps your were aware he had begun to harass a connection of ours. Fool.'

This appeared to be a word she liked, singular or plural. Abelard longed to question her but could not risk the delay. Where was the man with the Morris? Abelard took hold of the trolley handles. The woman moved swiftly again, slammed the door and stood with her back to it. 'You won't rob us,' she said.

He drove the trolley hard into her and heard Lucy groan at the impact. As the metal took her in the stomach the woman doubled and before she could recover Abelard left the trolley, held her by the arm and pulled her from the door, forcing her to a far corner of the room. He tugged the door open and pushed the trolley out and towards the shop, Lucy still snoring heavily. A middle-ged American couple were studying the bags. 'Someone may be along presently,' he told them. 'If not, feel free to help yourselves.'

'Is something… well… a little wrong?' the man asked.

'Wrong?'

'Do you need help, sir?'

'My friend here?'

'Certainly.'

'Thank you, no. You carry on with the handbags. I'm going to take her for a walk. Pity to waste such sunshine indoors.'

'Say, would you be Mr Nino himself?' the woman asked. 'I mean, the general... well... like *flair?*'

As Abelard crossed the shop he saw an old black Morris arrive and double park outside. A man he recognised at once as Richard Field hurried towards the shop. His trainers gleamed. Abelard pushed the trolley out of sight behind a display stand and went and stood close to the door, his back to it, as if studying the handbags. He drew the gun.

The woman whispered: 'Neil, darling, look. It's like home.'

The door opened, the buzzer called and, turning quickly, Abelard grabbed Field by his collar and tie, dragging him off balance into the shop. He changed his grip on the pistol and brought the butt down twice on Field's neat head. This could not be a straight policing operation any longer. Abelard regretted it. He felt split by his roles and confused about his methods.

Field collapsed face first on to the carpet and did not move. Abelard jammed the street door open with a beautifully soft ochre handbag and pushed Lucy out. 'Have a nice day,' he called.

People smiled and made way as he hurried towards his car. What did they imagine – a bet, the aftermath of a binge, a sponsored race? It was another mildly strange scene in a London street and nothing more. Just the same, he would prefer not to meet the police who *were* police. At the Escort he lifted Lucy on to the back seat and the move seemed to revive her a little. She wanted to say something. 'Later,' he told her.

As they drove down Sloane Street he saw the first of the blue lamps belting to Nino's. In case the Escort had a tail he did a big detour before making for home and near Charing Cross Lucy came to fully and started explaining. Some of it Abelard would have preferred not to hear. Most of it. 'Dick Field – alias the long-dead Abel Chandon, alias Burntenshaw, alias Squire, alias Nino – plus his bird Gabrielle were partners with Julian in the trade of course.'

'Of course.'

'Gabrielle's pretty hostile to me, not just because of the dough. I had a short, what you could call vivid, interlude with Dick Field.'

'Is that what I could call it?'

'What would you call it?'

'Degenerate.'

'OK, OK, maybe. I mean real short, about a week, when it looked like Julian had gone for ever. I thought he'd finally abandoned girls, settled for full-time gay, and I picked – well, consoled myself, I guess – with what was nearest. Gabrielle knew almost before it started. But it's mainly just a money matter now. They demand their slice. They wanted to hold me and negotiate with Julian.'

'Where is he, Lucy?'

'Oh, please, not back to there.' She sat forward in the rear of the car and put her face against his neck and chin. 'You know, Dick was at one of your major public schools, maybe Charterhouse, even Winchester.'

'Pushing does attract a nicer class of person these days.'

'Darling, don't despair of the likes of them and me. Especially me.'

He watched the mirror. It seemed clear. A radio news bulletin reported the death of the distinguished, British-born investigative journalist, Charles Tate, in suspicious circumstances after being hit by two untraced cars in a New York street.

14

TO HAVE BROUGHT Lucy home was a kind of victory, but what kind? They were back to where it began, waiting for Julian and, as far as Abelard was concerned, not even knowing whether he wanted him to show, because Lucy might disappear with him.

The three of them attempted to settle into peaceful life at the flat. Still fearing contact with the Outfit, Abelard rang Cadwallader to tell him he was taking a long due sabbatical. Verdun seemed entirely willing, although technically the job remained unfinished while Julian stayed loose. Abelard had the impression that the little man wanted to handle the whole thing himself now, deal with everyone who needed dealing with: Link-Mite, Judith, Turkey perhaps, and Julian. This prospect would stir him.

'Sabbatical?' he said. 'I must enter some project on the application form, Simon, for the bumf kings. What "research not necessarily related to normal duties" will you be following? Should I ask?'

'I thought, "Business ethics: their range and limits."'

'Nice. Get in touch if Julian tries to contact Lucy, won't you?'

'Who pulled the minders off, Verdun?'

'They're gone, are they? I expect it was tiresome having them loitering around your porch, anyway.'

Later, Mrs Abelard said: 'Sabbatical? What's that in the name of God? You turning rabbi? Ever heard of anything like this, Lucy?'

'Sort of study leave, ma. The Civil Service have always had it. Recharges the soul. I've suffered a lot of stress.'

'Gee,' his mother replied.

And the stress went on. Just before midday Judith Stewart arrived at the house in a taxi, still looking very drawn. 'Come to smash the place up again?' Abelard asked. 'How do you get rid of the guards?'

'Well, I suppose we all walk into one another's houses. But look, Simon, I'd like to forget all that now.'

'You're here to make a deal?' he replied.

'How are you Lucy, after the—?'

'You heard? How?' Abelard asked.

'Oh, Simon, we're in the information game.'

'I'm OK,' Lucy said.

'Grand,' Judith replied. 'You must be ready all the time now.'

Mrs Abelard came in with tea and a big home-made chocolate cake. 'You work with Si?' she asked Judith. 'He needs care. He went to Paris and came back looking like death.'

'French food?' Judith asked.

Mrs Abelard handed out the tea and cake, then left them.

Abelard said: 'Judith, you've got Bowling?'

'What is it you know?' Lucy asked her. Lucy's eyes seemed hooded after the knockout drop, her voice slow.

'I've had a whisper,' Judith said.

'Reliable?' Lucy asked.

Judith shrugged.

'She wouldn't come otherwise,' Abelard said.

'Sorry.' Lucy raised her hands in surrender, the kind of gesture Cadwallader used now and then. 'I forget I'm with heavyweights.'

Judith said: 'This tip comes to me before going to Verdun. But it *will* go to Verdun. We've only a short time.'

'For what?' Abelard asked.

'A business arrangement, obviously.' Today she was in a dull tweed suit, her office kit, perhaps.

'I don't understand,' Lucy said.

'I know I've no bargaining clout,' Judith replied. 'Sure, I could go to Julian and bring the two of you together, then demand a cut, but—'

'You really know where he is?' Abelard found himself almost shouting. Was it the thought of landing Julian that excited him – of finishing the assignment? Or was it the awareness of so much cash waiting? Had he caved in at last and become one of that mob whose only mission aim was to milk 'the current GB'?

Judith Stewart talked on: 'Who'd trust Bowling to keep his side of things if I did it that way? He never knew what it meant to play straight – why he was such a fine agent, before all this took over.'

'Jesus, don't talk as if there's nothing to the work but treachery,' Abelard said.

He saw she could not be bothered with fine points. 'So, I come here,' Judith said. 'You're my market. We need each other.'

'If you don't trust Julian how can you trust us?' Lucy said.

'I don't, not absolutely. Just more that I'd trust Jules,' she said.

'Do we need you?' Abelard replied. 'Julian will find us eventually. You did. Field did.' And Glass, but he left that unsaid.

'You don't understand,' she said wearily. 'There's no eventually, Cadwallader will be told soon. It could have already happened, making us too late. If we do a deal, that's going to be a gamble you accept. The dwarf is almost on to Jules, and in the cause of cleanliness the dwarf can be extreme, can be a throw-back, as you know, Simon.'

'Is Cadwallader honest?' Abelard said.

'Does it matter?' Judith asked. 'He means to get Bowling.'

'Yes, it matters,' Abelard replied.

As if speaking about Cadwallader had reminded her of danger, she stood and glanced from the window. 'He had a sort of surveillance on me. That was a surprise. At my house when I found Peter Graff dead in the bathroom – oh, did Simon tell you about this genial escapade, Lucy? – I decided then that I'd act broken, destroyed. At first I was going to have the body shipped out in a freezer, but then I thought again. I calculated that if Verdun believed I was in pieces he'd get to ignore me, and I could make my recovery. I sent the helpers away empty. But I suppose I should have known Cadwallader would still have me watched. I dropped the tail easily enough – some new kid, I gather, Lancing and Cambridge, – but they'll know it by now and start searching. This place will be on their list.'

Abelard said: 'So you're still trying to make your recovery.'

'How much would you want?' Lucy asked.

'Send me a present, if it works and you get the takings. Decide what it's worth. I've said I trust you. Or put it another way, I'm in your hands.' She looked appallingly weak and hounded. 'In a month or two I might be out of a job, or in something shitty especially cooked up by Verdun. He could make problems about my pension if he wanted to, and he will want to unless I play everything exactly as he says.'

'Sure, we'll send you an honorarium,' Lucy said.

'Sweet,' Judith replied. Then, with hardly a break, she added: 'Bowling is at 11 Home Place, a mews cottage near Brompton Oratory, alone, I think.'

She was eager to leave. 'Please make any payment to the Co-op Bank, Dagenham High Street, in the name of Dolores J Maidment. Pretty, isn't it? As a kid I always wanted to be Dolores. Anything for a speck of glamour. If the deposit could be cash, so much the better. Verdun has a way of locating secret accounts and discovering the source of payments. But I don't insist.' They phoned for a taxi and she left.

Lucy came with him to Home Place and they watched the house and the parked cars for a while from the little public gardens behind the Oratory. 'Looks deserted,' she said. There had been no movement, no lights, though the day was overcast. Had Verdun got there first after all? He frequently did get to key places first. 'I'll try it,' Lucy announced. 'Safer like that. He's not going to hurt me – not yet.'

Abelard protested, but while he was still arguing she

suddenly turned and, walking into the road, made for the cottage, out in the open, with no attempt to hide herself. He watched horrified, the Smith and Wesson ready again in his pocket, ready and useless at that distance. In any case, what if this was Lucy really dropping him at last, homing in on the cash in Home Place?

He saw her hammer the door and wait, but nobody came. She bent and peered through a small, leaded bay window, then returned to the front door. Taking something from her bag this outstandingly gifted embassy clerk fiddled with the Yale, opened it and went in. After a couple of seconds she reappeared and beckoned him. 'Empty,' she called.

It was furnished like a sentry post: a few chairs, a table, a bed, a camping stove. In the kitchen they found milk and bread, both reasonably fresh, and the *Daily Telegraph* for that day. They sat down. Perhaps she was not walking out on him after all, the everlasting imponderable.

'He's set himself up here while he tries to find me,' Lucy said. 'He can't get leaks from the Outfit any longer, so it would take him a time.'

'God, he could have found a cheaper spot than SW 3 for his camp.'

'That's Jules. Perhaps the cottage belongs to the family.'

'Not in the dossier.' Abelard had a good look over the place. If it came to a struggle he'd know the ground. It was the sort of venerable, pretty, undamp-proofed box you could have bought for £30,000 in a Cardiff back street, but which here would cost two hundred and fifty grand for the last few years on the lease. Wasn't it worth that for a view of the Oratory? The street door opened straight into a minute hall, which minutely broadened into a minute living room. At the back there was a minute, paved high-walled yard approached through a kitchen bare of equipment. He ignored upstairs. There would be no inverted Glass, and any fight would not reach the bedrooms.

'He'll expect you to bugger off to the bank, Lucy,' he said. 'Just you two.'

'The picture has changed. He'll see that. Don't fret. I won't be—'

Outside, a car drew up and stopped. Abelard grabbed Lucy's arm and pulled her away from the line of the window and they stood together against a wall, alongside the front door. Abelard drew the gun. For a second Lucy put her fingers over the muzzle but then shrugged and released her hold.

She said: 'I don't want him any more, but I don't want him dead. That figure?'

And those everlasting imponderables sneaked back.

In a minute a key scratched at the lock, but without turning it immediately, as if this, too, were a break-in. Then, at the fourth or fifth attempt, the door did start to open, and as it swung back Abelard yelled: 'Get your hands on your head. Do it now. Now.' He heard the key fall on to the stone flags, a classy feudal sound, and then Julian staggered into the hall past them and almost collapsed. Somehow, though, he reached the far wall and supported himself there with both hands.

'Jules, for God's sake, what's the matter?' Lucy cried.

Bowling hardly seemed to hear. He looked terrified, his mouth hanging open, uncontrolled. Despite their voices it was only when Abelard moved to close the door that Julian seemed to realise there were people in the house, and with great effort turned his head slightly. As he did, his hands skidded a few inches on the wall and Abelard saw a smear of blood spread across the paper. The small movement caused Bowling to sway and almost topple, and the two of them hurried to him. Abelard shoved the .38 back into his pocket. Taking an arm each they helped Julian to the living room and put him on a chair.

When he spoke his voice did not sound too bad, not too bad for someone dying. 'That little genius in the blazer.'

'Cadwallader?' Lucy asked.

'Did it in person. Clever as—'

He slumped to one side and did not finish the thought but, anyway, cleverer than Julian by the look of it when things turned to life and death. Bowling had on a trenchcoat and Abelard methodically checked the pockets for a weapon, then frisked his suit. As he undid the topcoat, he saw blood had spread from a wound high in the chest, almost the neck, soaking Julian's shirt and waistcoat and spreading down his arms. He groaned. Abelard found no handgun.

As if only now realising what Abelard had been doing, Julian muttered: 'I threw it away, empty. Christ, I hardly saw him and his assistant till it was over.'

'Where? How did it happen, Jules, love?' Lucy asked.

He concentrated and seemed about to reply, but then gave a small shake of the head, as if details did not rate. Here he was, near the end, and he would focus on that. 'I realised yesterday that our little friend was close. You can't enter this country without the bastard knowing. It was like the fucking OK Corral. I made it so damn easy for them, Lucy.' He paused for some air. 'Years ago he propositioned me once or twice. Three times. I wasn't interested. Never anyone older than myself – like Gore Vidal. I mean, Jesus, look at Verdun, even then! He did not forgive.'

Abelard said: 'I'll go and call an ambulance.' There seemed to be no phone in the house and he had left his mobile in the car.

Bowling stirred, hearing Abelard's voice this time and slowly put his full gaze on him. 'We were in a ditch together?' His eyes closed for a while, then reopened. 'This sod works for Cadwallader, Lucy. Are they bedmates? Are *you* two bedmates, now? Has he been with you all day? Possibly he was there, hidden, when this happened.' He moved a hand a few inches to indicate the wound.

'No, he wasn't there, Jules. He's all right.'

'Look, the only way a British black gets on in our game is by crawling to the boss.'

But what if this British black liked the boss because the boss seemed wholesome, this British black having been brought up to evaluate people against a collection of simple, rigorous Bible texts? Could Julian Bowling possibly understand that, even if he could hear it properly in his fading state? Probably he would ask what grown man could live by such stuff, and especially a grown man in their odd profession. Powerful objections. And Abelard would concede that these days the basic, foursquare teaching had to fight against other factors even inside him. But it was still there, still active now and then, even oftener. All Abelard said was: 'He propositioned me, too. Only once. Twice? I declined, so perhaps he'll turn against me, eventually.'

Lucy started to get Julian's clothes off to see how far the damage stretched. It was wise and it was pointless. No ambulance would arrive in time. Abelard might have helped her, but Julian snarled: 'Keep this bugger off me, Lucy. What are you doing with him? You should have let me kill him in France. You've gone sloppy.' With a bit of a groan he made himself sit up straight, or straighter, head and hands hanging forward. Blood thudded regularly on a thin Persian rug. 'Lucy, listen, none of the takings to my father, you understand? My mother? A little, maybe, but out of his reach.'

She tried to ease him back in the chair. They had the trench-coat off and Lucy was working on his shirt. 'I'll arrange everything about how the cash is split,' she said.

'I've covered the important bit,' he replied. 'A do-it-yourself WH Smith will yesterday plus a hand-over letter signed in front of a Commissioner for Oaths.'

'Fine.' She had no scissors but made a hole in the shirt with her finger nail and then began to tear it as gently as she could around the wound.

Julian said: 'The will witnessed duly and all that by the bloke and his wife in the paper shop. I did it and the letter just in case, and I was right. You're sole beneficiary. I hope those bloody Swiss will accept the instructions.'

'Yes, I know they will.' She dropped a large piece of blood-soaked shirt to the floor. The hole they found in Bowling was neat and small, when for a second they could stop the blood flow to look.

'You'd have done the same for me, Lucy,' he whispered. 'The letter and will.' For a moment he sounded as though he craved reaffirmation of their love.

'Sure,' Lucy replied. She kissed his forehead gently and he smiled and reached up with his right hand and touched her arm. His hand fell away.

'Sure,' he muttered. Now he folded back, eyes shut, his breathing very quick and faltering. 'Lucy, I can't tell you where the bits of paper are while this black valet's in the room.'

'I'll go and get an ambulance,' Abelard said.

'Yes, piss off,' Bowling said.

'Well, cheers then, Jules,' Abelard replied.

'Why?' Bowling said.

'Why what?'

'The leave-taking.'

'I'm going out,' Abelard said.

'Think I won't be here when you get back?'

'Cheers, Jules.'

'This could have happened to anyone, Simon,' he said.

'It has – to nearly everyone.'

'Not you,' Bowling said.

'Cheers then, Jules.'

On his way back to the house twenty minutes later, Abelard met Lucy hurrying along the street. 'He died,' she said. 'There were two other wounds. I have the papers. You didn't actually phone for an ambulance, did you? That would bring all sorts.'

'No.'

They took a bus. 'Am I turning hard, Simon? I couldn't cry in there. I couldn't even feel very much. He didn't seem anything to do with the man I used to know.'

Abelard forced himself: 'He obviously thought of you to the end.'

'The man I used to know got away with things. This one's shot down by a fucking gnome. A gnome with time to put three bullets in Jules.'

'A gnome with help.'

'Mr Carbolic. Do you think Cadwallader could be mad, Si?'

'Just honest.'

15

FOR A WHILE after the bank in Zurich accepted Lucy as sole surviving signatory to the account and released the funds, she, Abelard and his mother stayed in Switzerland and relaxed, eating at restaurants most days and going for trips in a hired car, like what Mrs Abelard called 'almost a proper family.' The bank did not actually come across with cash. Lucy had it transferred to more accessible accounts, one rating a cheque book and joint to her and Abelard. The total eventually made $13 million.

Things did not work out exactly as Julian would have wished, but close. Philip and Pamela Bowling of course threatened to contest Lucy's right to the inheritance. Fearing a court case would produce niggly questions about where the money came from, Lucy split a quarter share between them. She insisted it went in Pamela's name. A fortnight after the payment to her account they heard she had left Philip and gone to live in Portugal. From there she telephoned them once: 'My dear, dear boy bought his mother's liberty with private funds. At the edges of him I could always find fragrant traces, like only part-decayed meat.' Lucy put $100,000 into the Dagenham account of Dolores Maidment for Judith.

Why ever go home? Abelard's sabbatical had a few months to run and, in any case, the immediate job died with Julian. The prospect of other assignments did not excite him now he had seen the whole game reduced to cash terms, and had gained from that himself.

Even the persistent guilt he felt over Charles Tate's death had to be commuted. Abelard found that Tate had only one dependant, his mother, living in France, and he arranged for $100,000 to go to her, also. In previous days Abelard might have visited to sympathise and ask if there were other ways he could help. Now, though, the dollars by banker's draft must say the lot. Yes, changes had set in. He felt bewildered. Was he agent, cop, crook?

Lucy insisted on the joint account. 'I refuse to live with a kept man,' she said. 'Anyway, you did most in landing it.'

Not true. Or, at least, he had not sought the money deliberately. He had hunted a man because the Outfit ordered it, and because he had naively imagined at the beginning that the safety of the realm might be at risk, and because he felt needed to preserve the law. The cash had arrived by accident. But it was there now and he had grown used to it – was even growing used to idleness. He felt glad his father could not know.

Lucy liked Switzerland and his mother thought it wonderful. She could go out alone here and had faith in the police because they wore guns. Abelard was happy enough, too. All that crap about the facelessness of the Swiss and the dullness of their lives meant nothing. He preferred a bit of facelessness to what was readable on the faces of those who had pursued him and Lucy in France and Britain. She seemed to know Switzerland well – better than Abelard did – and was able to fix herself up quickly with a new coke supply: someone she and Jules had once helped and who longed to repay, for the right price. What more did they need?

Once in a while he telephoned his next-door neighbour at The Hawthorns in London to see things were all right there and he gave her a bank address for any mail that looked worth sending on. When it came a little nearer to the end of his sabbatical he might consider offering Cadwallader his resignation. He did not discuss that now, though. His mother would not understand how anyone could give up a job, even a job she despised so much. Money in the bank would make no difference to her attitude.

Nothing much came in the post. Then one day when Lucy and she did the bank run they brought back a large brown envelope with a 'Photographs: Do Not Bend' sticker on it, which the neighbour had forwarded. Abelard disliked the look of this and waited until his mother was out of the room before breaking the flap. He found two expertly done photographs, both of Verdun Cadwallader suspended something like Glass/Graff had been in the bathroom. He was clothed and his tie hung down over his nose. Abelard saw differences from Glass, though. Now, the setting was not a house. These pictures had been taken with the aid of artificial light in what appeared to be a metal tank, maybe the kind of container one saw on stilts in factories for fuels and chemicals. The other difference was that Cadwallader had obviously taken a thorough beating before he died, not just the death blows, as with Glass. They had sent two photographs so the bruising to both sides of the face could be appreciated, the tie making a dark border to each shot. Cadwallader had on his blazer, grey flannels and what could be rink shoes.

Lucy studied the pictures with him and stayed calm, as if she had seen things as bad or worse before: as calm as when Julian was dying. Then she took the photographs suddenly and would have torn them up and dropped them in the waste disposal unit. He stopped her. 'Why?' she asked. 'Integrity's always been a dangerous commodity. We don't need pix to tell us.'

'I wasn't even certain he had integrity.'

'I'd say he was mostly OK. This sort of thing happens to people who are mostly OK.'

'He was doing good work, putting things right,' Abelard said.

'He crossed someone. Judith Stewart?'

'Could be.'

'There are others?'

'That's how it looks: Link-Mite, Turkey.'

'Yea, I've heard of them.'

'He was hunting them all.'

'That's the world they're in.'

'It's the world *I'm* in, Lucy.'

She laughed: 'The difference is, you can buy yourself out

because we've been more successful at the dirty side than they have.'

'Thanks. What the hell is this thing Cadwallader's in?'

'Does it matter? He's dead. I've heard of such removals. An industrial acid container? There never was much of him, I guess. Now—' She put a hand over her mouth. 'Oh, Simon, I'm sorry. This is me putting on the shell. But I'd hate to see you sweating and worrying when we can't do a thing about it.'

'No?'

After this he made the daily trip for mail himself and decided to open anything dubious on his own before reaching home. Nothing else came, except a threatening notice about the rates.

One evening, after a very pleasant day touring by car, Abelard's mother said: 'This thing you're on, Si – this sort of holiday which isn't a holiday—'

'Sabbatical.'

'Is it still going?' She and Abelard were alone in the room.

'Of course.'

'Does it last for ever? Do they really keep on paying you for driving around Switzerland looking at mountains?'

'I'm considering a return soon,' he replied.

She brightened. 'Yes? Grand. All sorts of things need seeing to, you know. Guttering at The Hawthorns – things like that.' Lucy joined them. 'Simon's thinking of going home. Isn't that good news?'

'First I heard.'

'I thought you'd spot it,' he said.

'Well, maybe.' Nobody could have guessed she had lately landed a fortune: still the jeans, old tartan shirt and desert boots.

When Mrs Abelard had gone to bed, he said: 'They've got him out of the way so trading can continue.'

'Sure. So what? You're becoming Son of Carbolic, like Julian said? But can you be the great cleanser when you're a partner in his loot?'

'Tough one. I'll think about it.'

'But you want to go back, anyway?'

'Yes.'

She nodded. It could mean she thought he might be right, or it could mean, Christ, what would I expect from this mixed up dumbo? He waited for her to tell him he would be wiped out, too, if he took on a sentimental mission to avenge Cadwallader and gnaw away at rottenness. Gnaw away at some of the rottenness: not his own private helping.

'OK,' Lucy said. 'We all go. I never met the little guy, but what I heard I like.'

'This could be important. I'll be back to sort of policing. I'm looking at a crime, Lucy.'

'Yes, I said OK. You go, I go. That's how it is with us, yes? If we stayed you'd be thinking always of those fucking pictures. I guess if you could restore some hygiene in the Outfit you'd feel better about the dirty dough.'

'I don't feel too bad about it. Jules collected it from crooks. Fair game.'

'You're developing a sophisticated conscience even for a cop, Si.'

'Is that good?'

'Good in which sense?' she asked.

'Yes, I see what you mean.' Perhaps a sophisticated conscience was the only sort he could expect given his type of life, even now, in these unclandestine times. Next day he rang Judith Stewart at home.

'I've been so busy, Simon. I should have sent thanks for that little infusion at Dagenham.'

'You found time to post the pictures.'

'As it happens, the need for that very kind gift to Dolores Maidment was not as desperate as I feared. One is still in work after all, you see. We've had a bit of an internal fight here. Office politics. You're wonderfully lucky to be away from all that tedium.'

'Where in God's name were those photographs taken?'

'Verdun Cadwallader disappeared,' she replied. 'Had you heard? Utter mystery. Yes, absolute exit. People are worried. But how would you hear – you're abroad?' Her voice went down. 'Yet I've a feeling you're coming back.' He did not reply. 'I thought so. Fond of Verdun, weren't you? I've heard folk describe him as straight. Bit of a giggle, that. But, Simon, he spoiled things for everyone. He thought the game should still be about secrets and the realm and understanding the Mid-East. There's a place for such people but not at the top any longer. I'm not sorry he decided to pack his bags. My own suspicion is that after the Jules death and all the shit that flew – as you'd imagine – Beal or someone bigger than Beal told him to exit quietly or face trouble, possibly prosecution. Probably with a pay-off. They've begun to get a feel for things now in the Foreign Office, Beal especially. As a result, I'm somewhat better placed. Things flow. I'll admit that being a woman helps in their book. And what other book is there, Simon, given their majority and with the rival crew shambolic? But it's not all women. Roger Link-Mite and Turkey are much more settled, too. Peaceful here. All in all, I do think it would be better for you to stay out there and just enjoy things. I'll be confirmed in charge later this week and could extend your deserved sabbatical for at least a while. More or less indefinitely, in fact. And Lucy can get her essentials? You haven't weaned her off yet? She's so resourceful.'

Yes, Lucy could get her essentials and, no, he hadn't weaned her. He would. There might be a better chance on home ground.

And so they were going back. He pondered what kind of chance he would have against Judith and Link-Mite and Turkey, perhaps backed by Beal and his chiefs. But when telling him to stay away she sounded nervous, talked too much and too quickly. Judith was afraid and that must be good. There had been a time when so many of them had regarded him as one of Nature's pushovers.

Yet if she feared him why had she or one of the others sent

the photographs, more or less prodding him to react, almost challenging him to come back? It would be pride, the kind of mad, impetuous burst of vanity that could mess up the cleverest people. Abelard had seen her apparently humbled and jibbering, even if she claimed now this was an act. She wanted to show him she could hit back. This need to crow her victory was a gross and promising weakness, and there would be others. Abelard felt almost sure he could cope with her and with the rest.

They went by train and ferry. On the boat Mrs Abelard said: 'I get the feeling, Simon, you've been recalled to duty. That's the phrase, isn't it, in the adventure stories I used to read you?' She made her voice deep and solemn. '"And to deal with this national crisis our hero was recalled to duty".'

'Along those lines.'

'What crisis?' she asked.

'Like law and order.'

'I'm in favour of them.'

The Do-Not Press
Fiercely Independent Publishing

Keep in touch with what's happening at the cutting
edge of independent British publishing.

Simply send your name and address to:
The Do-Not Press (Dept. SPLIT)
16 The Woodlands, London SE13 6TY (UK)

or email us: split@thedonotpress.co.uk

There is no obligation to purchase
(although we'd certainly like you to!)
and no salesman will call.

Visit our regularly-updated web site:

http://www.thedonotpress.co.uk

Mail Order

All our titles are available from good bookshops, or
(in case of difficulty) direct from The Do-Not Press
at the address above. There is no charge for post
and packing for orders to the UK and EU.

(NB: A post-person may call.)